To my mother, who said 'do it'
– and never doubted that I would.

Acknowledgements

It is an act of faith – to say nothing of slightly unattractive self-belief – to write a novel without a publishing deal, which is where I was when I wrote this story. It could have been lonely too – but I never felt it was, thanks to many, many people including: my long suffering husband, who always shows a polite interest; the Romantic Novelists' Association – with honourable mentions for Catherine Jones and Melanie Hilton in particular; my lovely friend Julia Silk at Orion Publishing; the wonderfully encouraging team involved in the Good Housekeeping Novel Award including Luigi Bonomi, agent, Kate Mills and Jemima Forrester from Orion, Joanne Finney, Books Editor at Good Housekeeping and the rest of the team who scooped my entry out of the pile and were kind enough to encourage me, and not forgetting my loyal friend Anne Roberts who nagged me to enter in the first place; then there are my drinking pals who promise to buy it, including Alex, Claire, Clare, Kate, Nancy, Carolyn, Charlie, Georgie, Sarah, Anna, Vicky, Kim, Helen, et al – you know who you are ... and finally, the fabulous Choc Lit team who are patiently teaching me to be a proper novelist. Special thanks go to the Tasting Panel readers who passed the book and made this all possible: Lisa B., Sue P., Louise, Linda Sp., Melanie, Georgina, and Sarah C. I salute you all.

THE TEN COMMANDMENTS
for a politician's wife

My name is Emily Pemilly. I know, catastrophic. Being of dubiously sound mind my advice would be never, under any circumstances, marry a politician.

However, if you insist, the only advice I can offer is this:

1. Thou shalt take thy husband's name – because this is expected, even if thou art then called something utterly ridiculous like Emily Pemilly which makes thee sound like the heroine of one of those silly children's books that would never have got published if they hadn't been written by someone famous.

2. Thou shalt give up thy career – which was the one thing that made thee feel like a proper adult. That and having a sensible name. Sadly, being a fearless and uncompromising mouthpiece for the truth – I was a journalist – is an impossible career choice for people with silly names anyway. As another option, you could consider the following commandment;

3. Thou shalt choose a career which makes thee look saintly – thereby casting a glow of sanctity upon thy husband by association. Looking after sick children would be good, although being a nurse is politically sensitive because of the union issues and being a doctor means thou art a bit too clever. Perhaps run an animal rescue centre or similar as being nice to small, furry creatures is definitely a vote winner.

4. Thou shalt give up the right to make even the simplest decisions on thine own – leaving such weighty issues as which supermarket to shop at, which car to drive and even names for thy children, to be endlessly dissected and analysed by a focus group which will tell thee precisely how to do absolutely everything.

5. Thou shalt gaze adoringly at thy husband at all times whilst in public – even when he is making the most boring speech in Christendom. Actually, especially then. And no yawning. Ever.

6. Thou shalt cheerfully attend an endless series of constituency fundraising events – where members of thy husband's constituency and team will talk about thee as though thou aren't there.

7. Thou shalt deputise for thy husband at all the constituency surgeries that he can't be arsed to go to himself – even though this involves sitting for hours in draughty village halls listening to old people moaning about waiting lists for hip replacements, the solution for which is entirely beyond thy power.

8. Thou shalt not beat thy children – as thou art required to be a far more perfect parent than anyone else in the world. This is mainly in case thy husband is called upon to speak in support of a smacking ban or some other entirely unrealistic parenting policy thought up by people who don't have children.

9. Thou shalt not allow thy children to misbehave in public – a particularly difficult commandment given the restrictions imposed by commandment number eight. By the way, thou needn't think drugging them into submission is an option either because this is also frowned upon by those pesky childfree policymakers.

10. Thou shalt believe that the end justifies the means – in practice this translates to a devout and unquestioning acceptance that how things look is considerably more important than how things are.

And this is the word of the Party.

Amen.

Chapter One

Even the combination of tiger face-paint and a generous coating of chocolate spread failed to disguise Alfie's gorgeousness.

'Daddy,' he announced, 'is a poo-poo head.'

'I couldn't agree more,' Emily muttered. 'I know you're disappointed sweetie,' she said, ruffling Alfie's hair. 'Daddy wouldn't have missed your party for the world if he didn't have to.'

He had still had a fabulous birthday, she mused. As a sociable four-year-old, his idea of heaven was a crowd of mates, opportunities to run around screaming like a banshee and endless supplies of party food made primarily out of artificial colouring. He had had all these since three o'clock that afternoon and fifteen pre-schoolers had trailed home two hours later, off their heads on sugar and additives and primed to put their parents through hell until bedtime.

The house had not escaped unscathed and, once again, Emily rued her lack of forethought in not giving birth to her children in the summer. How did the other parents of children with winter birthdays cope without the garden party option? Her husband Ralph – pronounced Raif, but frequently mispronounced, to his irritation – had thought the same. He'd had little patience for her in the first mind-numbing weeks when she was caring for the new-born Alfie who had arrived when Tash, then four, was at the height of her despotic infant powers.

'You should have waited for summer recess,' he had said, creating the impression that, in his view, Emily could have extended gestation to fifteen months rather than thoughtlessly sticking with the usual nine.

He missed the birth of course. A three line whip had kept him in the House to vote. Then he had turned up at the hospital, not with flowers and champagne but with his agent TJ along with Saul, TJ's celebrity photographer boyfriend. Saul's sleeveless leather jacket, worn over a naked torso, attracted even more interest in the maternity ward than Ralph, who was irritated at not being the centre of attention. The resulting arty black and white shots of father gazing into the eyes of his new-born son had been sold hard into the national newspapers. Columnists had twittered at length about the family-friendly face of the Party, edging ahead in the polls with their young, dynamic team of shadow ministers, of which Ralph was the newest and shiniest. He was Shadow Secretary of State for Children and Families at the time, being elevated to the top of the party at just thirty-eight, only four years into his career as an MP.

She gazed wearily at the post-party mess. If only she'd organised a press call along with the crisps and sausage rolls, he might have made an appearance. Mind you, as Alfie was a lot more vocal and less co-operative than he had been, it suited Ralph to play the sanctimonious 'my family life is private' card more often nowadays.

'Give us a kiss, gorgeous,' she sighed, holding out her arms.

Alfie's eyes narrowed. 'Okay, just one,' he said, offering a cheek, 'but no spit.'

Nessa and Emily were having a cup of own-brand instant coffee, the best the kitchen cupboards at the village hall had to offer. It was an unappealing reward for finishing the clothes sorting.

'Who donates their pants to a jumble sale?' asked Emily again.

'I know darling. Too ghastly,' agreed Nessa with a shudder. 'Never mind,' she added, 'just the books to go – thank heaven. Must be my millionth time ...'

'More, I should have thought. You're so kind to help, you know. I don't know what I'd do without you.'

The last words came out with a barely perceptible tremor and Nessa knew Emily wasn't just talking about gruesome jumble sale preparations.

'Darling, I wouldn't be anywhere else,' she replied, giving Emily a little squeeze and then busying herself with the coffee cups so they could both regain their composure. 'God knows, I'd still be doing this as an MP's wife if Arthur hadn't so selfishly dropped dead on us all,' she continued over her shoulder as she rinsed the cups and put them on the draining board. 'Mind you, it's been forty-six years of jumble sales and coffee mornings I worked out the other day. Horrifying isn't it? The truth is – despite it all – I'm not ready to hang up my constituency boots just yet.'

Emily could hardly believe her friend was in her sixties. She wore her age with an ease that made the thirty year age gap irrelevant. 'I didn't have a clue what I was doing when Ralph took Arthur's seat,' she reminisced. 'Thank goodness you were prepared to stick around.'

Nessa smiled. 'I was thinking the other day I've gone from MP's wife to a kind of honorary MP's wife's mother-in-law.'

'I can assure you, you couldn't be less like a mother-in-law.'

'You say the sweetest things. Also, the very thought of being Ralph's mother! I don't know who would be more horrified – him or me ... ooh look, porn!' she exclaimed, distracted by a grubby paperback with a naked woman on the front.

'So it is. Much pored over by the look of it too. Ugh. Shall I chuck it?'

'Absolutely not. I'll keep it under the counter and whip it out when the vicar gets to me. He likes a bit of smut.'

'No he doesn't,' giggled Emily. 'You are naughty. He's a clean cut young man with a gorgeous wife and three children, as you know perfectly well.'

'Ah, but appearances can be deceptive,' said Nessa,

tapping the side of her nose. 'Now this really is interesting,' she exclaimed holding up a fat red volume with gold tooling on the spine. '*How to Run the Perfect Household* by Felicity Wainwright,' she read. 'It looks like – oh yes, look at this publication date – 1953. Now those were the days,' she reminisced. 'It was only the mid-sixties that Arthur and I were married – I was a child bride obviously – and my, what a shock it was, too! I could have done with something like this.'

'Must be hopelessly old-fashioned nowadays though,' said Emily, holding out her hand for it. 'For goodness' sake, look at this, for example. Page one, chapter one, *"A young woman of refinement entering marriage today is likely to find herself running a household with the bare minimum of staffing. She will therefore be likely to have to take on the role of housekeeper herself, taking a close interest in the work of the maid and cook, to ensure standards are kept to a respectable level. This is essential if she is to do her wifely duty of maintaining the dignity of her husband amongst his peers."'*

She blew a sigh. 'It was another world wasn't it! Pipes and slippers for the men and domestic slavery for the women, albeit with "help". Thank goodness we made it to the twenty-first century before Ralph and I tied the knot.'

'Hello ladies,' announced TJ as he marched into the village hall, looking more than usually brisk and efficient. Behind him followed a bespectacled grey-haired man in pinstripes. 'Right,' said TJ rubbing his hands together, 'let's talk tactics.'

'Great,' said Nessa. 'They're my favourite ... Only the mint ones of course, those orange and lime things they brought out are just too horrid for words.'

Emily giggled. 'Tactics, Nessa, not tic tacs.'

TJ looked cross. He raised his chin and continued, 'In light of the ... er ... developments of this morning, central office are keen to ensure we are optimising the opportunities presented to us by the inevitable increase in media interest.'

Nessa shot Emily a look.

'What developments, TJ?' asked Emily, 'only whatever massive news has been announced, we've missed it.'

'True,' agreed Nessa. 'We've been buried in dirty underpants and porn all morning. Haven't heard a thing,' she added innocently.

TJ and pinstripes looked pained and astonished in turn.

TJ sighed. When Arthur had died, a tiny glimmer of hope in the general bleakness of the situation was that Nessa would be replaced by an altogether more amenable MP's wife that he could boss around. It had worked out, to a point. He was secretly and devotedly in love with Ralph, as well as being extremely fond of Emily, but Nessa's continued presence led her frequently into insurrection that TJ, as agent and therefore lynchpin in the constituency, could do without. Now, more than ever, unquestioning compliance would be helpful.

'So, he hasn't contacted you?' he asked Emily, incredulously.

She shook her head. Although he had been in the London flat since Tuesday night and it was now Thursday afternoon, they no longer called each other several times a day, just to hear each other's voices.

'Well,' TJ continued, flustered, 'I am sure he would have done if he could. It's been really mental. I happen to know he's in a shadow cabinet meeting as we speak.'

'So anyway,' said Nessa, 'cutting the crap – as it were – what the bloody hell is this huge news, TJ?'

'Oh, right. Well, in a nutshell, the government have done it. They've called a general election.'

Emily whistled. 'Ralph must be beside himself,' she said with awe.

'Well, we're all pretty excited, that's true enough,' conceded pinstripes, coming forward to shake the women's hands. 'I'm Gerald Mortimer, from central office as TJ said. Basically, I've been asked to come out and help get everyone on message, help out with profile management, that sort of thing.'

Emily nodded and Nessa looked amused.

'The thing is,' he continued, 'Ralph is obviously a pretty key person as far as the presentation of the party is concerned. We will want to be using him – and you,' he flashed a grin at Emily, 'to show the electorate what we represent.'

'Which is …?' queried Nessa.

Gerald looked as if it was the pinnacle of his life's ambition to be asked such a question. 'Well,' he began, 'the main thing to get across is probably going to be the whole traditional family values thing.'

Emily threw him an enquiring look.

'You know,' he continued, 'like supporting the nuclear family with the introduction of a tax framework that rewards the single wage earner, allowing the other parent the choice to manage home and childcare meaning better educational attainment and a future workforce with inherent personal social responsibility and a valuable skill set …'

Nessa yawned extravagantly. Emily was sure she was putting it on. 'So, my role is …?' she queried.

'Ah,' smirked Gerald, 'You would be the go-getting, ball-breaking alpha woman, with the high-flying career and the househusband, obviously …'

'Really?' said Emily, flattered that her gossipy column in the local lifestyle magazine plus the odd feature article in a national broadsheet was considered 'high-flying'.

'Erm, no – sorry – I was joking,' he replied, embarrassed. 'We rather had you down as the "perfect home-maker, photogenic family, dedicated wife, charming consort to the powerful man" type of role actually.'

'Sounds like not much has changed,' Nessa observed. 'I've done rather too much "charming consort" stuff myself over the years.'

'Really?' said Gerald, a little too incredulously for Nessa's liking.

'Yes, really,' she said. 'I am relieved to say that role is

behind me – and I can assure you there is nothing less diplomatic than an ex-diplomat.' Emily noticed TJ nodding fervently. 'But surely,' Nessa continued, 'we should be allowing Emily a little more freedom than I had?'

'Yes, sure … I mean, erm, no,' said Gerald, confused. 'That is, Emily is an asset,' he beamed at her, 'and we feel she has an important role to play in enhancing the appeal of the party to the electorate. She and Ralph are a package. That's the point.'

'So she can continue being her charming, supportive, delightful original self?' pressed Nessa.

'Oh yah, absolutely,' said Gerald. But he didn't mean it. Emily could tell, having been mugged by the central office mafiosi before, not least when they insisted that she turn down a parliamentary sketch column – the would-be pinnacle of her journalistic career – because of a "conflict of interest". In other words, it "conflicted" with Ralph's "interest" in becoming the youngest member of the Cabinet.

'Anyway,' said Nessa, tiring of her TJ baiting game, 'I'm off.'

'I'll call you later,' she whispered in Emily's ear as she gave her a goodbye hug. 'And I think you might be needing this,' she added as she pressed something hard-edged and heavy into her hand.

Bringing it up to her face, she didn't know whether to laugh or cry. There, in her hand, was the copy of *How to Run the Perfect Household* by Felicity Wainwright, 1950's housewife extraordinaire.

Remember, your husband will be looking forward to returning home and off-loading the stress of his day. Even if your own day has been wearing, don't make the mistake of burdening him with your problems. Instead, prepare to amuse him with an entertaining snippet or two.

FELICITY WAINWRIGHT, 1953

'Tash has got nits again,' she said to Ralph as he took off his coat.

'Really? What glamour, what hedonism you enjoy when I'm away,' he joked. 'D'you think it's the school? Maybe we should send her private ...'

'The village primary's fine. She'd still get nits in a snob school.'

'Ah, but posh nits though. A better class of nit, if you will ...' said Ralph, giving her a hug and a glancing kiss on the cheek. 'Nothing for it though, the village primary it must be. Better for the image don't you know?'

She did. 'How was the surgery?'

'God, what a ghastly crowd,' he groaned. Fresh from the excitement in Westminster, the weekly constituency surgery had seemed even more parochial than usual. 'Can you believe that horrific old crone from Maybury showed up again to rant about double-yellow lines with her photo album of badly parked cars? Do you know, she actually goes around with a measuring tape to get evidence? One can only hope she'll get squashed by a lorry...'

'Did we not get a reply from highways on it? You remember we decided to ask them to do a study on it to see if the parking restrictions should be extended to help the flow of traffic?'

'Did we? To be honest I don't have a clue any more,' admitted Ralph, running his fingers through his hair, rubbing his scalp hard as if his head hurt which it probably did, to be fair.

'Tea or wine,' she offered.

'I'm not sure either of them are going to do it, have we got any gin?'

'Sorry. Gin, yes, but tonic, no. I forgot to put it on the list.'

'I'll have wine, as long as it's not that filthy stuff we got in for the cheese and wine do last week,' he conceded, but not before Emily had seen his irritated look at this failure in the domestic machinery which was, of course, her fault.

Emily rummaged for the corkscrew, eventually turning out the whole drawer onto the kitchen table, but then realised it was a screw top anyway as they almost always were nowadays, even the decent stuff which Ralph now insisted on. She recalled the days when any old plonk would do.

The day they met – her newspaper had sent her to do a profile on him as one of the chief architects of the new party – their business lunch had run into the evening and then through the night, with Ralph insisting on ordering another bottle of wine and then another before repairing to his Westminster flat where he talked her into bed. She had been ripe to be impressed by him. Flattened by the series of painful events that preceded her meeting with him, he was ten years older than her, successful, dynamic and in no way plagued by the self-doubt that crippled her.

Ralph, in turn, was totally bewitched. It was not just her petite frame, which belied her strength, or even the way her bright, brown eyes flashed with passion when she expressed her views on political issues. She was so genuinely earnest and charmingly unaware of her own physical attractions.

'I love your naive idealism,' he told her. 'I have to assume it's your youth.'

'Yeah, probably,' she had replied, unimpressed. 'I suppose I'm bound to have turned into a dried up old cynic by the time I get to your age.'

Not used to taking any woman seriously, let alone a younger one, Ralph found her enchanting and vowed to have her. When she fell pregnant just weeks after they met, he received her nervous announcement with the same decisiveness that he applied to his professional decisions. They would get married, he said. It would all be fine. The timing was ideal as he had been advised to find a wife before standing for Parliament – no-one was so stuffy as to care if the bride was up the duff nowadays – and the wedding would give him an excuse to invite all the people he wanted to cosy up to.

It had worked. He was rewarded for his loyalty to the party with a safe seat, although she had been disappointed it was in Sussex where she had no friends or family nearby. He had been elected to parliament when Tash was just a new-born and Alfie not even thought of, but the move to the country and downgrading of career for Emily had meant that she, quite naturally, had taken an interest in Ralph's constituency work. Initially, he had been driven by the desire to make things better for those whose votes he had relied on. Lately though, the glamour of Westminster and his rise within the party to shadow Home Secretary had replaced that passion with cynicism and a waning interest in local matters. Emily had tried to take over out of genuine concern for righting wrongs but found she was depressingly powerless to help.

'So, how are the boys at central office reacting to the election announcement?' she asked.

'Excited. Feeling like the PM's made a bit of an error calling it now, given that we're riding so high in the opinion polls but who are we to complain?'

'Who indeed?' smiled Emily.

'But then, what choice did he have? Looks like things aren't going to go their way over the next ten months and then they'd be forced to call an election anyhow. They obviously thought waiting until the last minute would be even worse.'

'Will we win then?'

'There's a good chance. As long as the key people can be persuaded to keep their noses clean over the next couple of months anyhow. It's all going to be on personalities. You could barely get a fag paper between our policies and everyone else's.'

Emily nodded. This had been her main angle when writing her political commentary even before Alfie was born and nothing much had changed since then.

'Yeah,' continued Ralph, 'as we've been saying, it's all

on personalities now, so we just have to make sure we are offering what the voters want.'

'Perfect, shiny, happy families then?'

'Well, yes,' he conceded, 'that's us. Then we've got the cool, cosmopolitan gay guys who are obviously Charles and Ivan, the steady older bloke with business experience, Alan – we need him to be the PM in waiting of course. In any other economic climate we'd be fielding a younger man as leader ...' he trailed off, rubbing his forehead with fatigue and thwarted ambition.

You would have been the 'younger man', thought Emily, who knew how painful it had been for Ralph when last year's leadership battle had led to his narrow defeat, despite the party nearly splitting in half over the battle to decide between him and Alan. He had been persuaded behind closed doors to stand down and back Alan, reuniting the party by publicly and vociferously stating his satisfaction with the role of shadow Home Secretary.

The phone rang.

'Ralph Pemilly,' he answered rather too loudly. Emily smiled to herself. However shattered he was – and he frequently was – he always answered the phone as if he had just been interrupted doing something important and dynamic.

'Yep,' he said, 'absolutely – no, you're absolutely right Gerald,' he was saying.

So it was pinstripe man, thought Emily. Judging by Ralph's manner with him, Gerald was a major cog in the machine. She supposed she ought to have been more appreciative that he spent so much of his time and energy on her and TJ yesterday.

Now Ralph was smoothing back his hair, checking his reflection in the darkened kitchen window. They were not overlooked and Emily rarely lowered the blind. Funny, she thought, how people tended to groom themselves when they were on the telephone. Almost like videophones were an everyday reality. And thank goodness they are not, she thought, given the number of times she had answered the telephone to constituents naked. Well, she justified, they did seem to think it was fine to call whenever they had a mind to.

'Okay, yeah, definitely,' he was saying now. 'Just tell him to contact the constituency office when he wants to come down.'

'Everything okay?' asked Emily when he put down the phone.

'Great, actually,' said Ralph, still arranging his hair. 'That was Gerald saying he's managed to get a Sunday Times magazine feature on me.'

'Wow,' said Emily.

'Yeah, well, they wanted Alan,' he admitted, 'but he was tied into an exclusive deal with the Telegraph just before the election announcement, so no-one else is allowed to do anything on him 'til it comes out. The Telegraph have landed on their feet of course, getting a print exclusive with the next PM.'

'Their loss is your gain though,' pointed out Emily.

'Yeah, well, Gerald did a good job of getting them to go for me instead,' he said with a humility Emily was sure he didn't feel. 'The leader of the party's more of a coup, obviously. Actually, they've not just decided to write about me, they want the whole thing; you, the kids, the whole family man thing.' He looked at Emily anxiously.

'Sure,' she reassured him. 'That's fine. It's not like it's a sleazy tabloid rag doing an exposé of your drug-taking, hard-drinking, and rent boy habit.'

'Nor yours my sweet,' he said, tapping her on the nose for her cheekiness. 'He'll probably be here on Monday to start getting a feel for everything at a constituency level. I said he should call TJ and go from there. I expect he'll want to spend more of his time in Westminster all told. That's where the action is really.

'I think he's probably quite good, this journalist,' he continued. 'Don't know if you've come across him at all in your former life? Bloke called Matt Morley?'

Emily froze. After a moment, Ralph looked at her enquiringly, waving his hand in front of her face.

'Earth to Emily! Have you heard of him?'

'Certainly not,' she snapped and then caught the puzzled look on his face. 'Sorry, what did you say?'

'Heard of him? This Matt Morley bloke?'

'Erm,' Emily thought fast, 'heard of him? Yes, sorry, I thought you said "had I *had* him" whereas you actually said "had I *heard* of him" ...' she trailed off, giggling nervously. 'So yes, the name rings a bell. I think he's reasonably good,' she added, blushing because, in that minute, for the first time in their marriage, she had just told her husband a big fat lie.

Chapter Two

It is a huge mistake to let personal standards
slip once you have that ring on your finger. Your
husband will still expect his wife to be the neat
and pretty woman he chose, so always make sure
to leave time, after the housework, to change your
apron for a clean frock, comb your hair and perhaps
apply a little make-up before you expect him home.
FELICITY WAINWRIGHT, 1953.

The children soon cottoned on that their mother was not fully present that weekend. Instead, Emily drifted around in a daze, saying yes to all sorts of rarely permitted treats, even allowing Tash to bury the homework that needed doing deep in her schoolbag and take herself off on a sleepover with her best friend Rosie. Alfie settled for telly watching, even in the morning when it would normally be strictly forbidden. He was delighted to be watching Scooby Doo, having also managed to score a packet of cheesy biscuits. With both children happily engaged, and Ralph out playing golf with a local rich party supporter, Emily at last had the peace and privacy she had been craving since the bombshell the night before.

Matt Morley – the man whose brief but passionate acquaintance overshadowed her early twenties, and whose success she had watched with fascination and longing ever since. Not only had she adored him as a lover, she'd idolised him as a journalist, watching his stratospheric career trajectory as his stern professionalism and tenacity secured him more and more prestigious staff positions on the national newspapers. His high profile meant that Emily, who had dropped out of his sight when their affair had ended so catastrophically, had been able to watch him invisibly (she fondly imagined) from the sidelines over the ten years since her hasty marriage to Ralph. Each glimpse of his by-line caused a twist in her guts that she could not decide was pleasure or pain – or just straightforward lust. And now she would see him again. Even more disconcertingly, he would see her. Of course, with just a day or two until they met, there wasn't much she could do about the sensible MP's wife wardrobe, the extra twenty pounds she weighed or the pedestrian lifestyle that he would surely despise in comparison to his own life. At least she could do something about the superficial grooming.

When Ralph came home, Emily was lying on the bed stinking of fake tan and wrapped in a towel, her freshly painted toenails separated by tufts of cotton wool.

'Can't talk darling, my face will crack,' she said without moving her lips as she got up and went over to the basin.

'What *is* that stuff?' said Ralph incredulously. 'You look like a mummy.'

'I am a mummy,' she replied, as she splashed her face with warm water, the clay mask dissolving into sludge in the basin. 'That's the problem. Children have rather made me lower my standards, personal refurbishment-wise ...'

'But I like you a bit scruffy,' protested Ralph.

'Oi, watch it. I never said "scruffy", I just feel I could gloss things up a bit. You know ... be the trophy wife for you a bit more. Make blokes fancy me.'

'Oh yeah?' he teased. 'Anyone in particular, because you do realise you're not really TJ's type, don't you?'

'Not anyone in particular,' Emily replied, blushing and feeling her X-certificate thoughts were written all over her face. 'No, actually,' she continued, improvising wildly, 'I was thinking about Gerald and, like he said, boosting your image, and – stuff.' She smiled triumphantly. 'I need to support you by making people lust after me. In a dignified, respectful way, obviously ...'

'Right. OK, well I have to say, I'm all for it,' he agreed, nuzzling her newly de-masked neck.

She wriggled out of his way, feeling ashamed for doing it but she didn't want to be touched. Not by Ralph anyway.

'Sorry,' she smiled at him. 'I must go and get supper on.'

Matt, too, was preparing for meeting Emily again. Although it would never occur to him to review his grooming routines he'd had the office prepare a cuttings file so he could track media coverage of Ralph's career and was working his way through it in date order. He tried to suppress his tendency to pay more attention to the stories where Emily was mentioned, and – better still – pictured. Not to say that he hadn't seen most of it before. You couldn't call it stalking, just a general 'keeping an eye'...

Matt lingered over a recent photo of Emily at her local village fete. Her face was a little rounder and her figure fuller than when Matt had known her. The sweet smile he recognised but there was something else – a complacent, implacable demeanour which was new. Despite himself he remembered returning to their little flat one night to discover her sobbing over a biography of poet Sylvia Plath.

'Don't you think committing suicide is a selfish thing to do?' he had suggested. 'It's an act of violence against the people you leave behind, I've always thought.'

'She didn't do it to hurt people,' Emily had insisted. 'She killed herself because the love of her life fell in love with someone else,' she said, waving her hand at the book in explanation. 'Look, she says it here: "*When you give someone your whole heart and he doesn't want it, you cannot take it back. It's gone forever,*" How could she live without her heart? Tell me you won't ever do that to me.'

'Your heart is safe with me,' he had promised, smiling. Later, he stumbled on an early copy of Sylvia Plath's poetry collection in a second hand book shop. It wasn't a first edition but, because it was signed, it was still a big chunk out of his young reporter's salary. He paid happily, added his own inscription and handed it to her when they were in bed one morning. He wondered if she still had it. Probably not.

He had loved her tendency to relate to other people on such a visceral level. It had made her a good journalist, he remembered, but vulnerable too. And then, just when he thought he knew her inside out, a rough patch in their relationship had turned rapidly and unexpectedly into a breakup. She announced she was pregnant just before he was due to travel to Kazakhstan. She asked him to cancel his trip, and – like an idiot – he went anyway, sure they would sort things out when he returned. Instead, Matt's face hardened at the memory as he recalled her phoning to say she had got rid of their baby. He had been staggered and appalled. By the time he returned she had moved out of their flat and he had never seen her again. *Where is the girl I loved?* thought Matt, staring at the picture in the paper. She wasn't that person now. Perhaps she never had been.

Shaking himself he picked up his notepad and returned to the cuttings. There was very little on Ralph early on apart from a brief mention of his wedding to Emily in the society pages. This had come just months after Matt's return to the UK, when he had discovered Emily gone. Seeing the cuttings caused Matt more than an echo of the bleak despair he had felt then. In the wedding pictures Emily's bump, which later turned into Tash, was extremely evident. No-one – in the media at least – had possessed the temerity to comment on the speed of their wedding, or hazarded a guess on the reason for it. Matt had worked out the dates in his head many times but he had never known how many weeks pregnant Emily had been with his child when their relationship ended. He didn't know because, like an idiot, he hadn't thought to ask.

At about the same time as the wedding some political commentators mentioned Ralph being the 'one to watch' amongst the newest and most dynamic group of MPs. Soon after his marriage, you could see the spin doctors swinging into action by the press cuttings that resulted. By then he'd had a junior ministerial post and was consistently and prolifically presented as a family man and doting father – champion of the aspirational middle income family. Emily was the adoring wife, her arm perennially tucked into his as if she was barely able to stand unaided. There was only one brief mention of Emily's early career and no suggestion that she struggled with the usual childcare versus career dilemmas. Matt had wondered about that at the time and he did again now. Emily, when he'd known her, had been fiercely ambitious. Although she'd loved children, he conceded, and of course they had never themselves had the conversation about combining work and family life, he remembered with another lurch of regret. He shuffled together the cuttings, stuffed them back into the folder and chucked them into his briefcase with a sigh.

Unusually, Emily and the children weren't running late that Monday, despite her taking a lot more care over her appearance than usual. She dropped off Tash in the playground and gave her a big kiss.

'But there's no-one here yet,' complained Tash, looking around at the near-empty playground.

'Yes there is darling, and look – Mrs Simpson's in the classroom. She'll let you in in a minute,' replied Emily persuasively. Tash pulled a face but luckily made no more fuss.

She hustled Alfie away, breathing a sigh of relief. Her main ambition was to get out of the school before any members of the mummy mafia turned up. The PTA members were the worst, all making arch comments about any television appearances Ralph had made, looking her up and down to give her outfits and general turnout marks out of ten and –

worst of all – pestering her to ask Ralph to cut a ribbon or draw raffle tickets. He was always appallingly grumpy about it, nearly divorcing her when she failed to prevent him from being railroaded into calling the numbers at an evening of fundraising bingo. On this particular morning she was well aware that her more than usually groomed appearance would excite impertinent comment and she doubted her ability to brush off unwanted remarks without blushing and looking guilty.

Dumping Alfie at preschool was even quicker than getting rid of Tash. Within minutes, Emily was back in the car heading for the constituency office with an entirely uncharacteristic eagerness. Even the depressingly narrow and smelly stairs leading to the offices, which were above a betting shop in the least salubrious part of the town centre, barely registered, although TJ made noises about their lack of ability to offer disability access to the offices. To Ralph they were ideal, being consciously low budget, showing he didn't waste taxpayers' and local supporters' money. Emily just loathed the shabby brown carpet and wished it didn't smell permanently of cabbage and mice.

'Sorry lovie,' said TJ, 'but basically, as usual, no one tells me anything. What's his name again?'

'Oh, er, Matt something or other,' she replied disingenuously, sure that he knew her insouciance was an act. 'It's fine,' she continued, 'I think Gerald only fixed it up on Friday so that'll be why you haven't heard. Anyhow, what can I do to help?'

Nothing depressed her more than helping out in the constituency office, but she could hardly turn tail and leave again. Also, maybe Matt would call while she was there, and then, after a weekend of agonies, she would at least know when the unsettling moment of meeting would arrive.

'Well, I don't know if you fancy folding these leaflets?' said TJ without enthusiasm, kicking a box at their feet. 'Central

office decided to save money by getting them delivered flat.'
Her heart sank.

'Or,' he offered, 'I know it's really my job but you could write and sell in a press release about Ralph's constituency visits this week?'

'Gosh yes, okay,' she said, relieved at being excused the leaflet folding. Thank goodness TJ recognised and used her journalism experience whenever he could. She threw him a fond look. Maddening though he and Nessa found each other, Emily was grateful for TJ's presence in her life. Heaven knows, she probably spent more time with him than she did with Ralph.

'I suppose at least we'll see more of Ralph now parliament's dissolved for the election,' said Emily forlornly, remembering that, actually, Monday was usually a constituency day. Instead he had left at the crack of dawn to get to yet another meeting at central office.

'You think? Now he's the Home Sec in waiting the constituency will barely see him. Let's face it, as parliamentary seats go, we're kind of a sure thing.'

Emily nodded. His seat was probably one of the safest in the country. 'No, he'll be sent to all the marginal constituencies now,' explained TJ, 'trying to swing the vote. Frankly we're lucky to get him here at all this week.'

'Ah well,' she said, rolling up her sleeves, and sitting at the computer to write her press release. 'What's his itinerary?'

'It's Thursday we've got,' explained TJ, 'so I thought we'd do a whistle stop tour, starting here in town and then bombing through the Downland villages, finishing off at Corfield for a rabble-rousing speech and Q&A in the town square.'

'Corfield?' She pulled a face. 'Ralph always hates going there.'

'Me too,' agreed TJ. 'Nice people on the whole but, heavens, the disasters that befall the place, no wonder everyone has such a long face. You don't want to stay there too long for fear you'll start wanting to kill yourself. I swear, the place is cursed. We call it "the village of the damned",' he said, disappearing into the kitchenette to put on the kettle.

Emily giggled, then screamed as a deep male voice close behind her said 'Or you could say the "Curse of Corfield", I suppose.'

She spun her swivel chair around and found herself face to crotch with the owner of the voice. Scanning up, she didn't need to see the face. The voice hadn't changed a bit, that authoritative but faintly amused drawl still had the power – she discovered in that second – to send a shiver down her spine.

While she could picture the naked body she used to know so well beneath the clothes – still the tapered waist, wide shoulders and broad chest – the face had changed. Lines from nose to mouth had deepened, more hooded eyes added to the dangerous, watchful look she knew of old and streaks of grey at the temples had done nothing to undermine the beauty of that thick, black, wavy hair.

'Hello Emily,' said Matt.

'Sorry. You made me jump.'

'Actually,' he replied, with a lopsided grin, 'I think I made you scream,' he paused for a beat, 'but then I've always had a knack of doing that with women – call it a gift ...'

'You can't just turn up you know,' she snapped, recovering. 'You were supposed to call.'

'Sorry. Still, I'm here now.'

'It might not be convenient.'

'Well, is it?'

'It'll have to be, won't it?'

Astonished and horrified at Emily's inexplicable rudeness, TJ all but elbowed her out of the way, holding out his hand to Matt.

'You're the Sunday Times guy, welcome,' he said. 'It's great to have you here. Can I get you a coffee?'

'Please,' replied Matt. 'Thanks.'

'You're welcome,' said TJ, handing him Emily's coffee and dragging him away to the little meeting area by the window.

'Now,' said TJ efficiently. 'I don't know what central office have been able to give you, but we run a pretty dynamic constituency operation here. I look forward to showing you the ropes.'

'No need to go out of your way. What I really need is a chance to soak up the ambience, observe from the sidelines. Just pretend I'm not here and carry on as normal.'

Emily groaned to herself. She had as much chance of ignoring Matt as she would be able to ignore a huge, hairy spider in the corner of the room. Even though she'd had the weekend to prepare, her heart was racing, her face was burning and her eyes were magnetically drawn to him. TJ was clearly keen to monopolise him, she couldn't have been more delighted to see.

She decided to draft the release and distribute it as quickly as possible. By then, she could plead she had to collect Alfie from preschool and get away. With any luck, the next time they met she would have Ralph with her – that should cramp Matt's style. But even though she had finished the release, the men were still chatting. She didn't want to stand up and draw attention to herself, so she kept occupied doing a spoof version to make TJ laugh. Calling it 'Corfield, village of the damned' she dropped in a couple of weak jokes about the Church Council being infiltrated by devil-worshippers and a coven of witches running the Village Hall Committee before bunging it over to him on an e-mail. Just as she was giving her real copy a final check, TJ hailed her. 'Hubby on the line, love. Can you grab it?' Emily quickly selected the local media e-mail list, attached the document and pressed send before picking up the phone.

'Hi, darling. Sorry I snuck off so early this morning,' said Ralph. 'TJ tells me this journalist bloke has showed up with you so I'd better get myself home tonight after all.'

Emily would have been more pleased at his unexpected return if he had expressed a wish to return for the sake of his family rather than his latest publicity opportunity.

'That's lovely darling,' she said, dutifully.

'Yeah,' he agreed, 'so can you fix something nice for supper and sort out the guest room? He was booked into the Seven Stars but there's been some cock up with the reservation. His office has tried to get him in somewhere else, apparently, but everything's booked up. I've persuaded him to stay with us. Nice for him to see the reality of family life close up and personal.'

'Er, yes,' she said, doubtfully. He saw so little of his own family life she wondered if he had a rather romanticised view of it.

'Tell you what,' he added, 'I'll bring Susie down too. After all, we've got lots to discuss, and then Matt will have met all the key people.'

Great, thought Emily, dinner for the five thousand and with no notice. Plus, try as she might, she couldn't help finding Ralph's parliamentary assistant more than faintly annoying, which meant that keeping up the necessary and expected charm took just a little more effort when she was around.

Alfie wasn't thrilled about being dragged around town after preschool just so that she could pick up the ingredients for a light but perfect supper. She had become well trained over the years. It seemed another life when she used to invite friends for supper and then end up grabbing a pizza on the way home to give them all. It had never mattered. This time, as always, she visited the delicatessen for Ralph's favourite cheese. She didn't get it for him very often because it made the larder smell like she was harbouring a rotten corpse. Then she went to the baker for fresh rye bread plus croissants and pain au chocolat for breakfast. Crab meat from the fishmonger and steaks from the butcher sorted out the starter and main course before Alfie staged a sit down strike and she gave in. He can bloody well make do with bought ice-cream for pudding though, she thought. Matt would still be absolutely astonished she told herself. When she knew him before it was a standing joke that her entire cooking repertoire from A to B consisted of spaghetti bolognese or – if she was feeling flash – the same thing nominally reinvented as lasagne.

She was doubly irritated that Ralph had invited him to stay too. It was all very well for him, she thought as she lugged cardboard boxes out of the guest room and piled them into the corner of their already untidy bedroom. The boxes were mainly Christmas decorations and winter clothes. Stuff she had been nagging him to put into the loft for months. Luckily the facilities in the guest room were basically okay. Just fresh sheets plus a jug of water by the bed and they were there.

She surveyed the scene, pushing hair out of her eyes. A bit dusty but otherwise fine. The guest room was charming, spacious and peaceful. She would show him what an accomplished home-maker she was now and he would be bloody amazed, she was determined. Better still if she could have shown him a sparkling career path instead but that was an opportunity denied her by Ralph's ambitions and her dedication to his job at the expense of her own. She felt sure Matt would see that. And be unimpressed too, which was a shame because, more than anything, she admitted to herself, she wanted to impress him.

Only to show him what he had thrown away, of course.

Chapter Three

It is the role of a hostess to make her guests
feel comfortable. The most important
component of this aim is to appear relaxed and
in control, although the author appreciates
this is not always easy, the appearance of
effortless entertaining is the aim …
FELICITY WAINWRIGHT, 1953

'No you may not stay up,' screeched Emily at Tash for the fourth time. 'You've had your supper, we are not eating until late, it is a school night and your father and I need to have some adult time with our guests,'

'Sounds great,' came a deep voice which made them both jump.

'I'm all for "adult time",' said Matt, coming in carrying a backpack. 'The door was open,' he added, kissing her on the cheek. She was furious at being caught out a) shouting and b) before having had a chance to put her make-up on.

'I hope I'm not too early,' he continued, although clearly, she thought, he knew he blooming well was.

'And you must be Tash,' Matt added.

Tash bridled becomingly and put on an excellent impersonation of delightful nine-year-old, as if the previous few minutes had never happened. 'How did you know?' she said, archly.

'Because you are just as beautiful as your mummy,' he explained 'and also because I am an excellent journalist so I've done my homework.'

'Oops, homework,' said Tash, with a stricken look.

'Tash!' roared Emily in exasperation, 'you have been home for hours, why didn't you say?'

'Just kidding! I handed it in this morning. Will you read us a story?' she added to Matt.

'No,' said Emily, 'he will not.'

'I promise I'll go to bed right now ...'

'Devil child!' exclaimed Emily, throwing an apologetic look at Matt, but he was already nodding. 'Sure I will,' he said with a smile. 'What about your brother?'

Right on cue, Alfie's head appeared, upside down, around the bend of the stairs. 'My Daddy sleeps with no clothes on,' he informed Matt solemnly.

'So do I,' replied Matt with equal solemnity.

'My Daddy likes wrestling with my mummy in bed.'

'So do I ... Ouch!' exclaimed Matt.

'Poor you,' said Emily innocently, hoping no-one had seen the swift kick. 'Did you tread on one of the children's toys?'

'Something like that,' he replied, giving her an aggrieved look. 'Anyway – as I was saying – so, do I get a book from downstairs or are they all in the children's bedrooms?'

Emily used the brief respite to charge into the bathroom and slap on some make-up. Matt was doing a surprisingly good job. They had chosen *The Gruffalo*, and he was producing an impressive range of voices. It struck her that she had no idea whether he was a father. For all she knew, he too was married, although, somehow, she thought not.

Hearing him reaching the climax of the book, accompanied by shrieks of delight from the children, she ran downstairs, checked on the supper – all fine, although Ralph and the others needed to show up soon or the crab pancakes would be ruined. She poured herself a huge glass of wine and arranged herself casually against the edge of the counter.

Smiling brightly at Matt as he returned to the kitchen, she endeavoured to adopt the mantle of 'perfect hostess'; calm, in control and hospitable in a manner designed to encourage absolutely no innuendo or – God forbid – flirting.

'Gorgeous,' he said slowly, looking her up and down. She tried and failed to resist the temptation to suck her tummy in. 'You've matured wonderfully,' he continued. 'Rather like that wine I'm rather hoping you are going to offer me a glass of.'

'You haven't tried it yet,' said Emily pouring him a glass. 'It might be absolutely vile.'

'Not likely,' he replied, 'you look as if you've developed a taste for the high life since we last met,' he said, quite unnecessarily stroking his finger along the back of her hand as he took the glass from her.

'You're right in a way,' replied Emily waspishly, snatching her hand away. 'I don't know about the "high life", but you could say I've raised my standards,' she added, giving him what she hoped was a crushing look.

'Ouch,' he said, holding her gaze. 'I've thought about you,' he added softly, staring at her mouth.

'I haven't thought about you,' she lied.

'Darling,' said Ralph as he let himself in with Susie in tow. 'I'm sorry it's so late. Is our journo chap here?'

'I am,' said Matt, coming forward and holding out his hand. 'I've been entertained by your charming wife and now,' he said smiling at Susie, 'I look forward to being entertained further by your equally charming assistant.'

'They're an impressive pair of women,' said Ralph proudly slipping his arm around Emily's waist and giving her a kiss. She reciprocated warmly, wrapping herself around him with far more enthusiasm than usual, meeting Matt's eyes triumphantly and hoping Ralph wasn't looking too surprised at the unexpected attention.

Ralph and Matt vied with each other to compliment Emily's cooking in between taking turns to show off for Susie who simpered and fluttered her eyelashes at them both. She was a pretty woman, slim and petite although with a regrettably big nose, accentuated by her unfortunate habit of wearing velvet headbands. Blonde and well-bred, she was used to being admired by men but had no serious relationship as far as Emily was aware. She was also intelligent and had benefited from an expensive education but chose to pretend feminine stupidity in a way that Emily found intensely irritating.

'Of course Ralph's position in the party was assured, long before he stood for election,' she was saying to Matt, holding Ralph's forearm proprietarily. 'He was already acknowledged as one of the key architects of party policy. Really, we were keen to have him stand so we could make the best use of his talents.'

'My biggest strength, as you can see,' simpered Ralph, 'is the loyalty of those around me. Susie's been an absolute rock since I was elected,' he said, giving her an admiring smile. 'I was lucky to have her.'

Matt raised an eyebrow. 'To have her?' he queried archly.

'Ooh, you naughty boy,' giggled Susie. 'You know he didn't mean that.'

Emily knew different. Matt always said exactly what he meant.

'Tell me about last year's leadership contest,' said Matt, relaxing back into his chair.

'Tell you what about it?' asked Ralph, but he knew what Matt was referring to. 'You mean the contest between me and Alan?' he continued. 'Yeah, well, you know how it goes. There are often a couple of front runners but the main thing is to get the party to unite behind just the one. You know that.'

'I understand getting the party to stick together was a bit of a challenge,' Matt probed. 'Rumour is there was a bit of a pact – a pay-off, promising power for you in return for you stepping down and backing the other man.'

'You might very well say that. I couldn't possibly comment.'

'I'll take that as a "yes" then, shall I?'

'Okay, well ... Alan will see me right, true enough,' admitted Ralph. 'It seemed to be what the party wanted,' he added with false modesty.

'A go in the hot seat then?'

'I wasn't aware there was a vacancy,' joked Ralph, but didn't deny it. 'Let's not forget, I may be the youthful contender, but Alan's hardly on his last legs is he? He's got a few good years in him yet.'

Emily was wringing her napkin through her hands, appalled at Ralph's bravado and indiscretion. God knows, it wouldn't be the first time his ego let him down. He was so easily flattered into saying more than he should and she was furious he was giving the impression of being so close to the leadership. Although Matt had no notebook or tape recorder handy, she knew he would be squirrelling away background for his story, and working out angles. Unbidden, memories returned of watching him gain the confidence of a bunch of Rwandan guerrillas, drinking beer with them as they lounged with their machine guns, all of them murderers but some of them no more than children. She knew all too well how he could feign comradeship and relaxation but really be sharply tuned to danger and the scent of a story. She wished she could warn her husband to be careful and tried hard to catch his eye.

Matt noted their interaction with amusement. Emily was right, he had done his homework and knew what questions to ask, but his secret weapon in the early stages of a story like this was simply to sit and watch. Flirting with Susie had been entertaining enough. She was willing, confident and responsive but as soon as the attention was off her he noticed it was Ralph she fixed her eyes on, not himself. He also noticed how she had flushed with pleasure when Ralph had praised her loyalty earlier. Matt was willing to bet her loyalty knew no bounds. She was Ralph's for the taking and Matt wondered idly if he had.

While Ralph's easy charm and undoubted charisma bought him the adoration of all around him, Matt suspected his Achilles heel was his vanity and that was a fault which could lead him into big trouble. There was nothing so destructive as a woman scorned ...

And what about Emily? he pondered. She must surely suspect Ralph and Susie were too close? In the past she would have come straight out and accused them both. She had been fearless, feisty, a loose cannon who spoke first and thought second, he remembered, the corner of his mouth twitching up in a smile. He had fond memories of her fury at a man in the park who dared to kick his dog in her sight; despite his being several inches taller and twice her weight, she had berated him with a stream of such articulate invective, it left him blinking and bemused, stammering an apology and hurrying away with frequent glances behind him. Matt had had to physically restrain her from following him, buying her an ice cream to take her mind off it.

And here she was now, suave and attentive, the perfect hostess. Dirty plates magically disappeared, wine glasses were filled and pertinent comments dropped into a conversation, all intended to commit to no particular opinion but to deftly place Ralph in the centre of the spotlight. Time to see how unshakeable she truly was, he thought.

When they were lingering over the last of the wine and the especially smelly cheese, Matt swirled his drink around his glass and announced casually 'Of course Emily and I were contemporaries when we were starting out as aspiring journalists. I remember her well.' Emily shot him a warning look, which he pretended not to notice. 'Oh yes,' he continued, enjoying her horrified reaction, 'we all had Emily tipped for the top, as it were.'

* * *

Emily froze, not daring to look at Ralph. That was possibly the second most gruesome thing Matt could have said, beating only the initiation of a discussion about how their passionate relationship had overshadowed her entire early career. Just in case he decided to raise that next, she dived in to pre-empt him.

'I'm rather tired darling, I think I'll go to bed if that's all right.' She stroked the back of Ralph's neck as she spoke, hoping Matt was noticing the intimate gesture.

'I'll join you,' said Matt, his eyes glinting dangerously. 'That is to say,' he added, 'I'm pretty tired too, if you could show me where you want me to sleep.'

Emily smiled brightly at him. 'Sure,' she said, but when they went upstairs together he followed her into the guest room, pushing the door closed behind him.

'Good God, Emily,' he demanded, his eyes opaque and unreadable. 'What the hell has happened to you? Are you actually still in there somewhere? What's the deal with the Stepford wife act? All this draping yourself over your husband ...'

'Exactly,' she hissed. 'My *husband*. That's what wives do, it's called being supportive. It's called commitment. I wouldn't expect you to understand.'

'Yeah, right,' he said, his face inches from hers, his body so close she imagined she could feel the heat. 'You should know all about commitment after what you did to me ten years ago. Then you scarcely knew the meaning of the word, apparently.'

'What *I* did?' whispered Emily furiously. 'That's really rich ...' She was rendered speechless with outrage for a moment. 'You *dare* to talk to *me* about being unsupportive ... Just tell me this,' she panted, her hand on her thumping heart, trying to calm herself, 'did you know I was Ralph's wife when you decided to do this story?'

'Of course I bloody did. I knew you dived straight into

a relationship with him as soon as you left me. I thought I should give you some space. Give us both some space, but the next thing I heard ...' he rubbed his forehead wearily. 'Mind you,' he continued, with venom, 'I can see the attraction. On the one hand you've got your slightly dodgy traumatised ex, having a bit of a tough time with the sheer bloody awfulness of the stories he's having to cover, plus – I'll grant you – a fleeting episode of commitment phobia over the woman he has fallen so passionately and totally in love with ...'

She gasped, but before she had a chance to interrupt, he ploughed on. 'And then, on the other hand, you've got a rather impressive up and coming politico by the balls, ten years older, sussed, panting after you and promising you a life of ease, where all you have to do is smile up at him every time he comes up with a particularly good sound-bite.' He paused. 'I just think you might have given it a bit more time. Thought it through. You loved me. I know you did. We fall apart and five minutes later you're married to this random bloke ...'

'It wasn't a rebound thing,' insisted Emily, knowing it was. 'I adore Ralph,' she went on. 'He's good for me.'

'And I wasn't?'

'What do you think? Just ... just, don't mess things up for me, I don't need ... complications.'

'Like this?' he grabbed her around the waist and drew her to him, sinking his mouth onto hers.

Paralysed with shock, she let him kiss her for several heart-wrenching seconds ... then she pushed him away with all her might. She swung an arm to slap him but he was too quick for her.

'Oops. Close, but no cigar,' he taunted as he grabbed her hand. 'Oh no you don't,' he added, grabbing the other one too before she had even consciously registered the intention. Grasping both her wrists in just one hand, he held them with no visible effort as she tried and failed to wriggle free. 'Now this is more the Emily I remember,' he observed. 'Passion, a bit of conviction ... just like old times.'

'Get. Off. Me.' Emily hissed, horrified at how slow she had been to reject him and knowing he had noticed. 'I am a happily married woman.'

'Ah, but are you though?' he asked. 'Only it seems to me you are just playing the part of a "happily married woman",' he went on. 'There you are, acting out the role of the dedicated politician's wife, the perfect partner, the charming consort ... you do it really well by the way. But all the while, you *know*...' he insisted, pushing his face closer, '... you *know* you've made a mistake, that you're living a lie, that you're just another member of the "Vote Ralph Pemilly" team. You *know* he doesn't really give a damn about you, don't you? Your place by his side is only as secure as the next focus group tells him it is ...'

'Shut up,' she whispered, her face blank with shock. 'It's not true ... Ralph loves me. I know he does.' As soon as Matt released her hands, she used them to cover her mouth, to press back the sobs that broke through her fingers. He regarded her sadly, for a moment, sighed and then gathered her up in his arms, cradling her head on his shoulder as the sobbing intensified.

'I'm sorry,' he whispered, rocking her gently to and fro. 'I'm sorry, you're right. It's not true. Of course he loves you ...'

'Mummy?' A voice intruded, barely audible over the blood pounding in her head. 'I've got a tummy egg.'

Matt groaned. 'You had better go to him,' he murmured, so close to Emily's ear she could feel his breath. She swayed as he unwrapped his arms. He steadied her, tenderly brushed her hair back from her tear-stained face and then, gently, pushed her away.

'Go,' he said.

And she did.

Chapter Four

Much as she disliked going to the constituency office, duty prevailed the following morning. There was the small matter also, that even folding leaflets was preferable to making polite conversation with Matt over the breakfast table.

TJ was looking grey-faced.

'Lovie,' he said when he saw Emily, 'bit of a balls-up on the media relations front.'

'Tell me about it,' said Emily, thinking about her behaviour with Matt the night before. On the other hand, TJ could hardly be expected to know about that. 'How so?' she asked.

'Village of the damned?' he said, raising an eyebrow.

'The Corfield release?' said Emily. Suddenly she gasped and put her hands to her face. 'Noooooo!'

'Oh, yes,' said TJ. 'I had a call from the Sussex Weekly asking if "Corfield – village of the damned" was an official rename or just the opinion of its MP. Then the radio guys called to ask if we planned to engage in some sort of exorcism or purification ceremony and, if yes, would the cost be covered by the council tax?'

'Ralph,' she said slowly and with grim certainty, 'will absolutely kill me.'

'Actually that's not true,' contested TJ, 'technically, he'll kill *me*. Publicity is my job after all.'

'You mean you wouldn't dob me in?'

TJ straightened up and stuck out his jaw. 'Certainly not,' he said, loyally.

'I'll tell him it was me, of course,' she said.

'I think the priority is to kill the story,' said a voice behind them. 'Leave the tearful confessions until later,' continued Matt, joining them.

She groaned. 'Not you again,' she said charmlessly. 'Do you always listen in to private conversations?'

'I'm a journalist,' he grinned, not remotely offended at her manner, 'it's what we do. Now,' he said briskly, 'who's it gone to?'

'All the media in the constituency basically,' she admitted.

'Okay, so that's a couple of weekly papers, local radio and the two TV station news desks who were probably going to ignore it anyhow. Lucky I've got contacts in low places.'

Matt sent TJ out to fetch them all some decent coffee – 'no offence mate but a cup of instant isn't going to cut it today,' – and then he hit the phone.

She had to admire his skill. Most of the contacts knew who he was by reputation and a couple appeared to know him personally, judging by the matey "how the hell are you" comments being bandied around.

The angle Matt went in on was simple. Printing the story would simply cause poor TJ to be sacked and alienate Ralph. As he had not even seen the release before it was sent out, any attempts to suggest that it reflected his personal views would fall on stony ground. In addition, they would ruin an otherwise fruitful relationship with Ralph's office which would be worth even more after the election, given that they would then have the Home Secretary himself in their constituency. He was sure TJ would make their loyalty worthwhile in the future. Finally he gave his word that if they spiked the story their competitors would spike it too.

The last point struck Emily as being particularly clever. 'Thank you,' she said, when he had put the phone down for the last time.

'You're welcome,' he replied, smiling warmly and draining his triple espresso. He had already sent TJ out for another one. Having barely slept after Emily left, caffeine – and plenty of it – was essential. 'Do you remember,' he said, 'when we were starting out, the only thing scarier than telling our editor we didn't have the story was him finding out that we didn't have it but our competitors did?'

'Oh yes,' she shuddered. 'Do you remember Brian? He was a sadist.'

'He was the editor from hell,' agreed Matt. 'I was livid with him when he made you call up the families of anyone who showed up in the obituaries that'd died young ...'

'So I could ask them what happened in case it was a gruesome story,' Emily continued, 'like being beheaded in a forklift truck accident or something ... I thought you were going to go in and wallop him.'

'I would have done, for you,' said Matt softly, enjoying how she smiled at the memory.

'Yeah, well,' she said, suddenly uncomfortable with their rapport. 'It was helpful really. It told me I was never going to cut it as a real journalist.'

'You *were* a real journalist. You may not have wanted to exploit grieving families but you were ruthless when it came to rooting out dodgy politicians. It just beats me why you went "poacher turned gamekeeper" on us all.'

'I didn't,' she protested. 'And also, I don't know what you mean, there's no dirt on Ralph. He's one of the good guys.'

'I really hope so. For your sake, I really do.'

She stared at him, aghast. 'Oh my God. You're here to do an exposé, aren't you?'

He shook his head but wouldn't meet her eye.

'You are,' she insisted, 'you want to dig up some revolting story to destroy my husband and his political career. Good grief, you really are bitter it didn't work out between us, aren't you? Even after ten years nothing would please you more than to reveal my husband as a sleazeball. You are unspeakable ...' she stopped, panting slightly.

'Do you think I'd have helped you out of this mess this morning if I wanted that?'

She had to admit he had a point.

'Listen if there's dirt to dig, I'll find it. That's what I do,' he snapped. 'I would be letting everyone down, the readers, the editor, my country, damn it, if I did anything else,' he paused. 'There was a time when you were the same.'

'I still am. I *am*. But ... my job is to support my husband now – and the party – and to raise my children. You know what? I really don't feel the need to have a career where I have to fight some sort of war everyday ...' she petered out, tears springing to her eyes.

Just then, they heard the door to the street slam as TJ returned with the coffee.

'I just hope for your sake that your precious husband is the paragon you think he is,' said Matt quietly before TJ came back in.

The next time Emily saw Ralph, she didn't have to confess about the balls-up with the release, as she had bribed TJ to admit it to him in advance. Luckily TJ totally understood, especially when she promised him a box of his favourite artisan chocolate truffles. Mind you it wasn't too much of a confession with no harm done after all – thanks to Matt's intervention. Trouble was, thinking about Matt reminded her about the other thing: Matt kissing her. There was certainly no need to mention that. No, the reason she didn't want to be admitting guilt about anything was because she was pretty keen to rip Ralph's head off over his indiscreet comments at supper with Matt and Susie. And she couldn't maintain the moral high ground if she had to admit fault first.

'I'm just saying,' she reasoned, after they had eaten supper together, 'from what I remember of my conversation with Gerald the other day, reminding key members of the media about the split in the party over the leadership is a very long way from being part of the current strategy.'

'He didn't need reminding,' Ralph replied. 'It was a

legitimate question, and the issue of the leadership contest is a matter of public record. As a journalist he's bound to ask.'

'You know perfectly well what I mean,' she continued. 'The whole pact thing – the pay-off for standing down. You're talking about being leader of the party again, even though,' she reminded him, 'we agreed after the last time, you wouldn't pursue the top job without us all deciding together. As a family.'

Ralph tried his charming smile. 'Come on darling ...' he wheedled.

'No,' she snapped. 'I don't agree. We haven't decided.'

'Yeah well,' he said, deciding there was no benefit to him in pursuing the conversation, 'pacts and promises notwithstanding, the fact is Alan's only fifty-eight, so the bugger's going nowhere. And anyway, there's the small matter of the election too. We haven't won it yet.'

Within a few days, election fever had replaced normal life to such an extent it had become normal life. Matt had gone back to London, where he was busy with other commissions, although he had promised to spend a few more days on the campaign trail and in central office before he wrote his piece. Emily felt both relieved and, strangely, flat that he had no plans to join them again in the constituency. Instead, all that was left from his visit was disturbing dreams at night and resurrection of bittersweet memories that overlaid all her daytime thoughts.

TJ had been right about Ralph being spirited away from home even more than before, with plans afoot for him to join the election bus for the vast majority of time in weeks to come, ensuring that the party presented a good selection of the key figures when campaigning in the marginal constituencies.

Emily slumped at the scrubbed pine kitchen table, cradling a cup of coffee. It was mid-morning and getting Alfie and Tash off to school had been wearing. Both of them were staying up late most evenings to try and catch a few words on the phone with their father. The previous night he was due home and Emily had made herself hugely unpopular by insisting that they went to bed without seeing him after they had stayed up to nearly nine o'clock. In the end Ralph had arrived after midnight, going straight to bed and disappearing the next morning before the rest of the family got up.

Not only were the late nights taking their toll, Emily was struggling to be sole parent. She would have valued Ralph coming back to lay down the law every once in a while, to say nothing of, only very occasionally, taking the children off her hands for an hour to give her a break. Not that he had ever done that very much.

She looked around her kitchen. Just spending time in it made her happy. Ralph had allowed her a loose rein and a generous budget when they bought the house in the constituency. She had obediently made the sitting and dining rooms rather grand to impress those people that MPs need to impress but Emily found them soulless spaces that had no role to play in family life. The children were not even allowed in unless supervised. By contrast, she had refused a posh handmade fitted kitchen, furnishing the large, high-ceilinged room with freestanding furniture she had picked up from the local auction room instead. Once she had painted it and rubbed it back artfully to make the most of its age and character, she thought everything looked pretty good.

Just when Ralph started to suggest she was going too far with the cheap options – being always mindful of the need to impress – she spent a horrifying amount on a brand new bright red enamelled stove that sat comfortably inside the huge hearth and kept the whole room cosy and warm. The scrubbed pine refectory table was her other favourite thing, surrounded by a selection of odd chairs, also repainted. The table top was positively enhanced – in Emily's view – by the embellishments of crayon, felt-tip and paint provided by the children over the years.

Brushing away tears that rose, unbidden and unexplained, to her eyes for the umpteenth time, she sighed, braced herself and grabbed the car keys from the dresser. Doing so, she noticed Ralph's mobile next to them. He would be furious to have left it behind. Then it occurred to her he might have thought he had lost it and be panicking about the security breach. After all, he had everyone including the future Prime Minister on autodial.

She picked it up and selected 'office' from the 'last number called' list.

'Darling,' came a husky female voice.

'Er ... hello?' said Emily, thinking she must have pressed the wrong button.

'Mrs P!' came a panicky squeak. 'I thought you were someone else.'

'Oh, hi Susie,' she said, recognising the voice. 'Likewise,' she added. 'I thought I had a wrong number. I just wanted you to tell Ralph I've got his phone. He left it behind this morning.'

'Oh sure. He hasn't mentioned it.' Was there even a note of criticism in Susie's voice? Then again, Emily found her husband's PA permanently mildly spiky. She ran Ralph's office with terrifying efficiency and a degree of imperiousness that he seemed blind to. On the contrary, Emily frequently had to tolerate Ralph's 'perfect Susie' eulogies.

'Yes, well, he probably hasn't realised yet,' reasoned Emily, slightly sharply.

'I'll send a car, we can't let it fall into the wrong hands.'

Emily swallowed her irritation that Susie clearly didn't think she was responsible enough to resist the temptation to – what? – stick it on Ebay? Sell it to the highest bidding tabloid newspaper ...?

'It's just a damned phone,' she snapped. 'He can have it back tonight.'

'He won't be home tonight. He needs to be here late for a vote, I expect he'll stay in the flat.'

'Right, okay, well, whatever you think best,' answered Emily, hanging up before she lost the battle with her temper and was unforgivably rude. Really, that woman needed taking down a peg or two. She seemed to think *she* was the woman in Ralph's life ...

And then Matt's words echoed in her ear. She, Emily, was only part of Team Pemilly until Ralph decided otherwise and who really knew what he was thinking or saying to the people around him?

Feeling nervous and undermined, she grabbed the offending phone and decided to drop it off at the constituency office to be collected from there. She was blowed if she was going to sit in the house all morning waiting for a car to turn up. She could have a coffee and a bitch with TJ in return for some constituency work. Gratifyingly, he was no fan of Susie's and could always be relied upon to take Emily's side.

Chapter Five

Pressing 'send' to file the copy of his latest article, Matt rubbed his eyes wearily, closed his laptop and then stretched, leaning back in his chair and staring at the magnolia ceiling of his study. Like the rest of his docklands flat, the room was furnished with a view to function rather than form. There was a desk with a reading lamp and floor to ceiling shelves along two of the four walls. The shelves were crammed vertically, horizontally and diagonally with books – mostly on the subjects of travel, politics and anthropology. Piles of those either acquired or used most recently had taken up residence on the floor. Among the books on a low shelf there was a decent but unobtrusive music system, the source of the Bach cello studies trickling into the room and drowning out the hum of traffic from the street below.

Matt had rented the flat several years before, basing his decision on nothing more emotional than its proximity to his newspaper offices and to City airport. The latter was a convenient portal in his frequent trips to the European parliament where he never failed to unearth a story of political corruption, greed, vanity or all of the above to serve up to his readers. His boss didn't require him to be in the office much. It was enough that he filed his copy, and that it was sharp, accurate and on time which it invariably was. Matt had little in his life outside of work to distract him.

This was not to say he lived like a monk. Plenty of women had seen his bedroom, which contained even fewer hints as to his personality than his study. He chose his partners carefully, mind you. It would be too easy to exploit all the breathless, eager young women whose heads were turned by his looks and his untouchable demeanour. These he kindly but firmly detached, flattering them so warmly they hardly knew they had been rejected. His choice, when his craving for companionship was too much to resist any longer, was the hard-headed and the hard-hearted women who knew what they wanted and were as happy as Matt was to move on the following day. Since Emily there had been a few of those. None of them reminded him of her though. That was the way he liked it.

His draft of the Ralph Pemilly article had been completed several days ago but it still nagged at his thoughts. He had come up with a perfectly workmanlike piece, exploring Ralph's meteoric rise through the party ranks and commenting on whether the country would be best served by such career politicians or whether the voters were looking for ministers who had more experience in the real world. It was a rather obvious and uninspired angle, but it would do. For now. There was still a while to go until he had to file it. He would wait. Sometimes a new angle would come to light and the work would be all the better for it.

An incoming text message pinged into his thoughts. Glancing over at his phone, he was surprised to see it was from Susie. As a professional courtesy he had given her his card when they met at supper not imagining she would use it.

She wanted to meet him, the text said. In private.

'How interesting,' he murmured, tapping his phone thoughtfully on the desk.

'How very, very interesting.'

After the 'village of the damned' debacle, TJ was scared of giving Emily any remotely challenging constituency work to do. She absolutely hated standing on doorsteps asking how people were going to vote and so mainly she was stuck in the office, folding leaflets and making endless cups of tea for the volunteers who bustled in and out being terribly self-important, the general election being quite the most exciting thing that had happened to them for years.

The one enormous upside was that Emily was seeing more of Nessa than ever. She was a frequent visitor to the office, wafting in glamorously in a swirl of floaty scarves and exotic perfume. Despite being at least sixty-five, as far as Emily could make out – she would never ask – Nessa made Emily feel dowdy in her smart but anonymous black trousers, worn with a selection of boring tops. She was reminded acutely and painfully of her early career, when she wore mainly vintage frocks, artfully altered if necessary, with an eccentric line in tights and a pair of trademark over the knee boots. And then the politician's wife's need for propriety had asserted itself. Abandoning her instinctive style had left her floundering without a look altogether. Somewhere along the line with pregnancy, babies and fatigue, Emily had given up taking an interest in her appearance.

'Nessa?' she asked one morning, as they stood over a chuntering photocopier together.

'Yes, my love?'

'You know when,' Emily paused. 'You know when Arthur first got his seat?'

'Yeees,' she replied, patiently.

'Actually, not then,' continued Emily. 'I mean yes then, but also when Arthur was first made a minister?'

'After the election, like Ralph will be?'

'If we win, yes. Were you – I don't know, it probably sounds really silly – but were you scared?'

'Mmm, I wondered when you were going to have an attack of the collywobbles,' said Nessa, putting a comforting arm around Emily's shoulders.

Tears sprang to her eyes again, and she brushed them away crossly. 'I just don't know what's the matter with me,' she wailed. 'It's what Ralph has always wanted, and now it finally looks like it's going to happen, I just – I just don't want anything to change.'

Nessa nodded and waited.

'I think,' she continued, slowly, staring unseeing at the wall, 'I think I'm scared because I thought I had made all the right decisions, and that I was happy with where we were going – together – me and Ralph.' She looked imploringly at Nessa, willing her to understand something she barely understood herself.

'And now?'

'Now ...? Now I don't know. Maybe,' she said, pushing her hands into her hair against her scalp and pulling it hard, 'maybe the truth is I made a really, really big mistake years ago and everything else that has happened since has been the wrong thing? Do you understand?'

Nessa smiled wryly. 'And "how", darling. And "how". But you don't mean the children of course. You don't regret them?'

'Heavens, no! I absolutely love and adore my babies with every fibre of my being,' she gabbled. 'How can I even say I have regrets about anything that might cause them not to exist? I'm a horrible person,' she concluded, slumping.

'Some people say I'm a wise old bird,' replied Nessa slowly. 'I'm not sure about the wisdom but I'm certainly an old bird, and in my considerable experience there is always the road you take and the road you could have taken ... It seems to me if it's not the children that you regret, it's something to do with Ralph and all that being married to him entails?'

Emily nodded reluctantly. 'That's a bit blunt, but, yes, I suppose you know better than anyone, you take on a lot with the whole politician thing ... it's not the person, Ralph's lovely ...'

'But it's a tough brief being a politician's wife.'

Emily nodded.

'And ... you're wishing you married someone else?'

'No!' squeaked Emily, 'Absolutely not!'

'Mm. I thought as much. Who was he?'

Emily shot Nessa a look. 'Well, it's all a bit academic obviously.'

'Obviously.'

'No, I mean "academic" because he didn't want me.'

'How can that be?'

'I know – bizarre,' she said, wryly. 'At least I didn't think he did. It was all a bit of a mess. A confusing time,' and heart-breaking too, she thought but didn't say.

'Look darling,' said Nessa decisively, 'we all play the "what if" game every once in a while, but, listen, you've got a pretty good life, two gorgeous children and a man with an amazing future ahead of him. Don't throw it all away on some adolescent "maybe". I know it sounds harsh, but you've made your bed.' She raised her eyebrows, and Emily nodded meekly.

'I'm fine,' she said, patting her friend's arm. 'Ignore my silly spells.'

'Talk to me about the wibbles and wobbles,' said Nessa, making Emily look her direct in the eye. 'I'm a safe sounding board. Not everyone is.'

Emily wouldn't have minded getting a bit of moral support from TJ too but, when they were both mind-numbingly stuffing envelopes later that day, she found him unusually morose.

'Wassup?' she asked.

'Ooh, nothing, really ...' he replied listlessly.

'TJ?'

'No, it's just...' he sighed, deeply. 'Well, it's all this,' he said waving a limp hand at all the envelopes.

'I know, it's really boring,' agreed Emily.

'Boring? No, it's not really,' disagreed TJ, surprisingly. 'I quite like all this sort of thing. The election, the new opportunities, all that promise and possibility ...' he tailed off, sadly.

'Ah,' deduced Emily. 'New opportunities. Come on, give.'

'Ralph said he'd put me forward to be on the candidates' list for a safe seat,' TJ blurted at last.

'He did,' remembered Emily. 'Still nothing?'

TJ shook his head.

'Well! Why on earth not?'

'Oh, well, you know …'

'No.' said Emily, 'I don't know.'

'He's pretty busy …'

'That's just so typical …' she fumed, the bit firmly between her teeth. 'Not that we want to lose you of course, but – for goodness sake – this is your career.' She knew that TJ had long wanted to stand as parliamentary candidate. He was incredibly able and had been a vital part of the Ralph Pemilly team machinery for several years, honing his skills and experience. He was going to be a superb MP. All he needed was for Ralph to help him take the next step, which he was well able to do. But he hadn't bothered and Emily was furious. Usually she struggled to stay cross for long but this time it was different. Her anger boiled up every time she thought of poor TJ and, by the end of the day, she had decided – for once – to take Ralph to task.

She heard the front door slam.

'Hi darling,' said Ralph blithely as he closed the front door and came into the kitchen, where she was chopping carrots for supper.

'Don't you "hi darling" me,' she hissed.

'Okay,' said Ralph, looking guarded. 'How about "hi sweetie"?'

'No.'

'"Hi gorgeous"?'

'No! Shut up.'

'Right-o.'

There was a brief silence while Emily fumed.

'Well? Are you going to keep your promise to TJ or not?' she blurted, waving the carrot knife threateningly under Ralph's nose.

'Er, yes I am,' he hazarded, nervously. 'Absolutely.'

'I should damned well think so too!' she said, the wind rather taken out of her sails by his immediate capitulation. 'That's all right then,' she added, lowering the knife self-consciously. She wasn't altogether sure she hadn't just stamped her foot. Hopefully not.

'Excellent. Good,' said Ralph, confident he was on firmer ground. 'Erm, what promise was that exactly?'

'Well that's just typical!' she shouted. 'You don't even know! You just carry blithely on, expecting us all to … to … do everything you say … and we do it don't we?' she squeaked, nodding frantically for emphasis. 'And you just think that all you have to do is … is … keep telling us all what we want to hear, don't you? Don't you?' she demanded, waving the knife again.

'Yes,' said Ralph, keen to agree. 'Actually no,' he added, on reflection.

'Yes you do,' insisted Emily. 'You do. All the time, and you just take it for granted. He's stalling his career for you. It's his life, for God's sake. All you have to do is make a call, have a conversation with one of your revolting cronies. TJ would make the most fantastic MP – a damned sight better than half the old farts the party has now, but no, you won't lift a finger …'

'Okay,' said Ralph slowly. 'I'm with you – at last … Look,' he said, raising his hands placatingly, keeping a wary eye on the vegetable knife, 'I did say I'd put in a word but – darling – you can't seriously expect me to do without TJ. Not now. There's plenty of time. He's barely thirty …'

'He's thirty-two actually. And you should bloody well know how old he is.'

'Okay, thirty-two, and you're right, I should help him,' agreed Ralph with relief. 'Right after the election. I promise you, next by-election that comes up he'll be on the list. I guarantee it.'

Emily wasn't at all sure she believed him. Matt's criticisms about Team Pemilly were still ringing in her ears and – she hated to admit it – they were looking increasingly accurate. Ultimately, for all his charm, diplomacy and wit, Ralph, she realised, always did exactly what suited him best. It was extraordinary how compliant they all were with him though. He only had to hint at what he wanted and, thanks to his sense of entitlement and casual privilege, the devoted little bunch leapt to attention. Susie, TJ, even Emily herself, she admitted. They were all as guilty as each other.

At least the photographer's visit meant that Ralph would be at home, she thought when she heard, although Ralph, who had been circling her nervously since their little chat, would probably have been happier to be elsewhere. The brief was for the photographer to shadow Ralph, just like Matt had done, recording in pictures every aspect of his life, from his role as family man with charming children – not sure whose children they were going to borrow to create that impression, she thought – through to his matey relationship with constituents and local supporters. Again, she wasn't certain where they were going to find constituents to tell that story – perhaps Equity ... and then there was his forthright, thrusting persona as Home Secretary in waiting, a key force in the new team set to run the country, if the polls were to be believed.

The photographer was charming. A South African called Kevin, who was delightfully playful and chatty, although she recognised his name and knew that he had done some very dark work in Rwanda, which seemed at odds with his Pollyanna attitude to life. A defence mechanism, she decided.

It was all a bit staged, with Ralph pretending to help Tash with her homework at one end of the kitchen table while Emily made chocolate hedgehogs with Alfie at the other. Ralph was looking handsome and modern in an open-necked shirt and jeans and Emily had made the children wear clean clothes – something Alfie was fiercely opposed to on principle. The overall impression was of a perfect family from a Boden catalogue.

'Have you heard of the curse of Hello magazine?' joked Kevin. 'It's the same with us. These pictures come out and you'll be divorced within the month.'

'You mean when the perfect politician, daddy and husband is exposed as a double-crossing fetishist with a penchant for kinky sex with small, old, bald men in leather masks and nappies?' asked Emily.

'At least it won't be a shock then,' he said, sighing in fake relief.

Later, she showed Kevin her computer so he could send his pictures to the office.

'So,' she said, casually, while they were waiting for the pictures to upload, 'do you know Matt well?'

'We work together quite a bit,' he replied. 'He's a sound guy.'

'Single?'

'Yeah,' he said, not showing any signs he thought it an odd question. 'Lots of women around him, mind you. Good-looking ones too, lucky bastard.'

'No-one special then?'

'Not in all the time I've known him. A shame really, when you think he could take his pick ...' he mused. 'There was someone once, I think. It messed him up pretty bad.'

'What do you know about her?'

'Bog all,' he replied. 'I can't get him to say anything about it, although I have to say we talk about everything else. Like I said, whoever she was, she messed him up bad.' He thought for a bit. 'Yeah, he's a good bloke though.'

'Good,' said Emily, feeling she had to explain her nosiness. 'Dealing with the press is – well – exposing.'

'Interesting choice of words! Something to hide?'

'Well, only the little old bald blokes in nappies, but why should *I* worry?'

'Absolutely,' he laughed. 'You of all people should know that stuff, though' he continued. 'Matt mentioned you were a journalist yourself in a former life?'

'Never a muckraking one, like Matt.'

'I'm sure not! You've got him wrong though ... He's good at getting the story, but he's not a sleazy bastard. Not that I've seen anyhow.'

'I think I'll be the judge of that,' she muttered.

Chapter Six

Emily palmed off the children onto friends for a play date and attended a constituency surgery where Ralph hoped to join them later.

A draughty village hall smelling of dust and Dettol was the venue. TJ was there to meet her. 'A couple of regulars, one nasty, one nutty, and an elderly lady who wants Ralph to get her young, fit boyfriend out of Ghana,' he muttered by way of a briefing. 'It's true love apparently.'

'Of course it is,' she said. 'Right, let's dive in.'

'He's a lovely man, your husband,' said Mrs Butterworth comfortably, shifting her bulk in the chair to take the weight off one of her puffy ankles. She wore a tweed skirt coated in white dog hair from the smelly little Westie that sat, sulking, under her chair.

'So I says to my friend Joan,' she continued, 'I says, Mr Pemilly won't let them change that bus route, I says, 'cos he cares about the people 'oo voted for 'im. He knows what side his bread's buttered don't he. So I told the man at the Council, I said "I'll have none of your lip, young man," and then I come 'ere,' she finished triumphantly.

Emily had reassured Mrs Butterworth that Ralph would write quite the strongest letter to the County Council on the matter, and had told another 'frequent flyer' constituent with mental health problems that Ralph was quite safe to vote for because he wasn't planning to switch his allegiance to the Zargan Democratic Union. This, Emily patiently explained to him, was not least because there had been no constitutional possibility of a political party from another galaxy being eligible to field a candidate in an Earth-bound election.

Then there was a further upsetting interview with a

constituent who was desperate about her son's failure to get into the best local primary school because they had recently moved into the area, were outside catchment and there were simply no places. Frustratingly, she was unable to offer her a lot of help but she thanked her lucky stars that the village school didn't really have a lot of choice about taking Alfie when he started in September because Ralph and Emily had made damned sure their house was nice and close to it. They won't know what's hit them, she mused, having been lulled into a false sense of security by Tash who was surprisingly angelic at school. As far as Emily could gather, from the glowing reports at parents' evenings, Tash saved her grumpiness and sloth for home time only.

And still TJ kept feeding them through to the main room in the village hall where the 'surgery' consisted of a couple of hard chairs and a small table in a draughty corner.

'I want to make a complaint about our MP – he's rubbish,' said a nasal, whining voice into her left ear.

She jumped and spun around, nearly falling off her chair.

'Hallo darling,' said Ralph, dropping a kiss on the top of her head. 'TJ tells me you've seen off hordes of whingers, loonies and charlatans.'

'Shush,' she said, looking around guiltily. 'That's an awful thing to say.' Ralph was always appalling about his constituents behind their backs. It worried Emily, who was irreverent but never cruel.

'Well, you're all done. Every last one, so we can go home,' he said, 'thanks to you.'

'Just say the word,' she replied, loyally. 'Anything I can do. You know that.'

'Great. Darling you're a trouper. Actually there is just one thing at the moment – could you possibly get Susie a present for me? It was her birthday today and I forgot.'

'Oops. Poor Susie,' she said, even though she didn't mean it. 'What sort of thing did you have in mind?'

'Well, she's got a cracking figure, probably about your size,' he said, looking Emily up and down. 'She's actually, a bit slimmer now I think of it. Maybe get her some silk underwear or something ... a negligee or whatever women wear these days.'

'A bit personal isn't it?' queried Emily, trying to ignore the casual "you are fat" implication.

'Nah,' said Ralph, waving away her protest. 'That's what everyone gets their staff these days. It doesn't mean anything.'

'I'll get two of everything then,' she said, personally unconvinced. 'That way you can give the same to TJ when it's his birthday.'

The next morning, thanks to Emily, Susie was delighted to have a large, expensive-looking box delivered to her. Unfolding the striped tissue paper within, she uncovered an exquisite oyster silk set of French knickers and camisole with a matching wrap. It contained a printed message card, supposedly from Ralph, thanking her for her hard work and wishing her many happy returns. Her lips pursed. Far from being too racy, the gift was a little less intimate than she had been expecting – or hoping for.

'Will we have to move?' said Tash, suddenly over tea.

'What, darling?' asked Emily, although she had heard perfectly.

'When Daddy's party wins the election. We'll have to go and live somewhere else won't we? In London? Where Daddy's office is?'

'I don't think so darling. Not if we don't want to.' She ruffled Tash's hair. 'We don't want to leave here, do we?'

'Nope,' said Tash, reassured and tackling her ice cream with new energy. 'We want to stay here. Daddy can just come home when he feels like it. Like now.'

'He would be here more, if he could, darling. When the election is over things will be better.'

'When I'm at big boy's school, will Daddy come to get me at home time?' said Alfie, flicking a glob of ice cream at a pigeon sitting on the windowsill. It splatted on the glass and slid down slowly.

'Don't do that, darling,' she admonished. 'I hope he'll be able to sometimes,' she added, without conviction.

Having got the children to bed at last, she poured herself a glass of wine and lit the fire in the poshest of the two sitting rooms to sit and wait for Ralph to come home. He had promised to make it back in time for a late end of the week dinner and – unusually – to have a whole day with the family the next day, although Sunday saw him back to the electoral grindstone, having to travel up to Cheshire for intensive lobbying starting early on the Monday.

She pondered, over her wine, recalling how they had planned, together, exactly how much he would do professionally, and how work would fit with family life. Somewhere along the line, the goalposts had been moved. The invitation to join the shadow cabinet had been the point where the joint promises had been forgotten. The time spent in London had increased and, when the leadership issue was being discussed, he had sounded her out on whether she would support him standing. Knowing that winning an election with him as leader would inevitably lead to moving the family to London – no Prime Minister had ever lived in his constituency – they had jointly agreed against it. In the end, the decision had been a bit academic with the party choosing to go for Alan, the man with the age and gravitas. Even then she had doubted the veracity of his assurances but had been soothed by the relatively low rating of the party in the polls at the time. When Alan won the leadership too, she felt she could afford to relax a little.

That was then.

'Will things change much if we win?' asked Emily, when Ralph had finally returned and eaten supper.

'What brings this on suddenly?'

'Tash was asking today. She's not brought it up before. Plus we got the letter today, confirming Alfie has a place at school for September.'

'We'll be here, darling, of course we will. Whatever, happens,' he said vaguely, his mind clearly already on other things. Then, she saw him drag himself back and he tried again.

'I will have to spend more time in London obviously,' he said, squaring his shoulders. 'We'll get more help in the constituency of course.' He glanced at her, checking for her approval. 'I hugely appreciate all the work you do for me here, but I'll need you beside me in London more often once we are holding the reins. There'll be events, ceremonial stuff. We'll have a grace and favour apartment. There are some amazing places to choose from ...'

'Sounds nice enough.'

'It will be. Once the children are older you can come and join me in town in the week. We can go to the theatre, the opera ... Whatever you want.'

'Will we really win?'

'The polls say we will. Mind you, there's still three weeks to go. Anything could happen'.

Chapter Seven

At around two in the morning the telephone rang, shrilling through the house like an emergency. In Emily's sleep it transformed into a nightmarish dream about fire alarms and trying to escape with the children through a house she no longer recognised, the familiar layout turning into endless corridors of smoke with no doors and no windows.

Eventually, although it must have been just seconds later, Emily awoke sweating to hear Ralph in bed beside her, talking on the phone.

'So, what's the prognosis?' he barked, as alert as if he had just drunk ten espressos and had eight hours sleep.

'Okay, well, keep me posted if you hear anything – anything at all.' A pause, and then, 'Sure. Send a car. Tell them I'll be there by – what?' she saw him check the luminous dial of the alarm clock, 'three o'clock, at the latest.' He paused again, while the other person spoke and then made his perfunctory goodbyes.

Before she had a chance to ask him anything, he was out of bed, switching on the light, and rummaging around for clothes.

'It's Alan,' he explained as he hurriedly dressed. 'Heart attack, an hour ago. He's still alive but it's not looking good.'

She watched him, dazed, as he moved around the room, gathering up his phone, wallet, car keys. His expression was grim, purposeful … excited.

Giving her a careless kiss, he was gone.

She lay awake, rigid, staring at the ceiling after he had left. Hours later, just after she had collapsed into an exhausted sleep, the children got up and were simultaneously squabbling and complaining of starvation. Wearily, she dragged herself out of bed and co-ordinated some breakfast. Of course she had heard nothing from Ralph and knew better than to interrupt whatever vital conversations were going on by calling his mobile. Instead, she flicked on the radio as she made a strong cup of tea to revive herself.

Almost immediately, she was shocked to hear Ralph's voice. 'Our overriding concern, at this time,' he was saying, 'is for Alan and his family. It would be wholly inappropriate to speculate on the General Election and the effect on it of Alan's sudden illness which has shocked and saddened us all.'

Turning off the radio, Emily switched to watching the twenty-four hour news on television where Alan's heart attack was either being discussed by a series of pundits or was scrolling across the bottom of the screen while they briefly covered the rest of the news.

Ralph's interview was repeated periodically, alternating with comments from the party chairman James, who Emily knew vaguely, stating that the party had no plans to consider a replacement leader at that time.

Rubbish of course, thought Emily. She had tried calling Ralph on his mobile but it was permanently on answerphone. She contemplated calling his office for an update but was reluctant to have to declare to Susie that she wasn't in the know. By teatime, still with no direct contact, she had no choice.

'Oh hello Mrs P,' came the chirpy, condescending voice. As always Emily resented being patronised by a woman barely a couple of years younger than her but Susie had always refused to call her by her first name. 'I really do think it is important to maintain that respect,' she had said to Emily when she gently invited her to do so. Respect, my arse, she had thought. Knowing perfectly well, as Susie did, that in fact, she was being put firmly in her place as a person to be tolerated and humoured – outside the circle of power which Susie considered herself very much a part of.

'Isn't it awful about Alan?' continued Susie, speaking slightly slower and clearer with the voice that Emily knew she saved specially for her. 'Of course now he's had the second one, things have changed here a bit.'

'A second heart attack? Are you sure? There's been nothing on the news.'

'Quite sure,' she replied, triumphantly, delighted to be in the know. 'Has Ralph not been in touch?' She didn't wait for a reply, knowing perfectly well that he hadn't. 'I'm afraid it's all over bar the shouting. There was a massive second heart attack a couple of hours ago. They're just keeping him on life support until his children can get there to say goodbye.'

Tears pricked Emily's eyes. How devastated they must all feel, his wife, his children – albeit that they were grown up with children of their own. It was too difficult to comprehend, for the poor man to be Prime Minister in waiting that morning and for the sun to set on the end of his life, just hours later.

'So, when will they announce it?' she said, at last.

'When they've decided what to say,' explained Susie. 'It's headless chicken central here at the moment. I should imagine they'll want to announce a plan at the same time as a memorial, for fear of losing the lead we've gained. We can't leave a ship without a captain, can we? Not with just three weeks until polling day.'

'I suppose not.'

'Of course it's terribly exciting for Ralph.'

'Why?' queried Emily, knowing the answer.

'Well ...' Susie demurred, 'it's the big opportunity isn't it? The answer to a dream for us all I'm sure, if we're honest. The PM post – and barely in his forties? Extraordinary really ...'

'I hardly think— '

'Absolutely,' interjected Susie hastily, realising she had gone too far.

'... and without us having discussed it ...' Emily continued, sure of her ground here at least. He would *never* allow such a thing to be announced without her agreement, whatever had gone before. And she wouldn't give it, of course, especially after the discussion they had had about it the other night.

Damn him, why didn't he call?

Suddenly, there he was on the screen, looking sombre, head bowed, with James at his side. They were both wearing black ties. She was pretty sure Ralph didn't own a black tie, which was probably an oversight on her part. Inconsequentially she wondered how he had got it. Probably that annoyingly efficient cow Susie had sorted it out for him.

The television presenter was saying '... and now, live, from party headquarters, is the statement we have been waiting for.'

James spoke first, announcing the death of their party leader, expressing sympathy to the family, paying tribute to his extraordinary achievements and then – within seconds it seemed – handing over to Ralph.

With unusual deference, he kept his head slightly bowed and eyes lowered as he spoke.

She stared at him intently, only vaguely aware of the words at first, tuning in eventually to hear him finish: '...with Alan having so recently taken over the leadership of the party, we are in the privileged position of being quite clear about Alan's wishes and the wishes of the party should a new leader be required as is now so suddenly and distressingly the case.

'And so, it is with the humility that is born of taking up the chalice from such an exemplary leader, that I pledge my energies to serving my party and – if the electorate wish it – my country.'

Emily screamed. And then when that didn't do enough to vent her wrath, she flung her mug at the television screen. Luckily it was empty.

Now, his face had disappeared from the screen anyway,

replaced by the anchor man burbling on about strategic rebranding and regaining the confidence of the electorate within the three weeks remaining until polling day.

She glanced at the clock. There was just twenty minutes until she had to collect Tash from her after school club and Alfie from his friend's house where he had, thankfully, been having a play date. She had to pull herself together.

Just as she took a couple of deep breaths to steady herself, the telephone rang. She leapt at it hoping to goodness it was Nessa. Now, more than ever, she could do with a dose of her common sense and wisdom.

'Hi, Emily.'

'You bastard!'

'Darling, I'm sorry. I meant to call you.'

'So I notice,' she said, scathingly. 'Have I unwittingly been waiting next to a broken phone all day? Was it inadvertently off the hook? Did I spend too long chatting to my mates on it, preventing you from involving me in quite the most massive decision of our whole lives which – mysteriously – you seem to feel is a choice to be taken entirely without my input?'

Vaguely, she was pleased with herself at managing to be so articulate – even sarcastic – despite the fact that hearing his voice meant that her chest was heaving frantically and she could barely catch her breath.

'Darling of course you're upset,' he soothed. 'We need to talk. That's a top priority of course ...' he sounded as if he was talking to himself now, checking off a list of problems to be solved. 'I'll get away just as soon as I can, it's completely mental here. Just hold on darling.'

She made a dismissive noise.

'Oh, and darling?'

'Hmm?'

'Don't make any comment to the media will you? Not until we've decided what to say.'

She gave a hollow laugh. It almost sounded like they

would be thinking up a response to the press together. Now she knew differently.

Minutes later, the phone rang again. Ralph. She let it ring, six, seven, eight times and then snatched it up, unable to bear the strident tone any longer.

'What?'

'Emily?'

'Matt!'

'Are you all right? A bit of a day for you both obviously.'

Not for the first time that day, she had an overwhelming desire to collapse sobbing.

'I – I can't talk to you.'

'Sure, no, I understand. I'm not calling for a quote.'

'You're not?'

'Actually no,' he replied. 'I just wanted to know you were all right,' he paused, 'and to let you know the magazine has stalled the story I wrote.'

'They did? You mean they've spiked it? Why?'

'God no, they're running it all right,' he replied. 'But what with Ralph being in the frame for the big job they've decided what they've got is dynamite.'

'Tell me about it,' muttered Emily. Just imagine what they'd think if they could hear the conversation she was going to have with Ralph the next time she saw him. That would be flipping front page stuff ...

'... so anyway,' he was continuing, 'we're going to need to keep following the whole thing through to the end. The editor wants to run a major profile, straight after the election – assuming Ralph wins of course. A kind of "fly on the wall" the making of a Prime Minister thing ... Emily?' he said, 'Are you there?'

'Yes,' she said, faintly. Just hearing the words 'Ralph' and 'Prime Minister' in the same sentence made her feel quite dizzy with fear.

'I've been told to stick to Ralph like glue – for the duration. Just thought I'd – well – warn you.'

'Great, yes, thanks. So … I'll see you around.'

She observed, with a peculiar detachment, that the promise of Matt's continued presence leading up to the election was reassuring. But somehow disturbing too.

Matt hung up and stared at the wall, thoughtfully. Of course, being in line for Prime Minister was plenty reason enough for his editor, Mike's, decision to run a bigger piece.

If he knew the other new angle Matt was suspecting his response could only be guessed at …

Chapter Eight

The next time Emily saw Ralph, she was giving Alfie and Tash tea.

'Daddy, Daddy,' they both clamoured. 'You're home at last,' Tash continued as if life had been unbearable in the inadequate care of their mere mother.

'You're lucky,' Emily hissed in his ear without them hearing. 'If we were on our own I would bloody tear you limb from limb.'

'Thanks darling,' he replied, cheerily. 'Well chaps,' he said to the children, 'isn't this exciting? Daddy might be Prime Minister.'

'Is that bigger than home secetrarary?' asked Alfie.

'Home Secretary,' enunciated Tash with crushing precision.

'Oh yes,' said Ralph, 'much bigger.'

'Dan's daddy's a policeman,' continued Alfie. 'Is it bigger than that?' he demanded with an air of triumph. Surely Daddy couldn't beat that, was the sub-text.

'Of course it is, stupid,' snapped Tash. 'Daddy's going to run the country.'

'If people vote for me,' he qualified, modestly.

'Well I won't be voting for you,' muttered Emily.

'Do try to resist the temptation to think out loud when Matt gets here won't you?' he snapped.

'Oh great, that's all I need.' She had assumed they might have a couple of days' grace to have a marital row without an audience. 'When?'

Ralph looked at his watch. As he did, the doorbell rang.

'Saved by the bell,' he sighed, and strode off.

She rubbed her face wearily. Great. She could hear Matt congratulating Ralph in the hallway. Bloody sycophant, she thought. 'And I look a right state', she told herself. And *yes*, she did mind.

'Hi Matt,' she said, as he came in, careful not to meet his eye. 'We're all in a bit of confusion I'm afraid. It's rather late.'

She hoped he would take the hint that his arrival was far from convenient.

'Sorry,' he said unrepentantly. 'Don't let me interrupt.'

'I'm going to get the children to bed,' Emily told Ralph. Chivvying the protesting children upstairs, she spent as long as possible getting teeth brushed and clothes changed, reading stories and sorting washing. Then, she ran herself a really deep, hot bath and soaked in it until she turned wrinkly. Still Ralph didn't come up to talk to her. Avoidance tactics if ever she saw them. Refusing, on principle, to go down and make polite conversation with her ex-lover and – frankly – a man she was currently happy to consider as her ex-husband, Emily put on her favourite, least alluring pyjamas and went to bed. She needn't have worried about having to fight off advances – from either of them.

In bed, her eyes pinned open with nervous exhaustion, she could hear the low rumble of male voices, Matt and Ralph talking late into the night. The general tone was obviously cordial, with appreciative laughter on both sides, but Emily's heart pounded in her chest as she strained to hear the content of their conversation, paranoid that either one of them was disclosing confidences to the other about her. Matt's Stepford wife taunt of the other night still stung and she felt judged and belittled for exactly the qualities Ralph knew her for. *Will the real Emily please step forward*, she thought, wryly, as she put her pillow over her head and, eventually, fell asleep.

Days later, she had still not had a chance to discuss things with her husband. She reckoned Ralph could have tried a little harder to make time. How else could she communicate that she was not speaking to him?

On the day of Alan's funeral they had no choice but to be in the same room. Even then, Ralph decided that Emily would have to meet him in Westminster Abbey as he would already be in London. Normally she would have asked Nessa to look after the children but, as she would have to attend as well, she had no choice but to ask Ralph's mother.

'But Mummy,' Tash had said, 'the only thing she ever talks about is how I'm doing at school.'

'Quite right, darling. At least she shows an interest,' said Emily brightly.

'But she makes us eat yucky sardines,' said Alfie. 'And she smells,' he added.

'She doesn't smell,' argued Emily. Actually she did smell faintly and unappealingly of lavender cologne and mothballs. Ralph's mother was old-school. Long ago widowed and rigorously slim, she was unforgivingly straight of back and strict of demeanour, living for church, mother's union and occasional lunches with similarly widowed old women with whom she spoke disapprovingly of 'the youth of today'.

'It's only for a few hours,' she wheedled. 'We'll get pizza tonight, shall we?'

'How about chips?' said Alfie, sensing weakness.

'Or Chinese?' asked Tash, pressing the advantage.

'Maybe. We'll see what Daddy wants to do, shall we?' she added, neither caring nor expecting that he would be around to ask.

To add insult to injury, Susie had made the travel arrangements. She had seen fit to organise a car for herself and Ralph to be brought from central office and another for Emily, collecting Matt and dropping off the children en route.

'Hi!' said Matt as he joined them, throwing himself into the back of the car and pressing his long thigh unnecessarily against Emily's as he did so. He looked with frank appreciation at her nylon-clad legs until she tugged her skirt down, scowling at him.

'Hello Matt,' she said, being icily polite for the sake of the children.

'Hey kids,' he replied, grinning widely and taking his eyes reluctantly off her legs.

'Hello Matt,' they both squeaked, disloyally, obviously delighted to see him.

'Are you coming to Mama Pemilly with us?' said Alfie.

'Don't think so,' he said, 'although it sounds fun.'

'It won't be,' Tash observed.

'You're covering the funeral I take it,' said Emily primly, attempting to turn things to a professional level.

'You bet. The king is dead, long live the king – and all that sort of thing.'

'Not quite king yet,' she pointed out. 'Two weeks to polling day, after all.'

'All right, the heir apparent is dead, long live the heir apparent,' said Matt, amenably. 'How are you?' he added, ducking his head down to meet her eyes. 'You're looking tired.'

'Thanks very much,' she said. 'You say the sweetest things.'

'You're welcome,' he replied, unmoved by her sarcasm. 'Hey kids, how about a game of I-spy?'

'Me first, me first,' said Alfie, bouncing in his seat excitedly. 'I spy, with my little eye, something beginning with … "tree".'

Tash gave a snort.

'Er, would it be "tree"?' hazarded Matt, clearly amused.

'No!' shouted Alfie. 'Lamp post. I win! I win!'

Matt was still laughing when they arrived at Emily's mother-in-law's Knightsbridge flat. The children were quickly despatched into her care and they continued, not speaking, to the Abbey.

The press pack outside were a tiered mob, with photographers at the back perched precariously on step ladders. Crush barriers separated them from the funeral attendees, who were being decanted from a stream of black limousines. Matt had peeled off immediately and Ralph was nowhere in sight, leaving her to walk in alone. The focus group people had been driving themselves mad over the question of whether or not she should wear a hat. Eventually it was agreed that she should wear a small fascinator – a plain black band with a token veil which made her feel a complete pillock. Actually, it went rather beautifully with her severe but sexily cut black suit with its nipped in jacket and narrow skirt that suited her curvy figure. She looked simultaneously youthful and elegant but felt self-conscious for having made such a conspicuous effort.

The twittering focus group had a reason for their even greater than normal indecision though. Alan, being leader of the opposition, was not even a former Prime Minister or cabinet member, meaning a highly formal state event was inappropriate. On the other hand, the great and good were petrified of seeming churlish or ungracious. Consequently, a service at Westminster Abbey had been hastily convened where all the right people would attend. The current Prime Minister was expected to give a flattering address and the cabinet of the dissolved parliament were to turn out in force, looking grave and respectful.

After the service the plan was for the coffin to travel from the Abbey to Alan's Surrey constituency. There it would be laid to rest in the churchyard of his tiny local church with only close family present – to Emily's relief as she found burials hopelessly gruelling and always cried buckets.

She was shown by an usher to her seat. She sat, keeping her head bowed, partly to avoid catching the eye of anyone she knew but whose name she couldn't remember. Looking up surreptitiously, she saw Ralph, standing next to Susie in a group milling around at the front. Even from twenty yards away, their backs were amazingly eloquent. His head was bent solicitously down to Susie as she, with her hand on his arm, whispered something in his ear. He nodded approvingly and gave her an admiring look. Emily tried and failed to remember the last time he had looked so warmly at her.

After a minute Ralph was led by an usher to join her, initially too involved with nodding seriously at people to acknowledge her. Then, probably mindful of the media and his image, he kissed her on the cheek, with half an eye on the bank of selected media who had been allowed into the service itself. At the end of the row sat Matt, looking impeccable in his dark suit and black tie although the formality of his dress contrasted oddly with his slightly too long shock of dark, wavy hair and his conspicuous five o'clock shadow. His eyes roved constantly over the congregation and occasionally he made a note on the lined pad resting on his knee. Emily had a pretty good idea he had seen their lukewarm greeting. She wondered if he had seen Ralph with Susie too.

After the funeral, selected guests were invited to attend a reception in the old Methodist Hall on the opposite side of Parliament Square. Thankfully the media was excluded and there was a palpable relaxation of the atmosphere as a result. Emily was relieved to see Nessa on the other side of the room, chatting animatedly. To get to her, she had no choice but to make polite conversation with a host of acquaintances, not least Alan's widow, Miriam. She was a sweet older woman who was kind to her but always made her feel lumpen and gauche.

'Mrs Williams, I'm so sorry,' she said inadequately, when she reached her.

'My dear girl, you must call me Miriam,' she said giving her a peck on the cheek.

'How will you manage?'

'I'll do very well, dear. Alan was a darling man, but high maintenance you know,' she said with a wry smile. 'I shall miss him terribly, but,' she continued, giving herself a tiny shake, 'I will find things to occupy me. My darling grandchildren, not least,' she said, gazing fondly, at her grown-up son and his wife, who stood sentry at her side.

'I'm so sorry,' Emily said, helplessly. 'It must be peculiar seeing Ralph take over so quickly.'

'Needs must,' Miriam reassured her. 'I wish you both all the very best and of course we all know Alan was keen that Ralph would take up the baton. It's such an exciting time for you.'

Emily wasn't sure about that. 'Did you really not mind Alan standing for PM?' she asked incredulously.

'Of course not,' exclaimed Miriam. 'It would have been hell of course, but Alan wanted it more than anything. I am only sad that he ran out of time ... He had so much else he wanted to do ...'

Emily was humbled. Miriam was truly a saint. Mind you, she qualified, at least her children were well into their twenties so she could reassure herself their father's career was not radically altering the course of their childhood like poor Tash and Alfie. She suddenly and overwhelmingly missed them both. They must be having a grim time with Mama Pemilly.

Keen to rescue them, she looked around for Ralph so she could tell him she was leaving. He was gone. Wandering out into the corridor, she glanced into an ante-room.

There he was, with Susie, the two of them, facing each other and framed by the doorway, as if posed there. Susie laughed fondly and raised her hand to straighten his tie, giving him a little pat when she finished. Emily cleared her throat to call him, but changed her mind. Instead, she turned on her heel and headed for the fire exit in the other direction. Pushing through the door, she was thinking mainly of how she would be able to remove her shoes and have a cup of tea. Rounding the corner, she gasped to be confronted by the phalanx of journalists who were previously haunting the entrance of the Abbey.

'Mrs Pemilly!' shouted several of them, clutching microphones and notepads.

'Emily!' yelled the photographers, 'Look over here.'

'How do you feel about your husband standing for PM?'

'Do you think the country will accept him?' asked another.

'Dead man's shoes, isn't it?' needled one bullying voice.

'I really can't – no – no comment,' stumbled Emily, before remembering that the image consultants told her never, never, to say "no comment" because it sounded as if there was something to hide.

'What is your husband doing now?' said one. 'Why is he not with you?'

'Bloody good question,' muttered Emily, a little too loudly, before a hand grabbed her elbow firmly.

'Come on you,' said Matt. 'Back in your box before you single-handedly change the course of the democratic process in a way your husband would not approve of.'

He hustled her down the street, putting his own broad back between her and the camera lenses. The door of the car opened as they approached and he more or less shoved her into the back seat, making to slam the door.

'Wait,' she said, putting out her arm, 'Aren't you coming with me?'

'Work to do,' he explained. 'Take care, Emily,' he added, as he closed the door and gestured for the driver to go.

She craned her head to look behind and saw him staring after her with an unreadable expression on his face.

Barely an hour later Matt was relaxing, or seeming to, whilst sitting opposite Susie in the bar of a discreet West End hotel. No venue near Westminster or the Docklands was suitable, with either parliamentary or media contacts likely to spot and report the liaison.

He had begun to think the meeting might never take place. After her text to him, Susie had cancelled twice before finally agreeing, in a rush, to meet after the funeral. Even then he had half expected her not to show up.

Her make-up was freshly applied, he noticed, and she was clearly self-conscious, sitting with legs elegantly crossed to show them off to best effect. He also noted how her coffee cup rattled as she replaced it in the saucer, and perspiration stained the underarms of her impeccably tailored dark grey dress which was both suitably formal for the funeral and sufficiently close-fitting to show off Susie's slim figure.

'So,' he said, after the obligatory few minutes of chit chat, 'To what do I owe the pleasure?'

At this, Susie threw him a nervous glance and wrapped her arms around herself as if she was suddenly cold.

'You're a respected journalist.'

He nodded, not demurring.

'I mean, I wouldn't disclose this to just anyone …' she continued in a rush. 'It's just that – well – I probably shouldn't say anything …'

'And yet,' Matt said acerbically, 'you clearly intend to.'

'Yes,' admitted Susie, chastened.

'It's about Ralph?' he queried.

Susie nodded.

'And the fact that you are having an affair with him?'

She gasped.

'Well, you are, aren't you?'

There was a pause. And then she nodded, hanging her head.

'And you want it to get out?'

She stared at her hands, which were now folded in her lap. A flush had risen from her neck, staining her face. She made no sign she had heard.

'Why?' continued Matt.

'Sorry?'

'Well,' he said, stifling impatience. 'You haven't brought me here purely to drink some of the worst coffee I've ever had so I'm assuming you want me – a journalist – to acknowledge, nay, announce to the world, the blindingly obvious fact that you and Ralph Pemilly are having an affair. Naturally enough I'm keen to know what you expect to gain from it?'

'It's in the public interest,' she muttered, still looking at her hands.

'Well, the "public" are certainly going to be mightily "interested",' acknowledged. Matt, 'but I'm not sure that's quite what you mean.'

'Ralph and I ...' Susie continued. 'It's important ...' she waved her hand, helplessly. 'People need to know that we ...' she fell silent.

'Do you want to de-rail his election chances?' asked Matt.

'No!' Susie shook her head, vigorously.

'You don't?'

'Absolutely not. Ralph will make a fantastic Prime Minister, it's what I've always wanted for him ... he'll need me, of course ...' Susie's eyes stared at the middle distance, a film strip clearly playing in front of her eyes, Ralph at the podium, acknowledging the electorate's decision, Susie standing to his right, perhaps he would turn and meet her eye, put his arm around her shoulders and bring her forward ...

Matt regarded her with pity and the beginnings of understanding. 'Did you tell him you were coming to see me?'

'God, no,' she admitted. 'He'd be furious.'

'Would he?'

'Absolutely. He keeps telling me – we need to wait, bide our time ... but I'm tired of it. Now, more than ever, he needs me to be – well – with him. Properly, I mean.'

'And the small matter that he's married?'

'Well,' said Susie with a dismissive laugh, 'obviously that wasn't his best decision was it? I mean Mrs P's lovely and all that but, really ...' she caught Matt's suddenly fierce expression and petered out.

There was a small silence.

'I'm just saying ...' Susie continued, sulkily, avoiding Matt's gaze. 'She doesn't "get it". She doesn't "get" how things work, how things need to look. How they need to be. Honestly!' she exclaimed throwing her hands in the air, 'as I always say, it's like herding cats getting people to behave. That's politics. Ralph always says I'm a natural. He says I'm his "secret weapon".' She tailed off, giving Matt a beseeching look, willing him to understand. 'I just don't see why I should be a "secret weapon" forever ...'

Matt regarded her dispassionately. She was Ralph's creature alright – a party political animal through and through. And she was quite an operator, he had seen that for himself at the funeral. With her savvy she was gold dust to Ralph and his career ambitions. She also had the capacity to damage him disastrously and her misguided determination to bring their true relationship out into the open now would horrify him, as Susie herself admitted. Mind you, Matt reminded himself, he didn't owe Ralph anything. Far from it. And there was nothing he wanted more than to challenge Emily's disastrous marriage choice.

But surely Susie realised the media frenzy that would result would damage her more than she could possibly imagine, sitting there with such misguided zeal to reveal the truth at any cost.

Matt sighed. 'Okay,' he said. 'I'm making no promises as to when, or if, or where I'll use it. But you'd better tell me whatever it is you want to tell me.'

Later, in his flat, he reviewed his notes. Far from being pleased to see how hollow Ralph and Emily's marriage had become, he found himself clenching his teeth in fury at how misguided her loyalty to her husband actually was. He may be a good politician, he may even be a good father, but he wasn't the husband Emily thought he was. And that made Matt angry.

As for how – or if – to use it? Well, he reasoned, the article he was commissioned to write wouldn't be coming out until after the election and – by then – hopefully any pressure on Emily would be less intense. Seeing how fragile she was, how distressed when he challenged her the other evening … he was worried she wouldn't cope with it going public now. That said, he had a number of contacts who would be more than happy to use the material straight away and would also be more than happy to pay the source. Morally, he should at least tell his editor, Mike. On the other hand, Susie was such a loose cannon he strongly suspected the story would leak out soon enough, with or without his help, in which case, allowing himself to be scooped by his rivals would earn him a right royal bollocking, or even a sacking …

He ran his fingers through his hair and massaged his aching temples with no effect on his headache whatsoever.

Checking his watch, he sighed, picked up the phone and dialled.

Chapter Nine

Unusually, it was not Susie but Ralph who phoned to summon Emily to the offices in Westminster. Stopping only to make sure Nessa could collect the children after school and keep them with her for as long as it took, Emily hopped on the train. Usually train travel gave her time to daydream, but today she was tense, her heart pounding and her palms clammy with a nameless fear.

Also oddly, Susie wasn't in her usual place in the outer office. *Curiouser and curiouser*, she thought as she pushed open the door to the meeting room.

'Ah, Emily,' Ralph said. He managed to give her a peck on the cheek without looking at her face.

'Gerald you know, I think.' He gestured at pinstripe man, who she hadn't seen since his meeting with her and Nessa three weeks before. It felt like years ago.

'Hello, Emily,' Gerald smiled thinly and gestured for her to take a seat.

'Coffee darling?' offered Ralph. Now this was really weird. When he mentioned coffee it was invariably a request, not an offer. In addition, Susie was usually around, simpering and fiddling with cups and coffee papers.

'Where's Susie?' she asked.

Ralph ran a finger around the inside of his collar as if it was suddenly too tight. 'She's taking a bit of a break at the moment,' he said, obliquely.

'Funny time to take a holiday with the election two weeks off,' she observed.

There was an uncomfortable pause.

'Emily,' said Gerald so suddenly he made her jump. He was leaning forward in his chair and looking remarkably animated.

'Gerald,' she replied, matching his tone.

'The truth is,' he continued, 'we have had to call you in today because we have a bit of a ...' he paused, 'well ... a bit of a media relations situation.'

He glanced at Ralph and then back at her. 'The journalist tracking you all – Matt Morley – he's got hold of a story we don't want out there. We've persuaded him to hold off on running with it, but we need you to back us up.'

Her mind raced. Surely he hadn't told them about their past relationship. Why would he want to do that? She failed to see how his editor would be interested in the previous love life of the would-be PM's wife. And anyway, she reasoned, telling everyone about how it ended would make him, Matt, look like a complete worm and she couldn't imagine why he would do that.

She became aware that both the men were watching her oddly, the scurrying thoughts in her head clearly visible on her face.

'Sorry, what was the question?'

'I – er – we were just saying,' stuttered Gerald, glancing at Ralph again, 'that he has made an undertaking to keep the story under his hat.'

'Right, good,' she said. 'That's okay then,' she added, making as if to stand up.

Ralph looked astonished and relieved. 'Well done darling, I knew you'd understand. These things just happen, they don't mean anything. You know that.'

'Well, I hardly think it's for you to say.'

'You're right,' he replied. 'I mean, I don't dispute that Susie may have felt differently ...'

Emily froze.

'I mean, men in my position, we are bound to attract female attention and – well – one is only human so, me and Susie, well ...'

Whack.

She looked at her hand, astonished, and then at Ralph's stupefied face. A white mark on his cheek was rapidly turning red and her palm tingled. She had never slapped anyone before and was amazed it really did make that whip-cracking noise you hear in films. She had always assumed it was dubbed.

There was a stunned silence.

'S-s-sorry,' said Gerald at last. 'You didn't know that Susie and Ralph were having an affair ...?'

'No. Did you?'

Gerald's face told her everything.

'Oh, so everyone knew but me then.' Although actually, her heart whispered to her head, she *had* known hadn't she? And she hadn't really cared very much either until now. 'So, I take it that's the story you are referring to?'

'It's buried,' said Gerald reassuringly. 'We have his word.'

'The word of a journalist though,' sneered Ralph, gingerly feeling his jaw.

'I'd rather have the word of a journalist than the word of a politician any day,' snapped Emily. 'I trust Matt and so can you ... but if your grubby little secret won't be hitting the papers anyhow, I am at a loss to know why we are having this conversation.'

Gerald and Ralph looked at each other, neither keen to speak. In the end it was Gerald who spoke up, 'It was a condition of his keeping the affair secret that we – Ralph – came clean with you.'

Emily looked at Ralph incredulously. 'So you're telling me about your sordid little affair with Susie, not because you are sorry, but because Matt told you to?'

'Oh come on darling. That's not the reason. I just didn't want to hurt your feelings – it was nothing serious, just one of those things. Matt, on the other hand, seemed pretty keen to hurt your feelings now I think about it. I can't imagine why. Did you piss him off when you knew him before?' he asked rhetorically. 'Anyhow, I would have liked to have spared you the pain—'

'Would've been better if you hadn't started shagging your secretary then,' she retorted, disliking his criticism of Matt very much indeed. 'And anyway, what's happened to her? She's not really on holiday I take it?'

'Well, it's sort of gardening leave,' explained Gerald. 'Susie is a much valued member of the team. After a period of reflection for all parties she will be offered an alternative role which suits her talents.'

'Interesting,' said Emily. 'Something which suits her talents would seem to be a role which has nothing to do with politics and more to do with soliciting. I know, perhaps she should be a solicitor. Maybe that's what you call it these days. What would I know?'

'That's enough,' snapped Ralph. 'Susie isn't at fault and I won't let you criticise her.'

Emily gave him a sharp look.

'What I mean,' he continued, in a more conciliatory manner, 'is that Susie has been a tremendous support to me. She has been extraordinarily loyal and I won't have her demonised.'

'You're right,' agreed Emily scathingly. 'We shouldn't blame her, *she* hasn't broken her marriage vows after all,' she pretended to think, 'Oh wait, *you* have though! I know – let's demonise you instead.'

Gerald looked uncomfortable. 'I should go,' he muttered. 'You both obviously have a lot to discuss.'

They didn't talk about it though. Instead, Emily used the second half of her train ticket to return home, and Ralph drove.

She was relieved to have the time alone, staring, frozen, out of the window until it got too dark to see out. Then, all she could see was her own reflection in the glass; a wan, pale face with (surely) exaggerated dark circles under the eyes. Curiously, prodding her psyche experimentally, she discovered her mood was ambivalent. Fury at his betrayal was certainly there – especially when she compared it with her own unquestioning and dutiful loyalty. On the other hand she had to admit to a germ of – what was it? Excitement? Anticipation? Let's face it, an affair in a marriage was either a catastrophe for the other party or, looking on the bright side, an opportunity for the other to bail out without guilt. What had Matt intended when he insisted that she be told? Was it a desire to hurt? Somehow she thought not. More like a chance to prove his theory that her husband was a rat bag. Perhaps even a way to persuade her that he, Matt, was the better man. Perhaps …

Returning home, she saw that Ralph was already there. His briefcase and phone were on the kitchen table and she could hear the shower thundering upstairs. His avoidance tactics had always involved long showers. She had joked once in the past he had a Lady Macbeth complex, needing to symbolically wash away his sins. He hadn't laughed, she remembered.

Plonking the kettle onto the hob and sinking wearily into a chair, she put her head in her hands. The uneasy excitement of the train journey had faded, replaced by a numb acceptance having neither the will nor the energy to move on. She dearly wished she could go to bed, go to sleep and wake up with everything back to the way it had been before, when she and Ralph had just muddled along, neither of them particularly happy perhaps but without the triggers destined to blow the studiously ignored faults in their marriage wide apart.

The mobile phone on the table started to buzz, turning a slow circle on the slippery table top. She eyed it dully. She could still hear the shower running upstairs. The display had a single word on it – 'Susie'. Emily picked it up and stared at it, her finger hovering over the answer button.

She pressed.

'Ralph?' Susie had clearly been crying.

Emily was silent.

'Ralph, are you there? Please say something,' said Susie again, ending on a distinct sob.

'It's me,' said Emily at last.

'Emily!'

There's a turn-up, thought Emily with a detached interest. No longer 'Mrs P', in fact she couldn't remember another occasion that Susie had ever called her by her first name.

'You know,' Susie continued. It was a statement, not a question. 'I – I'm sorry,' she added like a child forced to apologise for a misdemeanour they didn't regret in the least.

'Thank you.'

'I love him.'

'So do I,' replied Emily, calmly.

'No you don't,' said Susie crying audibly now. 'You aren't there for him. You don't understand his ambitions, his talents. Ralph is a great man and all you want for him is to be a rural MP and that would kill him. What he needs is me – not you.'

Emily reeled. 'I think not,' she said icily, and pressed the 'end' button.

Still shaking, she made her legs take her upstairs to the bedroom, where she could hear Ralph now moving around.

'Do you love her?' asked Emily, as Ralph rubbed his hair, his back to her. He stopped dead.

'Not like I love you and the children,' he said at last.

'She seems to love you.'

Ralph's eyes were misty. 'She's an amazing woman,' he replied. 'She doesn't deserve all this grief. I should go to her. Make sure she's all right.'

Emily could hardly believe her ears and yet, relief at postponing the moment when they had to address their problems flooded through her.

'Go,' she said flatly. 'Run off to your little mistress then. After all, she says she loves you ... and I'm not at all sure that I do.'

Chapter Ten

'What an idiot,' exclaimed Nessa with comforting outrage, when Emily carted the children around to her house the following morning. Ralph had not returned. After a sleepless night, she was dreading the weekend with no school to give her a break from caring for the children on her own.

'Here,' said Nessa, 'Let's get shot of the rug rats, and I'll pour you some of this,' she waved her glass of wine. 'There's soup and stuff for lunch later.'

'You are kind. What are we going to do with them?'

'Watch,' said Nessa with a wink. She plonked down her glass and grabbed a Waitrose carrier bag. Standing in the open kitchen doorway, she flung handfuls of its contents – little individually wrapped chocolate eggs – into all the corners of the garden.

'Children!' she hollered. 'Easter egg hunt. What you find, you eat.'

'Wow!' said Alfie and Tash together, scampering to the door. 'Can we eat them straight away?' asked Tash, slyly.

'Yes,' said Nessa.

'No,' said Emily, simultaneously. 'Oh, all right, yes then,' she added with a smile.

'Even before lunch?' replied Tash, incredulously.

'Yes,' said Emily again, ruffling her daughter's hair. 'And make sure Alfie finds lots, won't you darling?'

'Yeah, yeah,' complained Tash, but she took Alfie's hand, 'Come on monkey face,' she said. 'Let's go.'

'And so,' said Nessa, when Emily had told her everything, 'the man has behaved appallingly, and – as usual – the long-suffering wife has to take it on the chin.'

'I do?'

'Probably, yes. Or at least,' she added briskly, 'if you intend to leave him twisting in the wind, as it were, you need to know precisely the implications of your actions.'

'In other words?'

'In other words, you hold the future of your marriage in your hands,' she said, 'but you need to understand you hold the future of the country in your hands as well.'

Emily giggled hysterically. 'Well that's just great,' she exclaimed, 'far from being allowed to cut off the legs of my husband's trousers or give away the contents of his wine cellar, I actually have to ask, not what my country might do for me but what I might do for my country.'

Nessa held Emily's gaze. 'Oh my goodness,' Emily whispered. 'You are really not joking.'

'Remember the household management book? Not much has changed. Mind you,' she said, 'on a brighter note, if this Matt chap is to be believed, the whole thing is rather pointless if the story isn't going to come out in any case.'

'What!' shrieked Emily, sitting bolt upright, not even noticing that she had sloshed half a glass of wine into her lap. 'Not you too? You sound like them, the bloody focus groups and Gerald and – and – Ralph. They honestly believe that the way things look is more real than the way things actually are. It matters to me that Ralph and Susie cheated on our marriage. Everyone thinks it doesn't count if people don't know, but *I* know. I know he was unfaithful. Isn't *that* what matters?'

'In any other circumstance,' acknowledged Nessa. She fell silent, thinking. 'You know,' she went on, 'this isn't the life for everyone. It's bloody hard, you sacrifice your own life, your children's lives get turned upside down, you get the shitty end of the stick on every occasion, the husband gets all the glory and before you know it, they bugger off and die on you,' she paused, 'at which point you might just conceivably wonder what it's all been about.'

This was interesting. In all her friend's pep talks about sacrifice, tolerance, patience and diplomacy she had never, but never, raised the bail out option before. It was frightening to have someone else voice her darkest most lawless thoughts.

'Are you saying ...' asked Emily slowly. 'Actually, what *are* you saying?'

'Well, to play devil's advocate – you could leave him.'

Emily poured the remaining wine in her glass down her throat in one gulp. Immediately, Nessa replenished it.

'What I am saying is,' she continued, waving the bottle, 'if you are unable to tolerate the situation with Ralph as it stands, then I suppose you will have to make your move. Now.'

'With ten days until polling day?'

Nessa's volte face on the usual 'buck yourself up, stiff upper lip' pep talk made her think of those Doctor Who episodes she always found most disturbing as a child where characters suddenly took their faces off and revealed their true diabolical identity.

'Better ten days before than ten days after.'

'Really?' said Emily. 'Are you sure?'

'What do you think?'

'I think,' she said, slowly, 'that the issue of whether Ralph would be a good PM is, to be fair, entirely separate from whether he is capable of being a good husband and father.'

'Not what the majority of the electorate think,' noted Nessa. 'Wrongly, I'll grant you, but there it is. You're a package.'

'I don't want to be. I don't know what to do. I haven't even had a chance to have it out with him. Everything's about the election. Why can't it just be about us?'

'OK, suppose it was,' said Nessa. 'Just about you and Ralph, I mean. What would you do?'

'Kick him out.'

Nessa nodded. 'And then?'

'And then I'd wait. And then – eventually – we'd talk. We'd talk. A lot. And shout at each other, and have time to think ... Then, he could beg to come back,' she continued. 'He could woo me, make promises ...'

And he probably would, she thought, because Ralph, for all his carefully studied vigour and manly drive, was fairly rubbish at being on his own. Never without a girlfriend from the time he went to university to the day she met him, she was acutely aware he had segued smoothly from mother to wife, via stepping stones of a few – but not too many – attentive girlfriends who had all willingly volunteered to manage the practical, emotional and domestic side of his life.

'Mm. A visible breakup and then a fun reconciliation with flowers and forgiveness. Nice idea. Not really an option,' commented Nessa.

'I know,' snapped Emily. 'Heaven knows, at least I have the chance to keep the media from crawling all over it ... it's like people queuing up to jump on a broken leg,' she said.

Nessa winced. 'You only have a chance to keep the media out of your face if you don't do anything different to what you're doing now.'

'So kicking him out and making him beg for forgiveness as a way of deciding what to do is a luxury I can't afford.'

''Fraid not.'

And she was right. Emily was powerless and paralysed by the weight of everybody's expectations. Ralph had it good.

'And now,' Nessa announced as she topped up both of their glasses, 'I want to talk about me.'

'Let's do that!' exclaimed Emily guiltily. 'Which aspect exactly ...?'

'My love life. Or to be accurate, "the absence thereof". I've decided to launch myself into the brave new world of internet dating.'

'Why?'

'Because I'm lonely,' said Nessa, lifting her chin a little. 'I miss having a man in my life. I miss having someone to look after, to cook for, to talk to. I miss sex, for goodness sake!'

'Go, Nessa!' said Emily. 'In that case, I think it's a brilliant idea.'

'Good, because I need your help,' she replied, grabbing her laptop and plonking herself down next to Emily on the sofa.

For the next hour and a bit they were absorbed in creating an online profile. Nessa was keen to put in the bit about wanting sex but Emily managed to dissuade her.

'You'll attract all the sleazeballs and lowlifes,' she explained. 'All the married men who just want a bit on the side,' she added, momentarily diverted by a wave of hatred for Ralph, but pulling herself back to the task in hand.

'I have to be honest,' protested Nessa.

'Sure. Be yourself, but don't reveal too much. And don't end up suggesting something you don't want to suggest ... For example, see this bloke? He says he goes to the gym several times a week? Narcissist. Definitely.'

'I bet he's got a nice bod though ...' said Nessa wistfully.

'And some of these aren't real people you know,' continued Emily as they dismissed another handsome grey-haired model with a toothpaste smile who was looking, so he said, for a theatre and food-loving woman in her sixties for companionship and long term commitment. 'They just put them up there to hook you in to paying the fees. And then there's the other whole thing of meeting strangers. You need to be careful you know. Always meet them in a crowded place and never give out your personal details ...'

'I know, I know,' Nessa reassured her. 'I'm not Tash darling. I'm big enough and ugly enough to look after myself. I'll be fine, you'll see.'

Chapter Eleven

*Easter is a jolly occasion but even a public
holiday such as this is no excuse for profligate
expenditure. Charming decorations can be
fashioned from the humblest of scraps, with
vegetable dyed hen's eggs making delightfully
gay additions to the Easter breakfast table.*

FELICITY WAINWRIGHT, 1953

Emily prodded the eggs in the saucepan despondently. Despite using practically all of the food colouring she could find in the cupboard, and boiling them to the consistency of rubber bullets, the egg shells remained resolutely white.

Vowing to chuck them in the bin, she had already got Tash and Alfie using the food colouring neat, painting wobbly stripes onto the remaining eggs and onto everything else they touched besides. Alfie's fingers were dyed crimson right up to his palms, making him look like Lady Macbeth after a murder spree. Tash was more fastidious but, even so, Emily noticed a splodge of bright green on her new and expensive pink rugby shirt.

The book had recommended blowing the contents of the raw eggs out through two tiny holes before decorating them so the shells would be light enough to hang on sprays of winter jasmine and pussy willow. Feeling permanently queasy from the stress and from eating so little, she had been unable to face the prospect of putting her mouth anywhere near raw egg. Instead, she gingerly took the whole, decorated eggs, trying to arrange them artistically in a twiggy basket lined with florists' moss.

Standing back and looking at her table centrepiece through narrowed eyes, she personally thought the layer of moss, made the eggs look like they had sprouted elephantiasis growths of green mould.

Tash eyed her mother keenly. 'All right, Mummy?' she said.

'Yes darling, of course.' She smiled at her daughter and gave her a hug. 'Why do you ask?'

'Just … stuff,' said Tash, as inarticulate suddenly as the teenager she would become all too soon.

'What darling? Are *you* all right? Is it this whole silly election thing?' she hazarded, hoping desperately it was, and not the other whole elephant in the room issue – the marriage.

Tash considered, looking old beyond her years. 'Yeah,' she said at last. 'That's it.' She gave her mother another hug and pottered off to watch television, apparently oblivious to the mess on the table where she had been working.

Like father like daughter, Emily thought as, wearily, she began to clear everything away.

The table cleaned, she realised the rest of the day was hers and hers alone. Excused cooking the whole exhausting Easter lunch responsibility by Ralph who had – again – decided to spend the day with his campaign team, going over the polls and tweaking the strategies, she had little to occupy her, other than the children.

She collected the papers from the porch. There was a huge stack. Ralph liked all the papers to be delivered to his home every day so he could see coverage before his team faxed his cuttings. She dumped them on the kitchen table. Selecting *The Times* she pretended to herself she was carrying out research as she flicked quickly through to the lifestyle magazine. Here she saw Matt had contributed several pieces, his usual comment on the week, the TV reviews because the regular contributor was away and a six page article on the politics of abortion.

She made herself stop and brew coffee and then, sitting with a large steaming mug of it beside her, she settled down to read.

Despite the emotive subject, and her reaction to it – always even worse, Emily found, now that she had Alfie and Tash – she could not deny the incisive and dispassionate way that Matt had laid out the various arguments. He had started by framing the debate with the facts, quickly and coherently relaying the statistics, the history, and then exploring the various ethical positions with a detached clarity that she had to admire. Not that he had taken the emotion entirely out of the debate she noted. A case study detailing the experiences of a young woman who had terminated a pregnancy then regretted it had an immediacy and directness that caused tears of empathy to spring to her eyes.

She sat back and sipped. Subject matter apart, she had to admit, he was a superb journalist. Not that she had ever doubted he would be of course. When they were together he was already doing well professionally.

He was four years older than her, which had seemed a lot in their twenties. Of course Ralph was a full ten years older but, in many ways, Matt was the more grown up of the two men. He had been her mentor, champion and number one fan – until that last commission when he had returned from Serbia. Then he had been like a possessed soul, she remembered, angry and distant, refusing to communicate with her ... She had agonised endlessly afterwards about what she might have done differently. She could have talked more, made him get help rather than misinterpreting his psychological distress – in her youthful egocentricity – as being something about her. She was hurt that his attitude to her was less loving. She wished now that she had refused to let him go to Kazakhstan after yet another furious row sparked by his failing to say and do the right things when she told him she was pregnant. As a result her unplanned pregnancy and subsequent miscarriage had been faced alone while Matt fought his demons chasing yet more war stories overseas. She had resented him then most of all, for leaving her alone to cope with her grief while he empathised instead with the grief of strangers. But all that was too late now. The point of turning back had been passed many years before. The relationship irretrievably destroyed by her self-obsession – and his.

And then, Ralph had appeared, with his glamour, optimism and downright certainty about everything. Interviewing him on the day they met, when she was still reeling from the loss of her baby and the simultaneous implosion of her relationship with Matt, Ralph's confidence was appealing. The die was cast and things moved forward with breakneck speed as Ralph, quickly certain about his choice, drove the agenda. After her agonies with Matt, she was relieved to be no longer in charge, content to leave even the major decision making to Ralph and his team. She was sure the miscarriage and her rapid stress-related weight loss had made it impossible to conceive so she was astonished to fall pregnant with Tash the first time they slept together. They were married in months.

When Emily drifted back to the present, her coffee had grown cold. Feeling guilty about neglect, she called to the children who were both slumped in front of cartoons.

'Come on,' she chivvied. 'It's a beautiful day outside. In the garden with you both please,' she added, turning off the television at the wall.

They whinged, but they went.

She sighed, brushing away a sudden and unexpected tear. She couldn't ring Nessa to whinge again – it would be too much for the poor woman. She realised that there was, in fact, no-one else. No friends who she felt she could confide in. There were other mothers from the school of course, women she would meet for a glass of wine and a harmless gossip about things that didn't matter, but she wore her distance from them like a suit of armour. It was unthinkable that any of them should know what was happening to her, revealing an unfaithful husband who she should never have married.

The stripping back of the whole edifice of her supposedly glamorous life, successful by proxy, for them to see in all its chaos was too horrible a thought to bear. No, they were not her friends.

Another tear slipped down the side of her nose and ran into her mouth. She dabbed her eyes and took a deep breath. Nope, too late, a sob tried to escape and turned into an unbecoming snort.

Sinking down onto the sofa, she put her head into her hands and howled. Overwhelmed, she didn't even hear the knock on the door, or Alfie running to answer it before scampering, uninterested in the visitor, back to his game in the garden.

She had just got to the hiccupping stage and was in the middle of blowing her nose so hard her ears popped painfully when she heard the door to the sitting room swing open with its characteristic squeak. She had been meaning to oil it for months.

'Go outside darling,' she said brightly, turning away so Alfie or Tash wouldn't see her face and pretending she was rummaging in the pile of newspapers on the table 'It's too lovely a day to waste.'

'It *is* a lovely day,' came his distinctive deep voice. 'But it doesn't seem to be making you very happy.'

She froze, her back still to the door. Now Matt was here to witness it, her misery and humiliation was complete.

She didn't hear him move from the door to her side so, when he put his hand on her shoulder, she jumped violently.

'Shh,' he said gently, sitting down beside her, his hands either side of her neck. They were warm and dry, their heat radiating through her thin cotton shirt. He massaged gently, soothingly but the effect on her was far from relaxing. Trembling with the desire to run away or turn and throw her arms around him – she didn't know which – she stifled a groan and forced herself to stay still. After a minute, she relaxed and slumped back a little, imperceptibly, towards him.

'He lied,' she said, at last.

'I know.'

'And it was just his bloody secretary. What a cliché.'

'Actually it was his parliamentary assistant,' corrected Matt with scrupulous accuracy.

Emily looked at him. 'Bloody pedant.'

Matt gave a short laugh and handed her his handkerchief. She snorted inelegantly into it. They both looked at it and she decided not to give it back.

'You told him to tell me,' she said, but it was a question.

'I didn't want him to hurt you. But you – I – I wanted you to know ... I'm sorry.'

'I'm glad I know,' she said, giving him a wan smile.

'Good,' he said, staring intently at her. She became acutely aware of her puffy red face. Her nose must look all pink and shiny. It felt huge.

'It's no good,' he muttered to himself, and gathered her into his arms, pressing his mouth against her lips.

He had always been able to make her melt, to turn her body to liquid with lust that she couldn't ever remember feeling with her husband. Not even in the early days. In the end, it was her blocked nose that forced her to pull away, panting slightly. Even then, she couldn't resist the temptation to lay her head on his shoulder. His arms slipped around her easily and held her tight. She felt incredibly warm and comfortable there. She had been cold for days, tense and chilled to the bone.

'I can't believe you said you would bury the story.'

'Do you really think I could be that much of a bastard as to publish?' he replied, shaking his head. 'Anyway,' he continued, 'I only said *I* wouldn't publish it.'

He met her eye. 'I can't bury this one. It's a bit bigger than a dodgy press release about a few barking voters.'

'You mean it's coming out?'

'Not yet. But that's why I came. There's still stuff rumbling around. Rumours. No-one has the facts, or at least nothing their legal departments will let them run with, but ... the genie's all but out of the bottle. You should be ready.'

Emily nodded.

'If I could stop it I would,' he said gently.

She nodded again, and sighed. 'Wouldn't stop it being true.'

'No, but I'd like to save you the intrusion,' said Matt.

'Thank you,' whispered Emily. 'But that's my life now. Nothing is above – or below – public scrutiny.'

'What will you do?'

Emily sighed again wearily, rubbing her face with both hands.

'What do you think I should do?'

'Leave him, ruin his reputation, scupper the election, take the children and move in with me,' he replied. 'Since you ask,' he added as she stared at him incredulously.

'I can't,' she said, shocked at how appealing it sounded. 'I have a duty ...'

'Doesn't have to be that way! He cheated on you. What's to stop you bailing out and doing the same?'

'You know what?' she mused, 'if it does come out the chances are the scandal will screw up Ralph's chances of the PM role, and, much as I hate to admit it,' she said slowly, 'that's an interesting thought ...' She pondered, remembering her recent similar conversation with Nessa. 'He'd have to resign wouldn't he? Stand down as party leader ... That would be a blessing, for me and the children at least. But for me to actually give that fatal shove? No, I'm not going to do that.'

She was transfixed by the sight of Matt's hand on her arm as the confusion and emotion boiled up inside her. The affair, Matt's accusations of her selling herself down the river, the loss of the baby which she had faced without his support ...

Suddenly she leapt to her feet and began pacing the room, her fingers digging into her hair as she tried to think clearly.

'You!' she said, stopping in front of him. He sat, elbows on knees, dangling his hands between his legs. He was the picture of relaxation which enraged her.

'You,' she said again, pointing. 'You come here and turn everything upside down, telling me things I don't want to know about Ralph, messing around with me, my feelings, making me want you, telling me to ditch him. You make me just as bad as him. How is it different? I'm as guilty as him because of you ...' She found she was panting. She put her hand to her chest to feel her heart pounding and then dropped it again, feeling silly. Melodrama had never been encouraged in her family, and Ralph had no patience for it, unless it was him – which it usually was.

'Emily,' said Matt, reaching towards her. She longed for him to hold her again but he made do with putting his hands firmly on her shoulders. 'You're not guilty. As much as I'd like to,' he closed his eyes for a moment, 'we haven't done anything wrong.'

'Not yet,' she observed, wryly.

He said nothing, but his eyes bored into her face.

'No,' she said at last, detaching herself from his grasp. 'Don't. You should go.'

'Will you be okay on your own?'

'I'll *only* be okay on my own,' she replied, not daring to look at him, for fear her resolve would weaken. 'If you're right about the press I won't have long before I've got the party on my back ...'

At that moment, the phone rang. Emily didn't move. How easy it would be, she thought, not to answer. She could take the children, change their name, move to somewhere no-one knew them ...

Matt picked up the phone.

'She's here,' he said to whoever was on the other end. 'Just trying to help,' he said in reply to the caller's question. 'No,' he continued, 'I'm not.' He sounded impatient.

'It's your husband,' he said, handing her the phone. She stood up straighter, wiping her eyes and taking the phone gingerly as if it were a rattlesnake.

'Hello Ralph,' she said quietly.

'Don't talk to him,' snapped Ralph in a furious whisper.

'Hello Emily, how are you?' she said, sarcastically.

'What the bloody hell is he doing there anyway?'

'Shagging me senseless obviously,' replied Emily. 'Naturally enough, being given to believe that's the sort of marriage you and I apparently have.'

'Don't be fatuous. Now, we need to make a plan. There are rumblings in the press. They're starting to ask questions about me and an affair – not that anyone seems to know it's Susie, but their blood's up for sure.'

'Why don't we just let them run it then,' she said wearily. 'It's true after all.'

'Are you mad?' spluttered Ralph. 'And have the whole lot crashing down on us four days before polling day? You'd like that, would you?'

'Frankly my dear, I don't give a damn,' responded Emily surprising herself and Ralph with a giggle. She realised she was close to hysteria. The thought of just walking away from the whole sorry mess made her feel dizzy, and deliciously irresponsible.

As Ralph banged on, she returned to her daydream about running away. This time she had persuaded Matt to come with them. In her fantasy they were in a little white painted house on the beach. He and the children were playing together on the sand while she looked indulgently on. She was slim, tanned and naturally gorgeous. The children looked altogether happier and also somehow cleaner than in real life. It felt good …

She drifted back to the present as Matt put down the phone for her.

'They're coming down here. I should make myself scarce.'

Emily nodded.

'Ditch the bastard,' he added softly, and left as quietly as he had come.

Chapter Twelve

*A good wife should never let her own feelings or
indispositions get in the way of her being the perfect
hostess. One should present a pleasant demeanour
and gracious hospitality at all times ...*

FELICITY WAINWRIGHT, 1953

TJ put his hand on Emily's arm in a silent gesture of solidarity. He took the tray from her hands and led the way into the posh sitting room where Ralph, at home, did his formal receptions.

There, arranged in a tableau around the empty fireplace, were the usual suspects. Ralph was being bullish but avoiding her eye. Gerald was looking embarrassed but stern and purposeful. A colourless secretary had been drafted in to take notes. Clearly she was the replacement for Susie. Emily noted with distant interest that she was plain. Probably one of those terribly clever girls who thought a good Oxbridge degree and a stint as a parliamentary assistant would launch their political career. And perhaps it would, she thought bitterly, if they were prepared to sleep with the boss as well.

TJ offered around tea, coffee and biscuits with quiet diffidence as if he was at a wake.

'So, anyway,' Gerald was continuing, 'other than hoping for an even better story to take the heat off – which we are actively working on, I might say – our only real strategy is to confirm the rumours.' Ralph nodded, and then did a double take.

'What do you mean confirm the rumours,' he blustered, 'why on earth would we want to do that?'

'Er, because they're true?' hazarded Gerald.

'But isn't that what spin is for? Why do we pay you guys—?'

'You don't pay them,' snapped a voice from the corner. 'We do, and we don't pay them to lie for you. We're onto damage limitation now, Ralph. It's about all we've got left.'

Emily looked. There, in the shadows was James, the party Chairman. Emily hadn't seen him since the news reports announcing Alan's death. He looked tired, and older than Emily remembered.

'Hello Emily,' he said kindly, before continuing in a harsher tone. 'Frankly, my friend, it's a bit damned late for Saint Ralph now, the best we can hope for is disclosure, contrition and a bloody great statement of loyalty from your wife which, incidentally, you don't deserve.'

Emily practically had to sit on her hands to prevent herself launching into a round of applause. Ralph looked wounded but didn't answer back.

'So, Gerald,' added James, 'do continue.'

Gerald blinked a bit and straightened his tie. 'Erm, yes, so, the only way forward really is to confirm all the true rumours circulating before they get proved without our input and make us look obstructive. Of course we will be being obstructive as far as we can in not, obviously, providing any further facts – luckily these are pretty thin on the ground, at least at the moment. We just have to hope the whole thing dies of lack of oxygen.'

'No spin?' queried Emily.

'Erm, no, loads of spin,' Gerald replied with a hint of a smile.

'Luckily,' he continued, directing his remarks at James, 'none of the fishing expeditions we have received from the media seem to know *who* Ralph was seeing. We expect to be able to keep things that way.'

'You do?' said James, doubtfully.

'Susie is one hundred per cent trustworthy,' said Ralph with some pride. 'They'll get nothing from her.'

'Yes, well,' responded James doubtfully, 'let's hope not.

And we should certainly be keeping the woman very close to us indeed. Bring her under your wing, Gerald. Tell her it's to help protect her from the distress of press intrusion.'

'Which of course it is,' confirmed Gerald, gallantly.

James snorted. 'I don't want her out there, able to make contacts,' he continued. 'Not this side of polling day anyhow. Can't say I care much what happens after that.'

'Won't Ralph just have to resign though?' said Emily, genuinely puzzled. Since she'd had a chance to absorb the news she was rather hoping this mysterious leak would solve all her problems by getting Ralph out of the running altogether. She was sorry about his destroyed ambitions, or at least she would have been if he hadn't been porking his secretary.

'Well, one might think so initially,' explained Gerald, 'but I've been looking back at – er – similar scenarios in the past and, surprisingly enough, it seems to be the lying and denials that screw the MP's career, not the infidelity. Indeed it seems even fathering a love child isn't beyond the pale.'

Gerald and James both gave Ralph an enquiring look.

'Certainly not,' he blustered. 'Good God, no, Emily,' he told her earnestly. 'Absolutely not.'

Despite the sheer awfulness of it all, his face was a picture and she had to suppress the urge to laugh.

'Surely though,' she continued, 'his chances must be damaged.'

'God yes,' interjected James again. 'And the party's chances with them,' he added bitterly. 'But with so little time until polling day, we have no option but to go with him – unfortunately.'

'What are the odds though?' she persisted.

'Hard to tell,' said Gerald. 'Obviously we will be able to gauge the public mood once we've put our strategy into play. There are so many variables, so many other factors. We've just got to give it a go.'

James nodded and Ralph looked chastened.

'So,' continued James, turning to Emily, 'We have no right to ask this of you my dear, but whatever you think of your husband, and whatever your plans for the marriage in the longer term, I would implore you to help us repair the damage and give the party the best chance it can to put together a government. Our only hope now is to rehabilitate Ralph's image by fielding a loyal wife.' He raised his mug toward Emily in a gesture of salute. 'Are you prepared to do it?' he asked her solemnly.

She could feel Ralph looking directly at her for the first time that evening. Actually all eyes in the room were trained on her.

She wondered if her life was going to flash before her. It didn't, but her future did. First, there was the future where she and the children were taken away from the life they loved, thrust into the goldfish bowl of public life, and second, the dream of the little white house by the beach, anonymous and free. Matt was there.

She didn't know how long her mind had been wandering.

'I'll do it,' she said. As she spoke a heavy weight lodged itself in her chest. 'But only until the election,' she added. Ralph looked stricken. 'Only until then,' she said to him quietly. 'After that, I just don't know.'

The following morning, Emily woke late with a headache.

She had lain awake until dawn, staring at the ceiling, alone. Ralph had stayed downstairs for a long time after the team had left, but then she had heard him stealing into the spare room, where Matt had slept just days before. How life had changed since then.

Even a long, hot shower failed to remove the deep chill. She moved stiffly, and raising her arms to put up her hair was exhausting. She took care with her make-up, but – even after a gallon of eye drops and a tonne of blusher – the best she could do was to convert the face of a corpse to the face of a corpse gussied up by an undertaker with a heavy hand.

Breakfast was tense. Ralph adopted a hearty tone with the children, but Tash was sullen and Alfie grumpy from all the late nights, waiting for his Daddy to come home. Emily couldn't eat, but cradled a cup of tea, more for comfort than because she was thirsty.

Gerald and his team had been working hard overnight. They had set up a photo call that morning for half past ten. Statements would also be read and issued. Ralph had been adamant that the event should be held at the house. To her horror, Emily was required not only to offer the photographers a 'united family shot', but she had to read a statement which Gerald had drafted for her.

Ralph handed it to her wordlessly. By the time she had reached the end of it, she was paler still. Her jaw was clenched so tightly the pain of it added to her already aching head.

As she had pointed out before going to bed that night, they still needed to break the news to the children. She was grateful the Easter holidays meant Tash, in particular, would not have to run the gauntlet of the children at school as soon as the truth came out. If she was honest, she too was grateful Ralph's infidelity would not be the gossip fodder of the mothers at the school gates, until after the election. Whatever the outcome, today's story would hopefully have lost its freshness and intrigue by then.

'You talk to the children, darling,' he said nervously. 'You're better at that sort of thing.'

'Don't call me "darling",' she growled. 'Anyway, better at what "sort of thing"? Parenting?'

He had the grace to look ashamed.

'And we are damn well going to do this together,' she continued. 'Not just because this is all your fault – which it is – but also because the children are unlikely to be satisfied

103

by this charade of togetherness, unless we are – in fact – together.'

'Are we?' he ventured.

She gave him a crushing look but didn't reply.

For Ralph, talking to the children was clearly more nerve-racking than public announcements. Emily was surprised he hadn't discussed strategy with Gerald in advance. Actually, he probably had.

The two of them sat the children down in the kitchen and Emily made pancakes while Ralph tried to broach the subject tactfully. After several minutes of perplexing platitudes that left Alfie open-mouthed and Tash glazed with boredom, Emily brought the monologue to a close.

'What Daddy is trying to say, darlings,' she told them, 'is that when mummies and daddies have been together for a long time, sometimes they make mistakes and start doing the special thing they do together with other people. After this happens, people can still stay married and things can get better.' She looked at Ralph pointedly, and added 'and even if mummies and daddies decide they don't love each other any more, they still both love their children very much.'

'Did you make a mistake with another lady?' asked Tash, incisively. Emily smiled despite herself.

'Don't be stupid,' said Alfie. 'Daddy's going to be a pry mincer, they don't make mistakes because they have to rule the world.'

'Not that sort of mistake,' explained Tash patiently, 'Daddy made a sex mistake.' Ralph and Emily gasped in unison. 'Well you did, didn't you?' Tash interrogated. Ralph nodded. She gave a small smile of satisfaction. 'Told you,' she announced to Alfie proudly.

'What's sex?' he asked, but then Gerald poked his head around the door. 'Time to go,' he said, and Ralph breathed a sigh of relief. 'Come on gang,' he said heartily, rubbing his hands together. 'Our public awaits.'

The photocall was grim. The team at central office had done their job well and every major news media outlet was represented by the scrum outside the garden gate. Police stood by, quietly observing and ready to step in. Some of the photographers had brought step ladders to ensure they could get a clear shot. Emily was worried for the children, but they delighted in the attention and, by some unspoken moral code, or – more likely – by prior arrangement, the media mob kept a respectful relative silence and distance while the photos were taken. Emily smiled stiffly as they arranged themselves on the far side of the garden gate, the children both standing on the bottom rung with their wellies sticking out, and Ralph standing behind, with one arm proprietarily around Emily's waist and the other around the children's shoulders.

'Kiss me,' he muttered out of the corner of his mouth.

'You've got a nerve,' she hissed in return, but she tilted her head towards him. The noise of the camera shutters rose to a climax as their lips met. With enormous restraint, she stifled her instinctive recoil. Instead, she forced herself to meet his eye and smiled warmly at him. The camera shutters went mad again.

After a mercifully brief interval, the plain secretary ushered the children back into the house. When they were barely out of earshot, the shouted interrogation began.

'Mrs Pemilly, are you planning to divorce your husband?' shouted one. 'Will you stand down, Ralph?' demanded another. 'Can the country vote for a cheating Prime Minister?' screamed a woman hack, jumping up and down, waving her notebook to be seen.

Gerald appeared from nowhere, holding his hands up for silence.

'You have all had the press release. Mr and Mrs Pemilly will now make a brief statement. They will answer no further questions at this time.'

Ralph started and Emily found it relatively easy to go into 'listening with polite interest' mode. She had had a lot of practice at other occasions when he was making speeches. It was easier not to tune into what he was saying, but the occasional phrase filtered through and threatened her composure. He talked about 'his precious family,' and his 'darling, loyal and beautiful wife'. At this she maintained her polite distant smile, nodding supportively as if he was making some abstruse point about the prison system or crime statistics. He drivelled on, hanging his head and agonising about 'betraying the support of his colleagues' and 'bowing to the strains of maintaining the work-life balance which challenge us all'. This last point, she thought, was a bit rich, given that he could spend so very much more time with his family if he hadn't been choosing to spend it rogering his secretary – sorry – parliamentary assistant.

Then it was her turn. The only way she could get Gerald's words to come out of her mouth was to pretend she was doing nothing more than reading a shopping list or an instruction manual. She could feel the waves of disapproval from Ralph, irritated that she wasn't putting more into it, but the press seemed convinced, hanging on her every word, microphones shoved eagerly into her face.

'... and so,' she concluded, 'Ralph and I will continue to work on our marriage, for the sake of the children, and for the sake of my husband's career, in which he and I are equally committed to serving the needs of the country.'

How are people simply not vomiting at this sanctimonious rubbish, she thought, forcing herself to meet Ralph's eye and to smile as he put his arm around her waist and led her back inside the house. There was a cacophony of questions in their wake, and she heard Gerald telling them all where to get off as Ralph shut the door behind them.

Matt continued staring at the screen, long after Emily and Ralph had disappeared inside the house, replaced by a talking head back in the news studio. As a thorough and professional journalist with an important piece of new material he would be watching the clip several times, exploring every nuance. Watching it live, though, his attention was fixed on Emily. She had lost weight, even in the few days since he had last held her in his arms. The dark circles under her eyes were mercilessly revealed by the morning sunshine, despite her careful make-up which was heavier than usual, he noticed. He also noticed the twitch at the corner of her mouth as she smiled up at her husband, the slight tremor in the hands which held the statement she read out. She was tough, though, he told himself with a swell of pride. The old Emily he loved was still there all right, but the strain was evident, and he knew, with concern, she had more battles to face, alone.

Safely out of sight of the cameras, Ralph had quickly let go of Emily's waist and marched off to confer with his little gaggle of advisers and hangers-on who seemed to have taken up permanent residence in the posh sitting room.

Wearily, she trailed into the kitchen. She looked at the kettle but felt so drained she doubted her arms had the strength to haul it onto the range. In any case, she could hardly make herself a cup of tea without brewing up another gallon for the hordes and she didn't feel like doing them any favours at the moment. Instead, she wandered out into the back garden which was mercifully private. The bulbs she had planted the autumn before were the only splashes of colour.

How long ago, it seemed, that she and the children had planted them. That autumn, life had still been reassuringly predictable. There had been no election, no Susie, no terrifying prospect of being cast so very much into the public eye – and no Matt stirring up painful memories and complicated feelings.

She stroked a scarlet tulip petal thoughtfully. The grass needed cutting and the garden was littered with children's toys. Tash's pink bike was sprawled carelessly on the lawn and she noticed fondly that Alfie had inexplicably taken all his bath toys and arranged them amongst the pots of flowers by the back door. A rubber duck peeped out from behind some fading daffodils and his submarine nestled amongst some alliums yet to flower. She wondered if they would still be there to enjoy them when they did. She didn't believe Ralph's assurances that the family could stay in the constituency if he really did get the top job.

How odd, she thought, that she could singlehandedly ensure his failure in the election and safeguard her children's stability into the bargain, albeit at the probable expense of her marriage. Nothing seemed more impossible than to use that power, even though she realised, she was starting to wonder at whether the marriage was worth saving anyway. Maybe he would be better off with Susie, she thought. Perhaps somehow he could fulfil the Westminster part of his life with Susie at his side. She, Emily, could carry on working in the constituency, doing the job that he rarely had the time and the patience for any more. It wouldn't be the first time, she knew perfectly well, that a public figure had led a complicated personal life – although harder now that the media was so omnipresent and unforgiving. That said, the press appeared to have bought today's little charade with great enthusiasm. She seemed to have the capacity to keep everyone happy – everyone except herself that was.

She felt her mobile, which was on silent, buzzing in her pocket. Matt's name flashed up on the screen. She froze, staring at it for several long seconds. Then, in a flurry, she pressed accept, panicking that he would ring off before she answered.

'Emily?' came the comfortingly familiar voice.

'Yes,' she whispered, a lump forming in her throat.

'I wanted to ...' he paused. 'I was watching. Are you all right?'

'I think so.'

'I wish I could help you.'

'You can't,' said Emily, sadly, with infinite weariness. 'You can't help me, but – thank you.'

'If you need someone to talk to,' he continued. 'If you just need a friend ...'

'I know,' she replied.

'Emily?' called Ralph, as she hurriedly ended the call and shoved the phone back out of sight. 'Darling what are you doing out here, for heaven's sake? There could be telephoto lenses – can't be too careful,' he said, hustling her inside, looking suspiciously around the tranquil garden.

'I must see if the children are all right,' she muttered, keen to get out of his presence.

'They're fine,' he snapped. 'Nessa's here.'

Thank goodness for that, she thought, wondering how on earth she would ever be able to repay Nessa's efforts.

This was not a problem that seemed to trouble Ralph though.

'Hurry up darling,' he said, hustling her along. 'The team have been waiting to talk to you. We wondered where you'd gone,' he added petulantly.

'Here she is,' he announced as they went together into the sitting room, 'the hero of the hour.'

For a moment she thought they might give her a round of applause – a standing ovation even. But, thank goodness, even their capacity for condescension limited them to the type of smile you might save for a toddler who has just wiped his own bum for the first time.

They all glanced nervously at each other. On the whole

they seemed to feel that Ralph should speak but he indicated his reluctance with a tiny shake of the head and a fierce look at Gerald.

Poor Gerald, thought Emily stifling a laugh at their discomfort. They had a lot in common, her and Gerald. They should probably be friends. Belatedly she realised he was speaking.

'... so, with the superb response to the photocall and statement this morning,' he was saying, 'strategically, we need to build on that over the next few days,' he continued, making sure she was listening. 'You are such an asset to Ralph, as the dedicated wife and mother of his children. Now you have nobly accepted the – er – current situation, the eyes of the voters are on you as much as they are on Ralph.' He glanced at Ralph, and amended, 'well, nearly as much, anyhow. My point is, with only three days to go until polling day, we need to use every weapon at our disposal to ensure the country understands that Ralph is a worthy leader. A real person, battling with the same dilemmas as the common man, a flawed person – if you like,' he warmed to his theme not noticing Ralph's wounded look, 'a man who is redeemed in the eyes of the country by the steadfastness and loyalty of his devoted wife,' Gerald finished with a flourish, rendered moist-eyed by his own rhetoric.

'Don't I know it,' responded Emily waspishly. 'Wasn't that little chimps' tea party we all had to act out this morning precisely that?'

Gerald looked embarrassed and the meek but ambitious secretary earnestly made a note – presumably of the monkey reference – for future posterity. First, though, she gave Emily a conspiratorially sympathetic glance and seemed to be stifling a smirk at Gerald's discomfort. She'll go nowhere, thought Emily, with detachment. That is unless she learns to go along with the men's little games with the slavish admiration they expect.

'Well, hmm,' Gerald continued, 'the point is, we have discussed next steps, and I do think – under the circumstances – our policy with the media should be a rather more – er – confessional, personal approach than one we would otherwise have chosen. Less about the policies and more about the man, you know ...' he tailed off, looking hopefully at Emily.

'Abso-bloody-lutely,' she said, deciding she'd better chuck him a bone. After all it wasn't his fault her husband had turned out to be an arse. 'By all means shove Ralph on the telly anywhere you can. Bung him on the flipping Jerry Lewis show, it can't do any further harm now can it?'

'Jerry Springer,' said the secretary shyly, 'but that's American. I think you mean Jeremy Kyle.'

'Yeah, him,' replied Emily. 'Jeremy Kyle. He can wheel bloody Susie on and Ralph can choose between us live on air.'

'I do think you need to calm down a bit, darling,' said Ralph testily.

'Well, that's a bit rich under the circumstances,' she said, and Ralph made those infuriating 'calm down' gestures with his hands that always made her want to poke him in the eye. 'Anyway,' she added, suddenly weary. 'I said I'd go along with it, and I will, but don't think you need me to sanction every interview you want my husband to do.'

'Ah, well, that's where I need to explain the plan,' said Gerald, nervously. 'Strategically, we have had Ralph say everything we want him to say for now.'

'Tell me about it,' muttered Emily under her breath, wondering if he was aware how many times he used the word "strategically".

'Now,' Gerald continued, 'the most powerful weapon at our disposal is third party endorsement and – under the circumstances, as I was saying – that third party is you.'

Emily stared fixedly at him, which Gerald decided to find

encouraging. He continued; 'So we have decided to say yes to you appearing on "Daytime with Clarissa", "Women at large", "Breakfast time", and then, this weekend, on "Sunday, Sunday",' he finished, looking proud of himself.

'So, every magazine programme on national television and radio, then.'

'Yes,' confirmed Gerald with a satisfied nod.

'When?'

'Tomorrow,' continued Gerald. 'Well, except "Sunday, Sunday",' he said. 'That's on Sunday,' he added unnecessarily.

Emily sat blankly looking at her hands. He had, in one sentence, rounded up all the programmes she and Matt had jointly sworn they would never work on. 'Can't I at least do something proper as well?' she asked faintly. 'Like Woman's Hour or something?'

'Great!' said Gerald, sensing victory. 'They asked for you a while ago actually, but we were holding off to see what else we got.' He turned to the secretary. 'Give them a call and confirm, could you Rebecca?' Rebecca nodded, and took another note.

'We are also launching a Twitter account,' Gerald continued.

'I've already got one,' said Ralph.

'I know,' said Gerald. 'We need to keep that one fairly quiet for a while ...' he added with masterly understatement as he remembered scanning the torrents of abuse which had poured in as the rumours surfaced. The account had had to be suspended that morning.

'I actually meant a Twitter account for Mrs Pemilly,' he explained. 'Twitter will be one of the platforms we are using to get across our brand values of loyalty, domesticity, commitment to family values. We are already drafting a profile and will be tweeting content on Mrs Pemilly's day to day activities; baking for the PTA, taking the children swimming, and so on ...'

'I haven't got time for that,' said Emily, uncomfortably.

'No problem Mrs Pemilly,' Gerald assured her, 'our office staff will be generating the content on your behalf.'

'But how will you know whether I'm baking or swimming?' she asked.

'We won't,' explained Gerald, 'but that doesn't matter does it? It's just a tool. A means to an end. Nobody actually generates their own content nowadays.' He smiled at her reassuringly.

Chapter Thirteen

The breakfast time programme went by in a blur. To allow for getting there, and for make-up, the car had arrived to collect Emily at four-thirty in the morning. Determined to get their pound of flesh, and to make sure they retained their exclusive, the programme's producers had decided that Emily would be interviewed hourly from the programme's beginning at half past six. Mostly she was left sitting wanly in the green room, clutching a tepid vending machine coffee and looking without enthusiasm at a plate of stale croissants. On the screen in the corner she could listen to the presenters talking up her presence, making much of being the first television channel to obtain an interview with the would-be PM's wife. Every hour, she would be ushered over the wires and cables and plonked on the sofa. Weeks of poor sleep plus the early start had made her feel more than usually stupid. The presenters asked patronising 'safe' questions which had clearly been agreed in advance with Gerald. She tried terribly hard to be entertaining but their faces told her they thought her vapid and dull.

After that, the day was a simultaneously stressful and boring whirl of studios and taxis. Emily was accompanied by Rebecca who earnestly told her that her job title was 'external communications intern' and that her real ambition was to reach the heights of chief party spin doctor by the age of thirty. She didn't like to say, but Emily thought Rebecca was highly unlikely to achieve her goal as she gave the impression of being far too nice, with a tendency to think the best of everyone. She would get nowhere with an attitude like that, she thought. After all where had it ever got her?

No-one could accuse Clarissa of being nice and trusting. Having made a career out of being a sexy, earthy woman of the people, with her hugely popular day time magazine show, she hid a fierce intelligence under bottle blonde hair and curves, being disarmingly frank about her own tribulations, from the stresses of being a good mother, to the pressures of fame, no aspect of her life was off limits – and she expected the same of her interviewees.

Having softened Emily up with lots of predictable bonding over motherhood and flattering references to the embarrassingly prim fifties-style dress the party 'image committee' had insisted she wore, Clarissa went right in for the kill.

'So darling,' she purred, 'your loyalty to Ralph is an inspiration to all us women …' She paused infinitesimally and Emily braced herself for the punch, '… but what,' she added, smiling dangerously, 'exactly is it about your Prime-Minister-in-waiting husband that makes you prepared to tolerate his infidelity?'

'Well, it's not the "Prime Minister-in-waiting" bit, I can assure you,' replied Emily hotly. Clarissa merely smiled, her head pseudo-sympathetically held on one side, waiting for her to condemn herself from her own mouth. She duly obliged. 'I am simply saying,' Emily continued, 'that it is easy for other women to look at a man's indiscretions and decide what they would do under the circumstances but, frankly, until you are actually in that position …'

Clarissa was looking vacant, her eyes fixed not on Emily but on the middle distance as she listened to instructions from her producer.

'Right, right,' she said briskly, cutting right across her guest. 'It's time to announce the results of our viewer poll. You will remember girls, we asked you to tell us if Mrs Pemilly should forgive or forgo. Should she cuddle up or kick him out. At the start of the programme, seventy-two per cent of you advised Emily to forgive but now,' she paused, 'now a compelling eighty per cent want to see her kick him out, and a few of our ladies were keen to suggest precisely what she should do to a somewhat delicate part of his anatomy. Steady girls! So, Emily, what do you make of our viewers' advice?'

Emily gave her an incredulous look. She was exhausted, her eyes felt gritty and sore, the lights were making her sweat under the arms, almost certainly creating visible stains on her once crisp cotton dress, and her feet, in the clumpy high heels she had been told to wear, were starting to throb.

'Actually Clarissa,' she said, 'I can honestly say your viewer poll is the most fatuous, pointless, viciously conceived load of nonsense I have ever had the misfortune—'

'Anyway,' interrupted Clarissa rudely again, 'that's all we've got time for but stay with us for our 1950s fashion special, right after the news in your area.'

She beamed at the camera until the red light went off, her face dropping instantly into an expression of boredom. 'Thanks,' she said, waving vaguely at Emily, as a minion with a clip board led her away.

In the green room, she saw, not her minder Rebecca, but a shockingly familiar back view. The room had felt spacious before but, with Matt standing there it was small, cramped, even a little claustrophobic.

'Emily,' he said, turning to greet her with a wide grin. 'I haven't laughed so much in years. You *do* have a way with words.'

'So does that old cow, Clarissa,' she muttered, scuffing her foot petulantly on the carpet. Matt's amusement was irritating enough but Ralph and his little mates were going to do their collective nuts when they saw her losing her cool. As a matter of fact they had probably already seen, so she wasn't looking forward to returning to the office. Luckily she still had Woman's Hour and a couple of regional radio interviews to do.

'Where's Rebecca?' she asked, hoping to change the subject.

'She decided to jump off the roof when she heard your interview,' joked Matt.

She scowled even more. 'Anyway,' she continued, 'what the flipping hell are you doing here? Are you actively persecuting me, or just stalking me so you can enjoy my distress?'

'There is nothing enjoyable about seeing you in distress,' he said, suddenly serious.

She met his gaze. He had always been able to do that with her. To look into her eyes and make the rest of the world seem to disappear. Her head swam and she felt herself sway slightly. Time passed. Unconsciously, they moved closer. She could smell him, almost feel his lips on hers. She pined for his strong arms to slip around her waist. Her longing was so intense, the idea of being embraced so vivid, she imagined she could feel his touch as she stood, suspended between fantasy, reality and the painful memories of the past.

In the end it was Matt who broke contact.

'You should go,' he said, ducking his head and moving away. 'Before I do something you'll regret.'

'Quite,' she said, crisply, resolve fully restored. 'Although it's more likely to be something *you'll* regret. A smack on the chops is not beyond me. Ask Ralph.'

He chuckled. 'So I hear ...'

'Darling!' screeched a voice, and Clarissa charged in, pushing Emily aside to throw her arms around Matt. 'How completely adorable to see you. Where have you been you naughty boy?'

'Hello Clarissa,' he drawled, smiling apologetically over her shoulder to Emily, who was pressing her hands to her burning cheeks to cool them. 'Far from avoiding you, some of us actually work for our living. I've been busy.'

'Not too busy to come on the show today,' observed Clarissa archly.

'Ah, well, that's work,' replied Matt, smiling patiently. 'Purely a career move.'

'Oh yes, that,' said Clarissa, fluttering her eyelashes at him. 'Well, my researchers tell me you have unparalleled access to "team Pemilly" so I expect you to dish the dirt and earn your fee.'

'That's not the brief, Clarissa and you know it,' he replied, with steel suddenly in his voice. Clarissa blinked, disconcerted for once.

'Nice try though,' he added to mollify her.

When Rebecca came back to escort her to the next interview, Emily wanted to dig her claws in like a cat being kicked out into the rain. Life in the green room was strangely appealing – a hinterland outside real life where she and Matt could – well, they just couldn't could they …

If the idea of further interviews was painful, at least the delay in having to return to party headquarters was welcome. In the end, after Clarissa's startling approach, Emily almost began to enjoy herself.

On Woman's Hour, she only threatened to lose her cool when a question about the impact of Ralph becoming PM on her and the children was put in such an empathic, motherly way she was delayed in replying by an overwhelming urge to throw her arms around the woman's neck and burst into tears. Hopefully the little pause didn't register too much and, with radio, the listeners would have been unaware of her clenched fists and momentarily tear-filled eyes.

Matt, who had tuned in on his iPod while in a taxi from the Clarissa studio to his flat, was all too aware of the tiny catch in her voice and the distress he knew it signalled. He bowed his head and groaned in frustration. He had to appreciate the irony of being both the one who had – indirectly – put her in that studio, and the one who wanted most desperately to rescue her from the pain it was causing her.

Hours later he was still agonising. The way the party communications team had decided to handle the story infuriated him. Whilst he had personally decided not to admit to Gerald it was Susie who had told him, he made it perfectly clear that he, Matt, had the whole story, including Susie's identity. He had sworn – mainly to protect Emily – that he would not go public with it provided Ralph confessed to Emily. But that was then. Now the media had sniffed out the story anyway, Emily had been thrust into the full glare of the camera flashes. The heat would be off Emily if the press were pursuing Susie instead. Only they weren't. Because they didn't know who she was. He groaned again. A smaller issue was that his editor had been furious that he – Matt – had, apparently, been scooped by lesser journalists with the affair story. If he came out with Susie's identity he would simultaneously protect Emily and win back the trust of his boss. It was tempting. And yet ... his principles wouldn't let him do it. Not without Susie's permission.

Impulsively, he picked up his phone and put a call through to Susie's mobile. It rang twice and went to voicemail. Impatiently, he called again. This time he received a recorded message saying her phone was unavailable. She had seen his call and switched it off. Swallowing his irritation he tapped out a text instead and tried to distract himself with his current story. He was due to file it in a couple of hours. He had better get a move on.

His phone woke him. Glancing at the clock he saw it was just after two in the morning.

'Susie?' he said.

'Shh,' came the reply. 'I'm not supposed to be talking to you. They even wanted to take my phone away but I wouldn't let them ...'

She sounded hyper-alert, on edge.

'Well?' accused Matt. 'Are you going to come clean?'

'I can't ... I can't,' she whispered, desperately. 'They're watching me. This isn't how I wanted it to be.'

'No? Well, you're a fool if you think you can control the press,' Matt said. 'Or the PR team either,' he added, more fairly.

'They say they're protecting me, but really they're silencing me,' admitted Susie. 'There's someone with me all the time. They won't even let me speak to Ralph,' this last part was a cry of distress.

More likely he doesn't want to speak to you, thought Matt, but he was too kind to say it.

'They're parading Emily and Ralph around like love birds,' she wailed, surely risking waking up her minders.

'Shh,' Matt reminded her. 'Of course they are. It's three days to the election, they're hardly going to do anything else.'

'I do want people to know it's me,' said Susie, sulkily.

'Well, make sure you tell them,' he said, losing patience. 'As soon as you can.'

Later he felt guilty. There really wasn't anything Susie could do to influence how the team had chosen to manage the story. He would just have to wait and hope Emily had the strength to tough it out over the next few days. After the election they could all take a breath and then, hopefully, she would see reason, call time on her marriage and hand Ralph over to Susie once and for all.

Chapter Fourteen

'What the bloody hell was that all about!' snapped Ralph when Emily got back to the office from the Clarissa studio.

'If you actually look at the interview, I was defending you,' said Emily crossly. 'Goodness knows why, because despite my unfathomable loyalty,' she continued, 'I have been unable to persuade the majority of women in this country that you are not a complete arse, an opinion with which I am beginning to have some sympathy.'

Clearly unable to think of a reply, he turned to Gerald instead. 'What's the damage Gerald?'

'Well, I, erm,' he began with what Emily now recognised as his normal reticence. 'This morning's poll does seem to suggest that, erm, perhaps fortunately, the Clarissa show audience view is not entirely typical,' he said, pushing his specs back up the bridge of his nose.

'What, you mean the national official "Is Ralph a complete prat or what" poll is coming up with a different result?' questioned Emily.

'I, er, um, yes,' said Gerald, uncertainly. 'That is to say, the, er, poll didn't *exactly* ask that,' he said unnecessarily, 'but it did seem to indicate that a significant majority of the electorate found Ralph's human frailty and subsequent humility a positive boost to his standing.'

Humility my arse, she thought, but Ralph looked mollified, which was a relief. If she could convince him and his scary crew that she had done her bit maybe there was a chance they would let her go home to the children, who she hadn't seen since the previous night. She was especially worried that Tash might have had a tough day with her friends where she had posted her. Children could be cruel and their parents were often no better. She longed for the normality of tea and homework around the kitchen table. They should all make the most of it while they could.

Gerald was talking again. '… we've managed to uncover one source of rumour, turns out we've been a victim of a bit of a dirty tricks campaign, which is good news …'

'How the hell can that constitute "good news"?' exploded Ralph in disbelief.

'Well,' he explained, undaunted, 'it means we can start to get a bit of control over the news agenda. Rather than having to be on a back foot, having to confirm the rumours, we can go on the attack to suggest that the other parties aren't playing fair. Making the story about them, basically. With luck, I think we can get the front pages to concentrate on that tomorrow.'

'OK,' said Ralph slowly. 'And then, of course, we'll do more of Emily going on about how brilliant I am as well? No hint of anything other than devoted loyalty?'

'Absolutely,' confirmed Gerald.

Emily's heart sank.

'And the Twitter campaign is going really well,' he added. 'The media interviews have generated nearly forty thousand followers and loads of comments with sixty per cent broadly favourable according to our analysis. The tweet giving details of the dress Emily is wearing has been retweeted massively as well as generating coverage on several womenswear blogs.'

'So, I'm now officially more domestic goddess than human being,' commented Emily. 'I am simply an empty media construct – until after the election anyway,' she reminded them darkly.

They both gave her a wounded look which made her even more cross. 'Look, have you at least had your pound of flesh for now?' she said plaintively. 'Can I go?'

'Yes, yes,' snapped Ralph. 'She can go, can't she?' he added to Gerald who nodded nervously.

'Just stay in touch,' he said. 'Things are changing fast. It looks like we'll need you on the campaign bus tomorrow.'

'Surely not,' protested Emily. 'Who will look after the children? I'm running out of favours to pull in.'

'Mm, that's a consideration,' mused Gerald. Emily shot him a grateful look for his understanding. He hadn't struck her before as being a family man. 'Yes,' he continued, staring into space, 'it's a hard call as to whether it's strategically advantageous for Emily to be seen being loyal to Ralph, or to feed out the line that she's a devoted mother staying with her children.'

'Gerald has a point,' said Emily, 'although not for quite the reasons he gives,' she added pointedly. 'I actually do have to look after the children tomorrow and frankly I don't give a monkey's how it looks to the electorate.'

Ralph gave her an admonishing look. Really, thought Emily, she could absolutely murder him, so far removed was he from the man she remembered marrying.

'Of course!' said Gerald, excitedly. 'I have the perfect solution. Emily should come on the bus, and so should the children. What a chance to show Ralph as the dedicated family man, even the day before polling day.'

'I like it,' grinned Ralph. Then he looked doubtful. 'Isn't it the first day of term tomorrow? We had better not keep them out of school – doesn't look good, with all the stuff about education in the manifesto.' He looked pleased with himself. Clearly remembering the dates of the school holidays elevated him to the status of genius in his own eyes. Of course Emily had to do it all the time, but this was taken for granted.

'Tomorrow's an inset day,' muttered Emily reluctantly.

'What's that?' asked Ralph.

'Staff training,' explained Gerald, who really did seem to know everything. 'The unions negotiated it a few years ago. It's term time but the children have a day off so the teachers can do courses and things. Quite often they bung it onto the beginning or end of holidays, half terms and the like.'

'Good grief,' wondered Ralph. 'Don't they already have about fifteen weeks holiday a year for that? Anyway, they should already know what they're doing. There's one for reform when I get in. Take a note,' he added, waving at Rebecca, who diligently wrote something on her clip board.

'Anyway,' he continued, 'on the bright side darling, it means we can all be a family tomorrow, spend a bit of time together,' he said, smiling appeasingly at Emily.

'Make sure the media know,' he added to Gerald. 'I want to get a good turnout.'

By the time she finally made it home that evening, a family tea around the kitchen table was a lost opportunity for yet another day.

Nessa came out to greet her as she let herself in through the front door, slipping off her shoes with relief.

'Hallo darling. Wine or tea?'

'Cup of tea would be heaven, Nessa, I am *sooo* sorry,' she said, giving the older woman a forlorn look. 'I am hideously late.'

'I'm sorry too,' said Nessa patiently, but there was no criticism of Emily implied. 'They own you,' she added. 'I get it.'

'They want us all on the campaign bus tomorrow,' she said, taking a cup of tea and cradling it in both hands with a sigh of gratitude.

'Might as well,' observed Nessa. 'Not long now,' she added comfortingly.

Not long until things get even worse, thought Emily. It was funny how the horror of a positive result on polling day was starting – after the last few nightmare weeks – to be a comfort. A bit like starting to look forward to a horrible exam or even an operation because then the worst would have arrived and needn't be dreaded any longer.

'How are they? Are they both asleep?'

'I'm pretty sure Alfie is,' said Nessa. 'He was a bit tired, poor lamb. Barely managed his tea and pretty much fell asleep into his pudding.'

'Not like him not to want to eat,' commented Emily, concerned. 'And Tash?'

'Not talkative,' admitted Nessa, 'but I gather between the lines that she didn't have the best time at her riding lesson.' She paused. 'From what I can gather, "things" were said.'

Emily raised an eyebrow. 'About ...?' she prompted.

'Oh, you know, silly nonsense about Ralph and this daft Sophie woman.'

'Susie,' corrected Emily automatically. 'Anyway she's just "the other woman", they can't know who...' she added, jealous, again, that Susie was being spared vilification by her continuing anonymity. 'Poor Tash,' she went on. 'She'll be glad not to be going to school tomorrow then,' she observed, thinking that perhaps there was an upside to the next day's plan.

Come to think of it, with barely twenty-four hours until polling day, who was to say that Tash would ever go back to that particular school. Again, Emily's stomach lurched. How could they possibly uproot their lives? It was just so drastic. So violent. As if her brain was simply unable to handle any more overload, she found herself staring mindlessly into space. Vaguely responding to Nessa's goodbyes, she sat at the kitchen table to finish her tea.

When she finally looked at the clock, she was astonished to see it register nearly midnight. Clearly this was yet another evening when Ralph was not planning to make it home.

Earlier in their marriage, he had stayed over at the London flat rarely, making every effort he could to return home, even if, after late night voting, he only arrived in time for cocoa and bed. He delighted in the children running into their bedroom the following morning to say hello, jumping and rolling all over him like puppies. When he had stayed away, she tended to find herself imagining him in the little flat, picturing him cooking himself some supper, having a glass of wine perhaps, wishing she were there. Invariably he would telephone her late and they would share the little triumphs and disasters of the day.

Mostly now he didn't call.

Tash was excited when Emily broke the news about the campaign bus the next morning. Alfie, on the other hand was still pale and quieter than normal. He smiled when she told him they were to spend the day with Daddy but pushed his cereal around his bowl, eating little.

Even Emily had to admit being a little bit swept up by the adrenaline when they arrived at the constituency office where the bus was setting off. It was still barely eight o'clock, but the media was out in force, keen to record Ralph's every utterance and facial expression as the hours ticked by until polling day. The next forty-eight hours were the pinnacle of the campaign, and the team was bullish with the polls reporting a landslide despite – or perhaps because of – the fascination with Ralph's infidelities and Emily's grace under fire.

'Mrs Pemilly,' shouted the reporters crowding behind a barrier beside the bus, 'what do you think about your husband's impending victory?'

'I'm very pleased for him,' she replied, smiling. 'If it's true then it's good news for the party and good news for the country.'

Ralph was there as she climbed on the bus, pushing the children ahead of her.

'That wasn't bad darling,' he said, as he gave her a peck on the cheek, 'but don't go spouting without checking stuff past Gerald will you?' he added. 'We don't want any last minute boo boos do we?'

'I wouldn't imagine so, no,' she replied, giving him a bright, empty smile.

'Mummy,' whispered Alfie, tugging on her sleeve. 'I don't feel very well.'

'Don't you sweetie?' she said, switching her focus. 'Darling, you're not yourself are you?' Heavens, he really was pale, sickening for something to be sure. She pressed her hand against his forehead, but wasn't certain. He was a little warm perhaps.

'Why do people say "you're not yourself"?' he asked peevishly. 'I'm poorly but I'm still me, aren't I?'

'Yes, you are darling,' she reassured him. 'Now let's cuddle up at the back. You and Tash can look out of the window. That'll be fun won't it?' She chivvied them to the rear of the bus, passing Gerald and Rebecca en route. Turning to smile at Rebecca, Emily tripped and fell heavily in the aisle. She would have sprawled on the floor of the bus if a strong pair of arms hadn't shot out and held her up. Muttering her thanks, she steadied herself and looked up to see her saviour.

'Matt! What are you doing here?'

'Oh, let's see,' he said, putting his finger to his chin, pretending to consider. 'Is it because I am a feature writer for the Sunday Times, I'm lined up to do the definitive post-election profile on your husband in a matter of days and we are hours away from polling day where we will find out whether the world has any interest in reading my – rather good – article about him or not?'

'Yeah, yeah, okay. I thought you got your moment in the spotlight when you broke the infidelity story,' she whispered so the other journalists wouldn't hear.

'Not me, remember?'

'Oh yeah. You said.'

'Believe me,' he replied, 'when I break stories I like to get the credit. It wasn't me.'

'Okay,' she conceded, too weary for a fight. She knew Matt was a lot of things, but he wasn't a liar and, anyway, none of the snide, suggestive coverage actually identified Susie, so it looked like it was only Matt who knew that bit.

'How are you?' he said, staring at her intently.

'Fine,' she snapped, not able to meet his eye.

'You look rough.'

'Thanks.'

'It's destroying you.'

'What?' said Emily, throwing a nervous glance at Rebecca who was giving them both a curious look.

'This situation. That bastard. He's a turd. You should leave him,' he hissed fiercely.

'Shh,' she replied, glaring at him to shut up. 'Why do you keep doing this to me?' she whispered, glancing over her shoulder.

Luckily, Ralph was fully engaged, smiling winningly and shaking hands with great enthusiasm. He had a way of leaning his head towards the person who was talking to him. It gave the impression of his being fascinated with what he was hearing. She knew different.

Matt was still staring at her, his eyes burning with all the words unsaid and she was suddenly indescribably tired. She swayed and felt Matt's hands either side of her waist, steadying her.

'Muuummy,' came a wail from behind her.

'Gross,' added Tash. 'He's puked.'

'Oh, it's all right darling,' said Emily, hurrying to Alfie, who was sitting on the middle of the back seat, with a pool of vomit spreading at his feet.

'It's all right sweetie-pie,' she said, gingerly giving him a hug. 'We'll get you cleaned up, don't worry ...'

Luckily he had thrown up with a fair amount of responsibility – something Emily had trained both of her children in from an early age – and the clothing problem was sorted with a quick removal of his sweatshirt. The floor was another matter, but stoic Rebecca got stuck in with a miraculously produced mop and bucket. Emily really did feel that the poor girl was earning herself a promotion and said so to Ralph, who had appeared at the head of the melee, but only once the worst of the mess had been cleaned up.

'Can't you keep the children out of trouble for one day?' he said.

'Alfie is poorly,' she replied. 'They do that, children, unfortunately. I'm going to have to take them home.'

'No, Mummy,' wailed Tash. 'I don't want to go! I hate Alfie, he's always spoiling things.'

'He can't help it darling,' she reasoned. 'Maybe Daddy will let you stay with him,' she said, looking to Ralph for confirmation.

'Darling, I really can't,' he protested. 'It's polling day tomorrow for goodness' sake, plus I really need to have you here for the final publicity drive.'

Emily sighed. She regarded Alfie thoughtfully. His colour seemed a little better and he was watching the fuss he was responsible for with bright-eyed interest.

'How do you feel now, darling?' she asked him, putting her hand on his forehead.

'I'm okay, Mummy,' he said in a small voice.

Emily's heart swelled with love for him. 'Let's stay, shall we sweetheart?'

He did seem a little better. Maybe it was just something he ate.

'Great,' said Ralph, rubbing his hands together. 'Right, let's get this show on the road.'

Practically before they had set off from the constituency office, Alfie had dozed off.

The plan, Emily learned, was for a sort of triumphal parade, with frequent stops, from the constituency office to Westminster, where there would be a huge final press conference before the polls opened the following day.

More than one person likened it to the Palm Sunday return

of Jesus to Jerusalem. Emily seemed to be the only one who thought comparing Ralph to the son of God was a bit much. Also, she didn't like to remind people – least of all Ralph – that Christ had been crucified a few days later.

Now Ralph was sitting amongst the favoured journalists allowed a place on the bus. He was doing his 'man of the people' thing, Emily noted, giving the men matey claps on the shoulder as he sat down and then leaning forward, hands resting relaxed on his knees, to answer their questions. Matt wasn't part of the sycophantic crowd, she noted with approval.

He was still. Watchful. Moving only to scribble in his notebook in the accomplished shorthand budding reporters seldom bothered to learn now. He had always said that, while Dictaphone junkies would be stuffed when the batteries died, he would never miss a quote. He used to tease Emily when she struggled to read her own shorthand, she remembered with a smile, suggesting she might get further if she turned the book upside down.

Alfie was sound asleep when they reached their first stop-off point. Emily edged herself out from under him and took Tash out to join the spectacle. Her daughter was thrilled to be in the centre of all the action, and hung winningly from Ralph's hand, beaming huge smiles at all the little old ladies who cooed gratifyingly over her.

Like father like daughter, thought Emily wryly.

'Is she mine?' came Matt's voice, right next to her. She followed his gaze to Tash, who was oblivious to their joint scrutiny.

Emily gasped. 'Certainly not!' she exclaimed, jumping away from him, but a hand clamped firmly onto her arm.

'How old is she?'

'Nine, damn it,' hissed Emily. 'Barely nine, and you have no right to ask, after – after …'

'I know,' he said. 'You made that very clear at the time.' He released her arm so suddenly she nearly fell again.

Chapter Fifteen

'Try to look a little bit positive, darling,' muttered Ralph through a bare-toothed grin. 'You look like you've been slapped in the face with a big sack of poo.'

The poo would be a positive pleasure in comparison with this little charade, she thought, but gave him an adoring look for the cameras as he planted a kiss on her mouth. The camera shutters went mad.

'Emily,' shouted a scary bleach-blonde hack in a tight skirt, 'what is your message to other women with unfaithful husbands?'

'Vote for Ralph,' Emily replied dryly. 'As husbands go, he makes a pretty good Prime Minister.'

Ralph laughed but the arm around Emily's shoulders tightened painfully. 'As you can hear, my wife is one of my greatest supporters.'

'Didn't sound like it to me,' shouted the bleach-blonde. Emily warmed to her. Then, she read the banner held up by a gaggle of supporters. It said, 'Emily for Prime Minister'. She giggled and pointed it out to Ralph whose lips thinned in irritation.

'No time for more questions now, I'm afraid,' intercepted Gerald swiftly. 'Back on the bus for the final leg please. Ralph will be giving a full press conference when we get to Westminster.'

'How very convenient,' said Emily still grinning but seriously beginning to worry all this mirthless smiling and laughing was making them all look like gurning lunatics.

'I brought you along as an asset, not a bloody liability,' Ralph complained. 'Tash is the only one who seems to care about making a good impression.'

'I expect she'll be a politician when she grows up then,'

said Emily. It was true, Tash seemed in her element, holding court in the centre of a crowd of little old ladies. She was tossing her hair and peering out from under her fringe, charm turned up to gale force. The old dears were loving it.

'I must check on poor Alfie,' fretted Emily.

'Don't fuss, darling,' snapped Ralph. 'I hope to goodness he's not breathing his germs all over everyone. The last thing I need is for the whole team to be chucking their guts up for the whole of the next week.'

She ignored him. 'Come on Tash,' she barked at her daughter, 'time to go.'

'But I'm telling these ladies about when I was the Virgin Mary at school,' complained Tash. 'I was just getting to the best bit.'

'You've delighted them enough, my dear,' misquoted Emily, propelling her back to the bus with an apologetic gesture to the old ladies who cooed and waved gratifyingly.

Alfie was still sound asleep, his blond fringe darkened and plastered to his forehead with sweat. When Emily sat beside him and cuddled him close he partly woke and moaned, before settling back to sleep with his head on her knee.

'I need to get him back to his bed,' she told Rebecca who came down to ask if she would like a cup of tea. Rebecca looked around her as if the solution was somewhere else on the bus if only she could see it.

'Okay, er, we'll be in Westminster soon. I'll call ahead and arrange a car to take you home,' she said.

'Thank you,' said Emily, her eyes filling unexpectedly with tears at this tiny kindness. Rebecca saw and – being young – was embarrassed. 'Everything will be fine, Mrs P,' she said, earnestly.

'Susie called me Mrs P,' observed Emily.

'Oh gosh, sorry,' replied Rebecca, clapping her hand to her mouth.

'Is she going to be there?'

'I don't follow ...' said Rebecca, but she wouldn't look Emily in the eye.

Answer enough thought Emily, deciding not to torture the poor girl further. It was all the more reason to make herself scarce when they got to London.

She drank the tea Rebecca had brought. Then, with the soothing sway of the coach, and the after effects of her sleepless night, before she knew it her head nodded forward and her eyes closed.

The cessation of movement woke her. She glanced out of the window and registered the sheer, grey walls of central London, with their vertical acres of concrete and stone, dwarfing the pedestrians and cars at street level.

Tash was chatting excitedly at the front. She looked down at Alfie, still sleeping on her lap. She wondered if she could get him off the coach without waking him. He really did look unwell, poor little scrap, with his pale, sweaty skin and hectic cheeks, made pinker by the mottled rash dappling his face ...

Dark red pinpricks were scattered across his skin.

She grabbed his hand and held it up to the light. The pinpricks again, like blotches of blood just under the skin. On his palm several spots had joined together forming a brownish-red circle, the size of a kernel of corn.

'Alfie?' called Emily softly, giving him a little shake. He moaned but his eyes barely flickered. 'Alfie!' she said again, louder this time. Another moan, but his eyes were half-opened, staring unseeing into the middle distance. Still holding his hand she noticed it was icy cold, although slick with sweat. She put her other hand on his forehead. Boiling.

'Let me see,' said Matt, appearing suddenly in front of her. He quickly ran his eyes and hands over Alfie's little floppy body, taking just seconds to see what was frightening her.

'There's a car waiting to take us back home,' she said.

'No time for that,' he replied. 'We need to get him to a hospital.' Even as he spoke, he gathered Alfie into his arms and marched down the central aisle.

In seconds they were standing on the pavement, the seething mass of traffic in Parliament Square between them and the Houses of Parliament. Glancing up at the coach alongside, she saw Ralph staring open-mouthed at Alfie. He raised his eyes to meet hers as Gerald pulled at his arm, demanding his attention. For an endless moment, they stared into each other's eyes.

And then he turned away.

As he did so, another strand in the fraying cord of their marriage snapped for good.

'Where are we going?' said Emily, realising she was panting, her breathlessness making it hard to talk. The chaos of London life swirled around them, oblivious to her rising panic.

Without seeming to signal, Matt brought a taxi screeching to a halt beside them.

'A & E,' he said sparingly as he opened the door with one hand and swept Emily into the cab ahead of him. Emily sobbed at the sight of Alfie, paler even than before, draped lifeless over Matt's knee. The rash had spread within minutes, the pinpricks becoming blotches with malevolent speed.

'Keep it together, darling,' whispered Matt. 'He'll be fine.'

'You don't know that,' she said, desperately wanting him to disagree. He didn't.

The taxi took them right to the door of the A & E department. Although Matt was already carrying the still limp, unresponsive Alfie, Emily was grateful that he could spare a hand to support her elbow as she got down from the taxi. Her legs felt like they belonged to someone else and her body was trembling violently.

'It's like I'm an old lady,' she joked.

'You're in shock,' observed Matt curtly. 'The last thing we want is you falling over and breaking your neck.'

'I'd be in the right place though,' she observed.

Night was falling already and coming from the dusk into the brightly-lit hospital was like walking on stage.

Matt shouted for help even as they came through the door. Straight away a little flurry of staff gathered around and propelled him through a pair of double doors.

She glanced at the weary crowd in the waiting room as she shot through. Some looked as if they might have aged a decade or so since arrival. The dot matrix board announced a waiting time of five hours. But not for Alfie. Not for her little boy.

The urgency simultaneously reassured and terrified her.

Scampering to keep up, she dived through the doors and saw the group disappearing into a side room. She met Matt coming out, who fielded her in his arms and blocked entry.

'Come here,' he said, giving her a hug.

'What did they say?' said Emily shakily, detaching herself. 'What are they doing to him? I want to go in.'

He barred her way. 'Leave them to work. They'll tell us when they have some news.'

'He was fine this morning,' she sobbed.

He nodded. 'It happens like that.'

'Actually that's a lie,' she added, almost talking to herself. 'He wasn't fine. He was really under the weather. This time last year I'd have tucked him up on the sofa with his favourite teddy and some warm milk. Now, I bundle him into a coach and drag him off around the country. All for my husband's bloody benefit. What was I thinking?'

'It's a difficult balancing act,' sympathised Matt surprisingly. 'If it's any consolation I think you pull it off – admirably – with the same talent and dedication you apply to everything, in my experience.'

She blinked. She couldn't remember the last time someone whose opinion she respected had said something so admiring. He carried on, oblivious. 'Personally, I don't know why you bother. Not for him. I mean I wouldn't.'

'Lucky he didn't ask you to marry him then.'

'I just can't believe he asked you.'

'Thanks,' retorted Emily.

'That's not what I meant,' he explained, reaching for her hands, 'I mean you're too good for him.'

'But not too good for you?'

'Emily,' said Matt, his head in his hands, fingers gripping his scalp. 'I'm sorry ...'

Before he had a chance to say what he was sorry for, a woman wearing blue cotton scrubs and a stethoscope came out.

'Mum and Dad?' she queried.

Emily wasn't going to waste time explaining. 'Yes,' she said, getting to her feet but, on taking another look at them both, the doctor was clearly confused.

'Er, I have to ask,' she said, 'have I seen you before somewhere?'

'You don't watch "Clarissa" do you?' she replied, incredulously. Surely doctors were too busy to watch rubbish daytime telly. Obviously the humiliation she suffered – was it really only yesterday? – had a bigger impact than she had thought.

'Of course you've seen her,' said Matt, cutting across her. 'She's Ralph Pemilly's wife.'

'Heavens, of course you are,' said the doctor. 'I'm so sorry not to have realised.'

The doctor's eyes flickered nervously as she quickly reviewed whether anything that had happened so far was in contravention of treatment expected by the son and mother of the likely future Prime Minister. 'It's lucky you brought him in so quickly,' she explained at last, having clearly decided that the hospital had not yet let itself down. The name tag said Dr Llewelyn. She looked weary, with her hair hanging in limp strands from an untidy ponytail seeming to illustrate her fatigue.

'We are treating him for bacterial meningitis,' she went on. 'We won't have a definite diagnosis until the test results come back, but the progression of the disease is so rapid, it would be unwise for us to wait.'

'Bacterial?' said Emily. The doctor nodded. 'Well,' she said, 'that's good isn't it? Bacterial is good, right? You have antibiotics for bacterial infections. Viral would be worse wouldn't it? He hasn't got that.' Even to her own ears, she was aware that she was gabbling.

The doctor met Emily's eye. 'I'm sorry to say I would prefer, in this context, to be telling you it's viral. Mrs Pemilly, you need to understand, your son is extremely ill. We are treating aggressively but this is a rapidly advancing disease. I cannot, in all conscience, give you a guarantee that Alfie is going to recover fully. Or,' she paused, 'or if he is going to recover at all.'

Emily swayed, and felt, rather than saw Matt move closer to her.

'I want to see him.'

'Of course,' said Dr Llewellyn. 'I'll take you in to see Archie now.'

'Alfie,' corrected Emily quietly, but the doctor didn't hear.

Matt put his hand on Emily's back as they moved forward.

'Er, sorry,' said the doctor, barring their way. 'I'm afraid I can only let close relatives in.' She looked at Matt apologetically.

'Oh no, please,' said Emily desperately. 'I need him.'

The doctor looked at them both. 'Okay,' she said. 'Come through.'

Chapter Sixteen

Alfie was deathly quiet, looking tiny and defenceless on the high hospital bed. Emily was desperate to gather him into her arms, but with the oxygen mask, the drip going into his arm and the monitoring equipment she was too scared in case she dislodged something. Instead, she contented herself with pressing his little hand between both of hers. The bruises on his skin had spread like an evil tide, even in the last few minutes. Blotches on the backs of his hands had grown and Emily thought there were more pinpricks of blood under the skin on his waxen face. His blond hair had darkened so much with sweat now, it looked like he had just had it washed. Despite his sweaty face, the hand Emily was clutching to her was clammy and colder than ever.

'Where is everyone?' said Emily panicking. 'He's really ill, they should be ... someone should be doing something ...'

'They are,' Matt reassured her. 'Just be still, calm down.'

'How can I?' she asked, stroking Alfie's forehead distractedly. 'What are they doing for him? Why aren't they here?'

'Look,' said Matt reasonably. 'Here are the antibiotics going in.' He indicated the drip going into poor little Alfie's arm. 'These machines are monitoring his heart rate, blood pressure, respiration. If anything exciting happens they'll come crashing in here like the wrath of God.'

She felt a bit better. 'Alfie,' she whispered in his ear. 'Mummy loves you sweetie.'

For a moment, Alfie's eyes opened a slit and he turned his head towards her voice.

'Mummy?' he said, in a cracked voice.

'Yes sweetie-pie,' she said, squeezing his hand.

'I want Daddy,' he whispered, barely audible.

Emily realised she had not thought about Ralph since they left the coach. His presence or otherwise had been completely irrelevant.

'I know Daddy wants to be here, darling,' she said, remembering with cinematic clarity how he had turned away from her. 'I am sure he will come and see you just as soon as he can.'

'I suppose I'd better call him,' she said reluctantly to Matt.

'I'll sort it,' he said and let himself quietly out of the room. Shortly, he was back with a phone on a little trolley.

'Can't use mobiles in here,' he explained. 'I, er, I'll make myself scarce ...' he added looking back at the door.

'Stay,' she said, urgently. Matt nodded and went over to the window, gazing out, hands in pockets.

Needless to say, it wasn't Ralph who answered.

'Emily – er – Mrs Pemilly,' said Gerald nervously. 'How is little Archie?'

'Alfie,' corrected Emily, 'not good actually, I need to talk to Ralph.'

'Yes, of course, I'll ask him to call you just as soon as he can,' replied Gerald, trying to sound as if he was being terribly helpful whilst being precisely the opposite.

'No, Gerald,' she said, firmly. 'I need to speak to him now.'

'Ah,' said Gerald. 'Yes, right,' he added, clearly weighing up the options. He wisely decided to be more scared of Emily than Ralph. 'I'll get him,' he announced, and the line went dead for a considerable time.

Emily tried not to imagine that Matt's back was saying 'I told you so,' as she waited – yet again – for her husband to give his family the slightest priority ahead of his political ambitions.

'Emily,' came Ralph's voice at last on the line. He had that firm, dynamic tone that told her he was in a room full of people he needed to impress.

'Alfie's really ill,' she choked.

'In what way?' he immediately interrogated.

She explained briefly. 'He wants you to be here,' she added, imagining she ought to say that she wanted him there too.

Only she wasn't sure she did.

'Look darling, it's pretty difficult ...' she could hear the conflict in his voice. 'I want to be there, of course I do, but I am sure the hospital staff are all doing a fantastic job. I'll give the doctors a call – get an update – and then I'll get to you as soon as I can,' he said, trying to sound upbeat and decisive. And then he added – with just the tiniest hint of irritation – 'The polls are opening in just a few hours – in case you'd forgotten.'

Frankly, she had.

Chapter Seventeen

Alfie slept, peacefully it seemed, but secretly Emily wondered if he was unconscious. She dared not ask the intermittent stream of staff who came in to check the monitors. She didn't think she would be able to contain her panic if they told her something even scarier than what she had already heard.

Matt had tried to persuade her to go to the canteen to eat. She refused but allowed a kindly nurse to bring her a cup of tea. The young nurse was star-struck at Emily's presence and in awe of Matt, who she clearly found attractive.

Mostly, they just sat beside one another, Emily at Alfie's head and Matt at his feet. Emily found she couldn't take her eyes from her son, devouring the very sight of him like she remembered doing in the hours after his birth. She watched the marks under his skin obsessively. Were they spreading?

Without saying a word, Matt took a pen from his pocket. She looked at him curiously as he gently took Alfie's hand from Emily's and marked the edge of the largest blotch of browny-red. Understanding what he was doing, Emily said, 'but why don't they do that? Surely they should be watching him.'

'You heard the doctor,' said Matt, the voice of calm. 'They are treating him. I'm marking the line so *you* can see if it spreads. I know nothing else will reassure you.'

'What makes you think that'll reassure me?' she ventured shakily.

'Because the only thing that ever made you feel better about scary situations was knowing absolutely everything,' replied Matt. 'That was always one of the things I loved about you.'

'You loved me,' she said.

'You know I did,' he replied. 'I haven't stopped.'

Silent, they both gazed at Alfie, watching his chest go up and down as he took his too shallow, panting breaths.

'You left me,' she said at last. 'We needed to be together. To talk. And you just went away. Your work took precedence.'

'I know. I was an idiot. I'm sorry.'

She didn't reply.

'But I couldn't believe it when you told me what you'd done,' he added, after a long pause. 'I never thought – I was shocked.'

Emily was taken aback. 'What *I'd* done,' she hissed. 'We *are* talking about the bit where I told you I was pregnant and you buggered off in the dead of night to pretty much the only part of the world you couldn't be contacted?'

'I don't blame you,' Matt said, grabbing Emily's hand. 'It was my fault for not being able to cope. Actually I blamed myself for driving you to it. I've been blaming myself for the last ten years, wondering what she would have been like. Or he,' he added, looking at Alfie. 'Actually,' he admitted, looking searchingly at her for her reaction, 'I even thought you may have lied about it, just telling me that so you could end the relationship. Next thing I knew you were with Ralph and pregnant with Tash. I wondered if she was really mine, if you were just punishing me ...'

'Er, sorry?' she stuttered, floundering as every word he spoke deepened her confusion. 'What on earth is it you think I've done? And,' she added before he had a chance to reply, 'might I say it's a bit rich for you to accuse me of lying about whether I was pregnant, whether I wasn't pregnant...' she trailed away in confusion, 'when you were clearly appalled to hear I was carrying your child.'

'Not so appalled I wanted you to terminate it,' he snapped, before dropping his face into his hands and rubbing wearily. 'Sorry, like I said I'm not blaming you ...'

'Too bloody right you're not,' she said, after a stunned silence. 'Did you honestly think ...' Tears sprang to her eyes.

She didn't trust herself to speak for a moment. 'Did you honestly think,' she said at last, 'I would deliberately destroy our baby?' Her face crumpled.

He looked up, saw the disintegration and ten years of guilt and blame fell away. 'God, Emily I am so sorry,' he said gathering her in against his chest. 'I hurt you so much, I know I did. I suppose when you told me the baby was gone I assumed you had got rid of it because I had behaved like such an idiot.'

They both replayed in their minds that grim conversation, the line from Kazakhstan so poor that Emily heard everything Matt said twice, the repeat a second behind and coming from the far end of a long, echoing corridor. She had been determined not to show the depth of her distress when she lost first her lover and then, ten days later, her baby in an early and painful miscarriage. When he had asked after the baby she had snapped angrily that it was gone. Only now did she appreciate that she had provided no detail as to how and why. At the time her overwhelming feeling was anger that she had gone through the whole devastating event without the one person she wanted beside her. Still numb from the shock and betrayal, allowing herself to fall so quickly into a relationship with Ralph, and then becoming pregnant before she even thought it medically possible ... she realised she had simply let it happen, relieved to hand over thinking and decision-making to whoever was there beside her. And it happened to be Ralph.

Now, ten years later, the real comfort she craved was there at last. He rocked her gently as he held her, his body warming and soothing her distress as he stroked the back of her neck.

'Tash is beautiful, just like her mum,' he murmured in her ear. 'I would have been proud if you had told me she was mine.'

She choked back a sob. She could hardly afford to fall to bits but his tenderness, along with the sadness of her memories and worry over Alfie was breaking down her defences alarmingly.

'When I said I never thought of you, I lied,' she admitted, hiccupping slightly.

'I know,' he replied, sliding his hand into the hair at the back of her neck, kneading gently. 'I've thought of nothing else, how I ballsed everything up. Hurt you, and then lost you to that prat ...'

'Careful,' responded Emily dutifully. 'That's my husband you're talking about.'

He sighed. 'You hardly need to remind me. It should have been me.'

'You didn't ask,' she replied, sitting up and carefully wiping the tears from her eyes.

'Marry me,' he said, holding her tear-stained face in his hands so she couldn't look away.

They stared at each other for what felt like a hundred years.

'It's too late.'

'It's not.'

'Of course it is,' replied Emily, wishing it weren't true. 'Ralph and I have quite the most public marriage in the UK – at the moment certainly. I can't just bail out, much as I would like to ...' she added with honesty.

'What, because people you don't care about don't approve?' he challenged.

'No,' she said, although it was. 'It's about Tash and Alfie too – he is their father after all.'

'I wish I was,' said Matt intensely. 'I would love them, not just because they are fantastic kids but because you're their mother.'

'It's too late,' she said, 'don't do this.'

'You do feel for me though,' persisted Matt. 'You love me. I know you do.'

She did. And the realisation that her feelings were just as

intense as they were when he let her down in the past was no comfort, the impossibility of it all was greater than ever.

'Enough,' she said, remembering her promise to James. 'Matt, you must stop this.' She raised her chin determinedly. 'I am totally dedicated to my husband. There is no room for any possibility that you – we – can have any future. I need you to go.'

His face hardened. 'You don't mean that.'

'I do,' replied Emily sadly. 'I really, really do. And if you won't go, I will.'

The last word was a sob and she pushed him away reeling out into the corridor. Finding a little dark room filled with steel shelves of bedclothes and towels, she sank to the floor and sat, head in hands listening to her heart pounding, shutting her eyes to intensify the darkness.

In the end, she couldn't bear to stay away from her vigil with Alfie. Creeping back she was relieved to see that Matt had gone. In his place, a white-coated doctor, a man this time, was checking the chart at the end of Alfie's bed.

'How is he?' she pleaded, resisting the urge to pluck at his sleeve.

He jumped and turned, revealing a ridiculously youthful face that needed a shave.

'Hello Mrs Pemilly,' he said nervously. 'Try not to worry, everything is being done you know, and it's a real help that you got Alfie here so quickly. Also,' he threw her a disarming grin, 'he looks like a tough kid.'

She was tearfully grateful he had got Alfie's name right. 'He is,' she agreed, 'but what about this terrible rash?'

'It can look worse than it is,' the doctor replied. 'I wouldn't be at all surprised if he gets away with just losing his toes and fingertips.' He seemed to expect Emily to find this reassuring.

When he had gone she returned to holding little Alfie's hand and stroking his head. The biro mark Matt had made on his hand a couple of hours ago was being incorporated into a particularly big blotch, but Emily did dare to think the awful stain was spreading less quickly. It felt like days since they had set off that morning. Actually, as it was well after midnight, it was officially yesterday they had set off. Emily didn't know how she was going to survive until the dawn. She didn't even know what had happened to Tash but only hoped that someone had thought to take the poor child home and put her to bed. Now it was too late for her to telephone and find out. She would have to wait until morning only, being polling day, she seriously wondered if she would get any sense out of anyone even then. Not for the first time, she felt the desperate tug of being a mother not able to assuage her need to care for and protect both her children. Never had she felt more inadequate and more torn.

Her eyes were so gritty and sore, she felt they must be as pink as a white rabbit's. The reflection in the dark glass of the window told her the rest of the story. A wan, shiny face with lank, greasy hair looked back at her, the eyes so darkly shadowed they reminded her of the empty eye sockets of a skull. And then of course she reeked, not just with the usual stale sweat but the rank, piercing smell of nervous perspiration. *What a catch*, she thought ironically, *no wonder Matt couldn't keep his hands off me*. Recalling the hard expression on his face when he left her elicited a fresh rush of tears which she brushed away irritably. She felt so wired the continuous hum and clatter of hospital life outside the room grated unbearably on her nerves. A rattling trolley at the other end of the corridor sounded like someone dropping a hundred saucepan lids. She rested her head on the side of the bed and tried to close out the world. Incredibly, she slept.

'Mrs Pemilly, Mrs Pemilly.' Emily became groggily aware that someone was calling softly and shaking her shoulder.

Sitting up, she saw a sweetly smiling Irish nurse she vaguely remembered from the night before. She was holding

146

out a cup of tea. Emily would have preferred coffee but accepted it gratefully.

'Your husband's office called,' she told her. 'They say he will be coming in to see Alfie in a couple of hours,' she said excitedly. 'I hope it's before ten o'clock,' she added. 'That's when I get off duty.'

Alfie looked just the same. 'Should he still be asleep?' Emily asked the nurse anxiously.

'Sleep is very healing,' she replied, tweaking his blankets straight and, touchingly, brushing Alfie's fringe away from his closed eyes. 'Doctor will be doing her rounds soon. She'll be able to tell you more.'

Emily watched the clock anxiously. Eight o'clock came and went. At nearly nine o'clock there was a commotion at the door of the ward.

'Really,' came a familiar voice, 'I can assure you this child and his mother need to see me, and now, if you don't mind ...'

Emily nearly wept with relief as Nessa swept in looking comfortingly familiar but even more than usually glamorous.

'Nessa,' she said, her mouth trembling.

'Hush, hush,' Nessa murmured, sweeping her into a hug. 'Now,' she added after just a moment, 'chin up and tell Auntie Nessa all about it.'

'It is *so* good to see you.'

'Taken as read,' nodded Nessa, 'although not a sentiment shared by the dragon at the door,' she added.

'Takes one to know one,' shot back Emily cheekily, 'but still, I am glad you came. It's been a long night.'

'You've been alone?' asked Nessa.

'Matt was here.'

'Was he now?' she remarked thoughtfully, 'but no sign of the big man himself?'

'He's trying to get here – apparently.'

'Is he?' mused Nessa, looking at an elegant gold watch.

'And soon, I'll warrant, if he's planning to give the lunchtime bulletins something to cover.'

'Hark at you,' remarked Emily. 'You sound like Gerald.'

'Do I?' said Nessa, raising an eyebrow, amused. 'Funny you should say. Anyhow, you'll think I'm even more like Gerald when I admit I brought you some clean clothes to face the cameras in.'

'Thank goodness,' she admitted. 'I stink and I must look a sight.'

Nessa diplomatically said nothing, just handed Emily a holdall she hadn't noticed until then.

'You've been to my house,' commented Emily, burrowing through the bag and seeing, with relief, Nessa had thought of everything.

'I spent the night there,' explained Nessa, 'to look after Tash. I hope you don't mind?'

'Mind? Of course not – thank you,' said Emily. 'But where was Ralph?'

'Not sure,' she said blankly. Emily knew better than to interrogate her, but clearly her friend was unhappy with the situation and Emily didn't think it was her Nessa was cross with.

'Desperate as I am to get cleaned up, I don't want to go,' she said, gesturing at Alfie, who was still fast asleep. 'The doctor's coming in a minute. I'll miss her.'

'You won't,' reassured Nessa. 'I'll stay here with Alfie. You pop to the loos across the corridor. I'll come and get you if anyone turns up.'

As it was, after a lightning quick shower, the sheer joy of changing into clean clothes and even putting a bit of make-up on, Nessa and Alfie were still alone.

'That looks better,' commented Nessa approvingly.

'Good choice,' said Emily.

Nessa's efficiency was extraordinary. She had managed to

pick out Emily's favourite jeans, and a relatively smart grey cashmere sweater which was Emily's fall back comfort wear. She had even chosen matching underwear. She only had a momentary wobble over the thought of Nessa having to rummage through her far from organised knicker drawer. It was a bit like having your mum sort out your clothes for you, she decided.

The young doctor eventually returned, this time in the wake of Dr Llewelyn, who was either still on duty, or perhaps had gone and then returned.

'So, we meet again Alfie,' she said, smiling briefly at Emily and taking the offered chart from an underling.

After a brief perusal of the clipboard, she examined Alfie, who half opened his eyes for the event and even pushed her hand away irritably.

'A good sign,' she murmured. 'Hello Alfie,' she added, louder. 'How are you feeling?'

'My head hurts,' he muttered, eyeing her crossly. Emily stifled a sob of relief.

'I am sure it does,' said the doctor. 'You've been a poorly boy.'

'He's been?' interrogated Emily, no longer able to watch without comment.

'I would say he is on the way to recovery,' said the doctor, addressing Emily this time. 'It's been a tough night for mum,' she observed. Emily nearly dissolved at her matter of fact sympathy, and just nodded mutely.

'I'm pretty happy with him,' continued the doctor. 'We'll not get the result of the lumbar puncture for a couple of hours but he's clearly on the mend,' she said. 'We'll need to carry on with the antibiotics and keep a very close eye on him for now.' Her entourage all nodded in unison. 'He had his guardian angel looking after him that's for sure,' she added. 'The tragedy is when parents leave it too long before they bring their children in to us. Lucky you got him here so soon,' she told Emily who was just thinking she knew exactly who Alfie's guardian angel was, although she wasn't sure if Matt was the type for white fluffy wings.

'What about this ...' said Emily, gesturing at the dark blotches, lightening before her eyes, now she had received such reassuring news.

'His skin looks grim I know,' said the doctor, 'but in many ways it looks worse than it is. A bit like frostbite.' Emily nodded, not having the faintest idea about frostbite either. 'Will he lose his fingers and toes?' she said, glancing at the young doctor nervously.

'Not unless he has an extremely unfortunate accident with a lawnmower,' joked the woman, giving her underling a stern look. 'I understand this little boy has a very important daddy?' she queried.

'Hard to tell until tonight,' said Emily drily. 'Until then he's merely a shadow of his future self.'

'"Shadow", right, got it,' said the doctor appreciatively, 'that's good. Well, let's hope by tonight Alfie is a proper PM's boy, not a shadow PM's boy.'

'More a victim of a single parent family,' muttered Emily, which made the doctor give her an odd look.

'Talk of the devil,' said Nessa, who had been discreetly standing by the window out of the way. Emily went over to follow her gaze. She saw Ralph's car draw up by the main entrance, sweeping past a gaggle of media and a short row of smartly turned out staff. He got out of the car on the opposite side to where the cameras stood but, after a brief flurry of activity, the two women watched as, comically, he got back in the car, which then reversed a short way and swept in again. This time, he got out of the side nearest the entrance where the cameras could see him and, looking serious and concerned, shook hands briefly with the staff before striding inside.

'Ever the media tart,' said Nessa sourly.

Clearly the media opportunities continued because it took

an inordinately long time for Ralph to reach Alfie's room. Eventually, he rushed in as if he had run all the way, ruffling his hair to create the necessarily 'distraught father' persona which suited circumstances.

'Darling,' he said giving Emily a cursory kiss. 'What's the story?'

'It's been a tough night,' she said. 'The doctor says he's doing well.'

'Hallo trouble,' said Ralph affectionately ruffling Alfie's hair.

'Ow, Daddy,' he muttered grumpily in reply, making Emily cover her mouth to hide a smile. 'Don't, my head hurts.'

'Course it does mate,' continued Ralph. 'Mummy says you've been pretty poorly. But you're on the mend now. You can go home soon I expect.'

'Will you be there?' asked Alfie so plaintively Emily's heart swelled for him.

'Well,' said Ralph, 'I've got a lot on, mate.'

'No, then,' said Alfie with resignation, and sighed. 'I'm tired,' he added. 'I want to go to sleep.'

'You do that, sweetie,' said Emily. 'I'll be here when you wake up.'

'No point me hanging around by the looks of it,' said Ralph briskly when they adjourned to the corridor.

'None at all now you've given the TV stations their story,' said Emily daringly, but he seemed impervious to sarcasm.

'They should be broadcasting it by lunchtime,' he said looking at his watch anxiously. 'I wonder if I ought to offer a statement, something about the excellent work of the NHS, only obviously they'll have to deliver a bloody sight more when I'm in government,' he added, checking cursorily to make sure none of the staff could overhear. The nurses at the station up the corridor, who were paying close attention while pretending not to, grinned brightly at him and bridled at his returning smile.

'Now, darling, the plan is for you to come back to the constituency with me in a few hours, to wait for the results, obviously. In the meantime, I'll need you to look adoring at the lunchtime press conference.'

'No,' she said.

He looked so astonished she nearly laughed. 'I can't leave Alfie,' she explained.

'Okay, well, that's all very laudable, darling,' said Ralph with the ultra-reasonable voice that she found particularly annoying. 'But he is just going to be asleep isn't he? Not much point you staying here and watching him do that.'

Emily didn't bother explaining to her husband how the whole principle of her being a mother made it physiologically impossible to leave her son's bedside. Instead, she turned on her heel and went back into Alfie's room. When she glanced out through the glass door a moment later Ralph had gone.

Hours later, she had read Alfie a Thomas the Tank Engine story – five times – and had even seen him eat a reasonably good tea. Normally she wouldn't be keen on him eating nothing but chocolate mousse, but today she was thrilled when he asked for more.

'How are you feeling darling?' she said, stroking his hair.

'I feel tired Mummy,' he admitted. 'My legs are still poorly I think, but my arms feel better,' he said, waggling them around to demonstrate, but then flumping back on his pillow, pale with the effort.

'That's what made me decide to go into paediatrics,' Dr Llewellyn said, appearing suddenly at Emily's elbow and looking at Alfie approvingly. 'Children can be at death's door one minute and racing around the ward the next. You certainly know where you are with them.'

'Not racing around yet,' said Emily, although she was nearly tearful with relief at Alfie's recovery.

'Try him tomorrow morning,' said the doctor knowingly.

'You're doing well Alfie,' she said to him, 'but take it easy. You've been very sick – gave your mummy quite a fright.'

'And my daddy,' corrected Alfie automatically. 'Do I have to go back to school tomorrow?' he added, reluctantly.

'Not tomorrow darling,' said Emily. 'You'll need to stay in here for a bit, I should imagine?' The last bit was more of a question.

'I expect we'll let you go in a couple of days,' said the doctor, 'if you keep doing as well as you are now.'

Emily was amazed it was so quick. Also, she wondered where on earth they would be in forty-eight hours. If Ralph got his way, would they even be allowed to return home? She consciously calmed her panic, reassuring herself that, despite her best efforts to show her loyalty, James for one was highly sceptical the election could be won. Even if the worst happened, she had pledged her loyalty only until tomorrow. She had lied for Ralph, lied to Matt, and – one way or another – she would be able to put it all straight again. That was what Ralph had promised.

'What, Mummy?' queried Alfie perceptively.

'Nothing at all, darling,' said Emily. 'Just wondering how to keep you amused if you can't go back to school for a few days.'

'DVDs and cuddles on the sofa,' he said quickly, returning to the reassuring ritual Emily had established with both children when they were ill.

'With a blanket on?' she asked.

'Yes,' agreed Alfie, 'and popcorn,' he added hopefully.

'We'll see,' she smiled, stroking his feet.

Chapter Eighteen

A nurse had come in and put their television on for the teatime news. 'I expect you'll see your daddy,' she said, smiling brightly at Alfie and handing Emily the remote control.

First the presenter interviewed a commentator who talked in serious tones of Ralph's statesmanlike demeanour despite the stress of his child's illness and even made obsequious allusion to the dignity and focus of his behaviour since Alan's death. Emily was nearly sick. They didn't even damn well mention his affair. One sick little boy, it seemed, and old Ralph was Mr Goldenballs. Granted then, just to even things up, they had someone talking in support of the opposition, but the spokesman was too wily to try and score any cheap points against saintly Ralph, for fear it would backfire, like the accusations of dirty tricks over the affair had done. Instead he confined himself to casting doubt on the depth of Ralph's experience given his sudden rise to power. That wasn't nearly enough to scupper Ralph's chances thought Emily with irritation. He was so obviously a weasel-worded politician with a tendency to be led by the willy, she couldn't believe people couldn't see it. What was wrong with everyone? Still, reassuringly, she could imagine most of the women would see through the bullshit and they constituted half the electorate after all.

Despite the increasing tension outside, and her irritation at the media coverage, Emily felt comfortably cocooned from the events of the day. Time was marked out comfortingly in the hospital by meals, medication rounds and cups of tea. Alfie ate some ice cream for supper which delighted Emily and caused a smiling Irish nurse to suggest 'doctor' would order his drip to be disconnected in the morning – providing he continued to eat and drink, she warned, wagging her finger mock sternly.

Emily's only regret was that she didn't have Tash with her too. Nessa had promised to bring her in but, as the hours ticked by, Emily watched the doors of the ward with increasing impatience.

At last, Nessa pushed through the double door with Tash holding her hand. Jolted out of her usual insouciance, she looked young and vulnerable. She rushed to Emily and clung to her tearfully.

'Hello my gorgeous girl,' she whispered in Tash's ear. 'I missed you.'

'I missed you too, Mummy,' Tash replied in a near wail. 'Nessa's been really kind, though,' she added hastily, separating herself from Emily and giving Nessa a polite smile. The sudden flash of adult grace under pressure made Emily's heart swell.

'Tash has been the kind one,' contested Nessa, brushing Tash's hair out of her eyes. 'She's been terribly grown up and good, showing me where everything was.'

'Tash,' muttered Alfie weakly, waking from another of his profound sleeps.

'Hi monkey face,' said Tash, trying to sound laconic, but swiftly and impulsively leaning down to give him a kiss, before pulling a face to counteract the embarrassing display of affection.

'Have you had an exciting time darling?' asked Emily, trying to sound enthusiastic.

'S'pose so,' replied Tash reluctantly. 'Lots of grown-ups pawing me and telling me how clever Daddy is.'

'He is,' said Emily, loyal for her daughter's sake.

'I know,' replied Tash. 'But I'm clever too, so I already know. They just suck up to me to get to him.'

Emily blinked. Over Tash's head she saw Nessa stifle a smile.

'So,' continued Emily, clicking into mummy mode, 'have you had some supper? Heavens, it's eight o'clock already. Perhaps Nessa will take you down to the cafeteria to get something to eat.'

'Nooo,' wailed Tash, suddenly back to being the child she truly was. 'I want to stay with you, Mummy.'

'Of course she does,' said Nessa briskly. 'Now you *both* need to eat, so why don't I stay with Alfie and you go and get something. Tell you what, there's a Pizza Hut just around the corner, why not get properly out and have some fresh air too?'

Emily looked uncertain, but Alfie had fallen back into a deep sleep. He probably wouldn't even know she had gone.

'Come on, Mummy,' said Tash, 'I'm starving, although I'd rather have a McDonald's. We saw one of those too.'

Emily grimaced. 'I suppose so,' she said, uncertainly, but Tash deserved to have some quality time after their forced separation.

Nessa had already dismissed them, taking out a book and reading glasses from her capacious handbag and settling herself beside Alfie's bed.

There was a slight complication caused by a remaining gaggle of media outside the main entrance but that was sorted with a smart move by the hospital manager on duty who whisked out surgical scrubs for Emily, promising her that hospital staff frequently snuck out to grab a takeaway and that it would act as a sufficient disguise. Tash just put the hood up on her coat and then they were both smuggled out of the side entrance closest to the shops.

After a vanilla milkshake and a double cheeseburger with large fries Tash's chirpy nine-year-old persona was completely restored, although Emily was shocked how tired and pale she looked. Glancing in the now darkened window she was even more shocked when she saw her own reflection.

By the time they got back to the ward it was late and lights were being dimmed to allow the children to settle for the night. Nessa had not, of course, just sat quietly in Emily's absence.

'Now,' she announced, when Emily reappeared, 'we have hatched a cunning plan.'

'Why am I not surprised?' she joked, suddenly achingly tired now that Nessa was there to share the load.

Nessa bowed her head to acknowledge the compliment. 'There's a house nearby for parents to stay overnight – siblings can stay too,' she said to Tash who looked panicked at the thought of having to go home without her mother again. 'That said, there is rather a lot of interest in you, tonight of all nights, so you might prefer to stay within the hospital.'

Emily nodded wearily. She was also not yet ready to be very far away from Alfie, who did seem to be improving by the hour, but it was going to take her a very long time indeed to be relaxed about him again.

'The option I like best,' Nessa continued, 'is for you and Tash to bunk up in the side ward opposite, which is currently empty, by a miracle. The ward sister made a bit of a fuss about it being deeply unusual, but she saw sense in the end.'

'Nessa you are a star,' breathed Emily. 'That sounds great, doesn't it darling?' she added to Tash, who was sighing with relief at knowing she could stay with her mother.

'I wouldn't thank me too soon,' said Nessa swiftly. 'It's not the Ritz, but I should think you could sleep on a clothesline after last night.'

A quick perusal pronounced the side ward perfectly acceptable. The beds, there were four of them, all empty, were a little high and the side bars were disconcerting but, once the blinds were drawn to cut out the fluorescent light from the corridor, it looked very appealing indeed to Emily.

She persuaded Tash to get her pyjamas on and brush her teeth straight away. 'You can stay with Alfie for a bit and watch Daddy on television if you like, darling,' Emily cajoled, 'but it's terribly late and at least if you're ready for bed you can pop across the corridor and go straight to sleep whenever you like.'

When the sensible older doctor dropped in half an hour later, she found Tash snuggled up next to a still sleeping Alfie, her eyelids drooping. Emily, her arms wrapped comfortingly around her own ribs, was ignoring the television in the corner, gazing at her children instead.

'We need to get you and this little one some antibiotics too,' she said quietly. 'The chances of you getting ill are low but it doesn't make sense not to cover yourselves,' she continued. 'His father should probably take them too. Presumably they've been in close contact in the last couple of days?'

'Not really,' said Emily truthfully.

'Oh,' said the doctor. 'Well, he's been busy I would imagine,' she said waving at the television where a BBC presenter was pointing earnestly to some dull looking charts with pictures of the UK on them.

After giving Alfie a brief but thorough check and twiddling the drip going into his arm, she smiled and left.

Few staff were around now. The hallways were only dimly lit and Emily felt cocooned in the darkened room with her two children, like a lioness with her cubs. Her window to the world outside – not that she had the slightest interest in it – was the television in the corner. With the sound turned off, the expressions on people's faces were pure entertainment. Portly old men in blazers with brass buttons and earnest young, usually spotty, party workers, were shoulder to shoulder in church halls across the country.

As announcements were read silently, Emily was mildly diverted by letting the expressions on the faces of the candidates tell her the results. The losers were largely stoic, hiding their devastation with an almost immediate polite smile. Entertainingly, the winner, Emily noticed, would do the opposite, instantly plastering a deadly serious look on their face and accepting congratulations with the kind of pained expression that one would expect from someone going to the dentist – or perhaps the gallows. How frightfully British, thought Emily, amused.

Another source of comedy was all the live feeds from lowly regional BBC reporters who had probably never done telly before, so fazed were they by the complexity and confusion. The country was constantly broadcasting live from Little Snoring or some other backwater constituency where the local reporter was blankly unaware they were on air for several seconds. One was yawning hugely, another was chatting on her mobile and yet another was picking his nose with extraordinary thoroughness.

Her attention was snapped suddenly into gear when the cameras alighted on their own constituency. There Ralph was, surrounded by a phalanx of familiar faces and a much larger crowd of voters than at many of the other venues. Ralph was looking more unattractive than usual, his hair separating with a hint of stringiness over a thinning spot on the back of his head, his face greasy and redder than normal and eye bags pronounced. Emily was surprised the party hadn't sorted out some make-up for him. The usual crowd jostled around him, with TJ looking pained and anxious in the background and Party Chairman James adding sombre weight to the occasion. Emily scanned the faces, not admitting to herself who she was looking for. Then, with a lurch of shock, she saw Susie, right behind Ralph's elbow – the power behind the throne, she thought, sourly. What the bloody hell was that smug tart doing there?

Yet again she felt the twist of bitterness that Ralph's lover's identity had not been revealed in the press, despite fevered speculation. Ungraciously, she resented Susie being spared the full glare of the media's and public's fascination with the subject. To top it all, as she watched, Susie's puppy dog gaze was rewarded with a moment of attention from Ralph. He grasped her upper arms in both hands and spoke intently to her. Even in the small television camera picture Emily could see her competitor melting into an adoring heap at his ministrations. Fuming, she was glad when the camera panned, but then her bitter musings were arrested suddenly by the sight of another face.

Matt stood quietly on the edge of the crowd, watching. His stillness was compelling and his expression, as he too watched Susie and Ralph, was grim. Emily was disappointed when the broadcast returned to the studio for another tedious interview with a political pundit.

What amused her even less was to see the maps of the UK being gradually covered with the trademark vibrant orange stain of Ralph's party. By midnight it was clear that – against all the odds – it was to be the party of government, with him at the helm and his family dragged reluctantly in the wake. Through the night, the children snoring gently, Emily's mind skittered from one problem to another. As her second night without sleep, she knew no sensible decisions could be made but she was reminded of the Wordsworth poem – or was it Keats? – with the line "shades of the prison house close upon the growing boy" which seemed to perfectly sum up her increasing sense of entrapment.

And then another crushing thought struck her. Of course, Matt was producing his definitive piece on 'the Prime Minister the man' right after the election. That would be the Sunday after next, Emily reckoned. Even if he was putting the finishing touches to it over the next few days, she doubted very much if he would be in contact with her after their last conversation. She longed to be able to see him again and this time – having done her duty – to be honest about her true feelings to him at least.

After another couple of hours, she started imagining

things moving in the shadows, making her jump and glance nervously into the corners. Alfie was still sleeping soundly so this was her signal to at least lie down. Letting herself quietly into the room opposite Alfie's and closing the door softly to avoid waking Tash in the bed by the window, she slipped into the remaining empty bed. As she did so every muscle in her body started to ache, as they resisted her instruction to relax into the hard hospital mattress. Her eyes felt impossibly gritty, so closing them was a relief, but sleep would be bound to elude her.

Chapter Nineteen

When she woke, stiff and cold, she discovered Tash had crept into her bed.

Extracting herself carefully, so as not to wake her, Emily scooped a mouthful of water straight from the tap and splashed another handful on her face. Pulling her fingers through her hair, she sloped across the hall and snuck into Alfie's room. He was already awake and – she was relieved to see – looking reassuringly bored.

'There you are,' he said petulantly.

'Hallo darling,' she said. 'Better?' He nodded irritably.

'Is Daddy pry mincer?' he asked.

She nodded. 'Think so.'

'Are we going to live in the House of Commons and have a policeman standing outside the front door?'

'I suppose so,' she said, her heart sinking.

'I want to stay at home,' said Alfie. She saw tears welling in his eyes.

'Darling!' she scooped him up into her lap. 'Don't worry, we'll be together wherever we are.'

'Will we though?' contributed Tash as she came in, blearily rubbing her eyes, 'if you and Daddy get divorced?'

'Where on earth did you get that from?' Emily asked unconvincingly. 'Listen. Wherever you both are, I'll be there. And Daddy will be with us as much as he can – just like before,' she added.

'So you are getting divorced,' said Tash, razor sharp, despite having had barely any sleep.

'No darling, that's not what I said,' flailed Emily, 'but anyway, now is not the time.' Looking distractedly at the still broadcasting television in the corner she grabbed the remote control and turned up the volume. There, giving an impromptu press conference, was Ralph.

'So, later today,' he was saying, 'I shall have the privilege of visiting her Majesty in the hope that I will be asked to form a government, but first,' he smiled engagingly, 'I have an even more important appointment to keep,' he paused, 'with my wife and children.' Recognising the background on the screen, Emily ran to the window and there he was, just disappearing through the main doors of the hospital, a group of security men guarding the entrance from a rabble of journalists who tried and failed to follow him.

'Hullo everyone,' said Ralph as he came into the room, barely giving Emily a glance before Tash flew across and threw her arms around his waist.

'Daddy, Daddy you won!' she exclaimed.

'I did,' he said. 'Actually, we did, I could never have done it without you sweetie, what with all your canvassing work.' Tash positively swelled with self-importance.

'What happens now?' she pleaded. 'Is there going to be a big party?'

'Sort of, sweetie. Certainly we are going to be very busy, but the main thing is to get settled at Number Ten ...'

'No,' said Emily loudly, surprising herself, but not, she noticed, nearly as much as she surprised Ralph.

'Darling!' he said, unsure how to handle this unplanned for response. 'It's been a long couple of days, I appreciate ...'

'It has,' said Emily, smiling apologetically. 'It really has, and Alfie just needs to have peace and quiet when he gets out. He needs to go home to a familiar house,' she gabbled, convincing herself, more than Ralph. 'Tash needs it too.'

Tash looked mutinous but said nothing.

'It's going to look a bit odd,' said Ralph, musing on the public relations impact of the new Prime Minister's family just leaving him to it as he took up the role. Then, he brightened. 'Okay darling, you're right. Go back to the constituency for a bit. There's lots of time. We'll need to look at schools for the children and so on. Probably best to give it until the autumn, start of the academic year and so on … yes …' he mused, stroking his chin, 'we can do a whole "putting the family first" thing.' He smiled into the middle distance, but then snapped back to the present. 'You'll have to do without me a lot of the time though. I'll need to be in London.'

Emily tried to look as if she was weighing up the options. 'Right,' she said slowly. 'Of course, yes, well we'll just have to do our best.'

'I'll send someone in to sort out arrangements to get you all back home.'

'I'll be staying until Alfie is well enough to leave,' said Emily firmly.

'Absolutely,' agreed Ralph, making Emily blink with surprise. She studied him covertly. He was keen to avoid meeting her eye, she noticed. Far from being the confident and triumphant character she expected, he looked furtive. Nervous, even. Knowing him as well as she did, she sighed. Ralph was nervous alright. He was hiding something. Almost certainly from her, and she thought she could probably guess what.

It seemed extraordinary to Emily that the hospital staff could go from seriously concerned about Alfie to smilingly certain that he was well enough to go home.

'Really Mrs Pemilly,' the sensible Welsh doctor reassured her, 'he's fine.'

Emily looked at her son doubtfully. Granted he was jumping on the bed, whilst complaining about the relative lack of bounce, having polished off two slices of toast, a bowl of Weetabix and a boiled egg for breakfast. This was a mammoth amount even for him. To Emily, being the hypercritical mother, he had visibly lost weight and his skin was still pale, his face pinched and shadowed.

The doctor clearly followed her line of thought, 'He's fine,' she insisted again. 'It's nothing that a few days at home with his mummy won't sort out. Now,' she continued, 'you'll need to take him to his own GP for a check up next week. Give him this letter when you visit ...'

Chapter Twenty

Letting herself into the house, it felt lifeless. She could smell the dust in the air, as if it had been empty for months, rather than just a few days. Settling Alfie in front of a favourite DVD, she and Tash checked out resources. The milk in the fridge was just about okay but there was little else to eat. She would have to put an order in to the supermarket and said a silent prayer of thanks for grocery delivery services.

'We could get a takeaway?' suggested Tash hopefully.

'Good plan,' said Emily smiling. 'Find the menu could you darling, and see what Alfie feels like having.'

They ate pizza with their fingers while slobbing on the sofa in front of *Finding Nemo* and, once Emily had persuaded both of the children to go to bed, she poured herself a glass of wine and settled in the sitting room. Even after a long sunny day, the air was musty and chilled. She thought about setting a match to the fire laid tidily waiting. After only a few minutes reflection she vacated the uncomfortably hard and overstuffed sofa – one of an expensive pair lined up either side of the fire – and retreated to the kitchen. Curling up in the Lloyd Loom chair where the cat usually slept, Emily felt the anxieties of the last few days ebb away, leaving her aching and drained in their wake. A couple of tears escaped and dripped off her chin. Brushing away others as they ran down her face, she sniffed defiantly and rubbed her nose on her sleeve like a small child. Then she sighed and hugged her knees. God, the chair was uncomfortable. Heaven knows why the cat was so keen. She wiggled her fingers under the cushion to see if the basketwork had collapsed, but instead she found herself running her fingers along the edge of a hardback book. Hauling it out, she was disappointed to see it was Felicity Wainwright's *How to Run the Perfect Household*. Raising her arm to fling it across the room, it slipped from her hand and fell open on her lap. A little pen and ink drawing of a perfectly coiffed woman with a tiny waist getting a perfectly risen cake out of the oven caught her eye.

It was captioned, 'Home is where the heart is'. How bloody true, thought Emily – probably why Ralph was hardly ever there. It was perfectly clear his heart was elsewhere. Being brutally honest with herself, she had to admit she had not only been determined not to see that Ralph was messing around with Susie before Matt insisted she be told, she also had no proof he was carrying on misbehaving now that his sins had been found out. But she thought he probably was. And where did that leave her?

Divorcing him with a clear conscience probably, that's where. She was astonished to admit how relieved she felt at the very thought. But it wasn't that simple. He had been an arse, and was probably incapable of changing, but he was the children's father and she was honest enough with herself to admit that the most unappealing aspect of continuing her marriage with him was the impact of his new job and not any greater flaw in their marriage than most people tolerated. As the ghastly Felicity Wainwright put it, *"A wife simply cannot expect her husband to maintain the glorious romance of their early courtship, but must remember, he remains her provider and protector nonetheless."*

What would happen to the house if they divorced, Emily wondered. There was a big mortgage on it, she knew. Too big for her to pay on her own, but surely he would have to help with his big fat PM's salary? He would hardly need to buy another house for him to live in. As well as his London flat, he would have an embarrassment of residences to choose from now, not least Number Ten and Chequers.

There had never been a divorced Prime Minister before,

she thought. Either way, the election was now over. Whatever public duty she had fulfilled by standing by him so as to keep the voters on side, she had done it now and owed him nothing. Dreading the fallout from announcing her decision to him though, she decided to take a couple of days to weigh up her options.

The following morning continued its peculiar atmosphere. Emily couldn't decide whether it felt like a holiday or a siege, but, with police stationed outside it was probably more the latter. The groceries arrived so, with plenty of food in the house, she was absolved of any need to venture out. It was the weekend, not that Alfie was well enough to go to pre-school anyway, and the children were happy to lounge about watching television or mooching about the garden where the high walls and plenty of trees lent it an air of seclusion, more welcome now than ever.

TJ had tried to persuade her to allow security staff to be in the house as well as outside but she had refused, point blank. Keeping them outside allowed for the pretence they weren't there. At least for now.

The telephone crouched like a malevolent toad in the hall, Emily dared it to ring and promised herself, if it did, she would ignore it. For the same reasons she refused to switch on the computer, her heart rate rising at the very thought of reading her e-mails. Along with shoving the post in the hall table drawer without looking at it, she felt she had been relatively successful at going to ground. Being his home, of course there was always the possibility Ralph could simply walk through the door.

But he didn't.

In the end, it was TJ that broke the cordon, by turning up on the doorstep. He rang the doorbell, and when that didn't get a response, he rang it again, leaning on it for several seconds. Emily regretted not having installed a proper spyhole to identify callers. She peered through the letter box instead, which gave her a superb view of TJ's crotch. Luckily he was wearing his favourite chalkstripe suit, rather too wide in the stripe and cut snugly around the hips.

'I'd recognise that groin anywhere,' she said with a grin as she swung open the door.

'You and many others,' replied TJ. 'Not that I'm a tart, mind.'

'Heavens no. How's Philip?' she said, waving him in.

'Hmm. Don't ask,' replied TJ. 'Being a bit of a baby about the whole election thing, not giving him enough quality time, et cetera,' he admitted.

'I'm sure that's true. I just hope Ralph is grateful for all your efforts.'

'Hard to tell,' said TJ with just a hint of reproach. 'He's not been in the constituency since election night, but then,' he added, 'you know that. He's not been here has he?'

'Is that really a question?' asked Emily quietly, putting on the kettle.

'Actually no,' admitted TJ. 'What gives?'

She turned to face him, leaning her bum against the Aga for comfort as well as support.

'I'm not sure how to put it,' she said at last.

'Have a stab darling,' suggested TJ. 'I shan't quote you if it comes out wrong.'

'Okay, well,' replied Emily considering, 'it's just this whole marriage and keeping up appearances thing.' She paused. TJ put his patient face on. 'I'm just honestly not sure if I can be arsed with it all any more.'

'Right,' said TJ, his eyebrows shooting up. 'It's worrying that you feel so strongly about it,' he deadpanned.

'But that's it,' she complained, 'I just don't. It's divorce on grounds of apathy rather than adultery.'

'It could be on grounds of adultery though, couldn't it?' argued TJ doggedly.

'Or unreasonable behaviour,' countered Emily, 'on account

of him deciding to stand for PM without asking me,' she elaborated when TJ looked inquisitive.

'Mm, not sure that's a classic example – or at least not one that comes up too often,' he joked.

They sipped their coffee thoughtfully.

'How do you feel about the whole affair thing?' he asked, at last.

'I don't care – Ralph and Susie can do what they like.'

'Not him,' said TJ. 'You.'

'Don't know what you mean,' muttered Emily, unable to meet his eye. She was impressed though. TJ had grown in maturity since she had known him. He was always a bit of a laugh when he wasn't taking himself too seriously. Now she saw a new wisdom in him, a steadiness he didn't have when she first met him.

'Philip is good for you,' she observed.

'Don't change the subject,' he said, but smiled serenely. 'All I'm saying is people could relate to you kicking him out for carrying on with his lover.'

'He rates her,' said Emily sadly.

'He rates you,' said TJ.

'Sadly he doesn't,' she said, matter of factly. 'You know what though?'

TJ shook his head.

'The reason he doesn't rate me,' she explained, 'ironically enough, is because I tried to change myself. I tried to become the person I thought he wanted. The compliant, supportive, powerless, girlie female who pandered to his every wish and made him feel like the big swinging dick.'

TJ blanched. 'Sounds good to me,' he joked.

'Yeah, well, you'd think wouldn't you?' she continued. 'But the truth is he prefers Susie, the hard-nosed, ambitious, child-free career bitch. The woman I was, in fact,' she added slowly.

'I like you now,' said TJ loyally.

'You know the real me,' she explained. *Like Matt does*, she thought silently. The realisation made her chin wobble and then, unable to help herself, she started to cry.

TJ was horrified. 'Emily!' he exclaimed, tearing off several sheets of kitchen towel and bunging them at her awkwardly. 'Don't let the bastard get to you,' he said.

She nearly laughed. It was such a sublime irony that the 'bastard' making her cry was not her husband, as TJ thought, but her ex-lover who no-one knew about.

'It's all a bit of a mess,' she sobbed. 'Ralph and I have been washed up for years. I just thought everything would be okay if I tried harder to be a better wife. That if I did everything the party told me to he would love me, then maybe I'd love him and the children would be happy ...' she trailed off, staring into space hopelessly. 'I suppose I really do have to end it,' she said quietly.

'Why?' said TJ, desperate. 'There has to be a reason! I mean a proper one. Needless to say Ralph behaved like an idiot with the whole Susie thing, but we rely on you. You've always put up with all that rubbish – for the good of the party.'

'Oh please!' she exploded. 'Even now, does it have to be all about the bloody party?'

He looked surprised. Clearly it had never occurred to him that anything else could be more important. Emily groaned in frustration and despair. 'What are you telling me? That I not only have to break it to Ralph I want to end our marriage, somehow I have to divorce "the party" too?'

He gazed at her thoughtfully. 'All I'm saying,' he said, 'is that you may get an easier ride – more understanding – from the party, the press, even Ralph, if the big reason is something that's Ralph's fault.'

'Like his affair with that bloody woman,' she said.

TJ nodded.

'I don't know if she's still got her claws into him,' she admitted, grudgingly acknowledging to herself that the tender little moment she had witnessed on the election night hardly constituted forensic proof of continuing adultery.

'Then I suggest you find out.'

The thought stayed with Emily. TJ was right – but for all the wrong reasons. While she was pretty sure she wanted to get out of her marriage anyway, having a tangible 'hell hath no fury' reason for kicking him out just seemed altogether less complicated. It wasn't anything to do with Matt, anyway – not at all. In fact, Emily was relieved that Matt had not been in touch. A little surprised, granted. She rather thought that he might want to know how Alfie was. But no, basically she was relieved. Yes.

'So,' asked Emily, the next time Ralph called to find out how they all were, 'are you still having a thing with Susie?'

'Wow,' responded Ralph, 'that's quite a question to suddenly throw into the conversation.' There was a pregnant pause. 'I can't believe you asked,' he continued. Then he changed the subject, presumably not expecting her to notice that he hadn't answered. 'We've had a few journos sniffing around, asking when you and the children are moving into Downing Street.'

'Mm?' she responded, deliberately vague.

'Yeah, so, Gerald suggested we hold them at bay with the story we want the children to stay in their schools until the end of the summer term. That way we've got until the end of the summer recess to, er, you know. Resettle.'

'Good plan,' she agreed. 'Get Gerald to say that then.'

And that was the closest they got to discussing whether their marriage was still living and breathing or whether they had both implicitly decided it was already on the mortician's slab.

It took a fortnight for Alfie to go from dangerously ill to completely recovered. The interim time was tricky with him veering from demented with boredom at missing preschool to clingy and whinging, with the slightest exertion leaving him pale and listless. Tash was hard work too, missing her father and fed up with the interest from her mates at school who were not always kind about the change in status and positively cruel about reminding her of her father's infidelity.

'Take a break,' said Nessa one morning. She had dropped round on the way back from the constituency office, bringing chocolate biscuits and constituency gossip.

'To do what?' asked Emily.

'Whatever you like and wherever you like. I'll look after the children,' Nessa replied. 'You need to get out of this house, my love.'

She was right. Now that Tash was on an independence kick, she insisted on making the short walk to school on her own. Emily was quietly relieved, not wanting to face the school gate mums, but the upshot was that she had barely been out of the house at all for the best part of two weeks. During that time, she had seen nothing of Ralph, speaking to him on the phone just a handful of times. Nessa was right. She would go mad if she didn't get out. And she knew exactly who she wanted to see.

Chapter Twenty-One

*Whilst your role is to be there for him at all times,
it is important for a husband to have a life of
his own so don't be a nag and expect to know
everything about how he is spending his time.*
FELICITY WAINWRIGHT, 1953

She lied to Nessa, telling her the plan was to go out with some of the other mothers from Tash's school. She felt terrible about doing it and was sure Nessa didn't believe her, but she said nothing, just agreeing bed times for the children and making sure Emily had her phone with her, just in case anything went wrong and Nessa had to call. 'Although I won't my darling, because I am sure we are going to get on splendidly, aren't we children?'

'Can I come with you, Mummy?' Tash asked again.

'You know you can't,' sighed Emily, 'but you and I will go somewhere together this weekend. Maybe go shopping for some new clothes?' she added, pushing Tash's hair out of her eyes. 'You could do with a haircut.'

She groaned. 'I'm growing it,' she complained. 'Can we get nail varnish?'

'I'll think about it,' Emily said evasively.

Continuing to maintain the illusion of a boozy evening with the girls, Emily left the house in a taxi, but it took her straight to the station where she caught the train to London. The plan was vague. She would just have to make it up as she went along. One useful bit of intelligence was that there were no major votes planned in the House that night and the official engagement diary was empty. She knew that because she telephoned the office and asked. That was humiliating.

Surely, was the undercurrent, the wife should know what the husband was up to. It also struck her that, if he was – as she suspected – still carrying on an affair with Susie, the office would certainly know and would be colluding with him over it. Oddly, that thought made her angrier than anything else.

No, she would not only get to the truth, she would get evidence. Photographs she supposed. Then she, Emily, would be dictating the agenda at last. For a start she would take her evidence to Matt, she decided. He could do what he wanted with it, after abstaining from running the story the first time. Better still, she admitted to herself, the meeting would give her a chance to tell him at last how she really felt about him. After that, who knew what would happen. It could only be good things ...

So, anyway, she knew Ralph wasn't up to anything good, which meant it was likely he was up to something bad. Following him was too obvious though. She was cleverer than that. It was smarter to follow Susie surely. If her suspicions were correct, Ralph would turn up soon enough. Then she could have 'the conversation' with him, and she would have the upper hand for a change.

The trouble was, she didn't know where Susie lived exactly, although she knew it was somewhere in Chelsea, a posh flat, presumably funded with family money as the salary of a PA working for a member of the opposition would hardly be high enough for that. Of course she would probably be doing better now he was PM. Emily had no doubt the favoured ones would be benefitting and she had no illusions over whether Susie continued to be 'favoured'.

She nearly missed Susie leaving Portcullis House, seeing her at the last minute, scuttling out of the side entrance with a tidal wave of other office staff, all heading en masse to the tube station. Susie stopped at the edge of the pavement though, and hailed a taxi instead. Luckily there was another taxi just behind. Flagging it down so furtively the driver nearly didn't see her, he screeched to a halt just past her, forcing her to run after it.

'Follow that taxi,' she said breathlessly as she clambered in.

''Fort no-one would ever ask me that,' said the driver good-humouredly. 'Will do, darlin'.'

He was as good as his word, tailing it so closely she was sure Susie would think it odd, but neither she nor her driver seemed to pay the slightest attention. After just a few minutes, they drew up at Cadogan Square and Emily fumbled for her money to give her an excuse to stay in the cab until she saw Susie disappear safely in through the grand main door.

She gave the cabbie a hefty tip and set up camp opposite the building. There she stood, partly hidden by a small stand of trees, watching carefully. There were so many windows, most of them still unlit, although the evening darkness was intensifying by the minute. Just when Emily was starting to wonder if Susie's flat was around the back of the building, she saw a light snap on in a room on the fourth floor. She watched carefully, trying to make sense of the brief flashes of movement she could see inside. Then, suddenly, Susie came to the window and stood staring out. Emily shrank further into the cover of the trees, feeling exposed. Was Susie looking for her? Perhaps she had noticed she was being followed after all. She held her breath. After a few seconds, Susie disappeared and a light in the room next door came on.

It was the kitchen, she could see, and she watched Susie moving about purposefully, opening cupboards and drawers before appearing in the window again, holding a glass of wine. Her heart quickened but this time with anticipation. Susie was clearly unaware of Emily's presence but the obsession with what was happening outside did appear to suggest Susie was waiting for someone and Emily reckoned she knew who.

Rehearsing what she would say to Ralph the next time she

saw him, "you're busted mate – I saw you," was probably a phrase worth contemplating. She also quite liked "You dirty cheating rat bag", and the chance to say "I suppose you told her your wife doesn't understand you," was definitely an opportunity not to be missed. Not that she was vengeful. Why would she be? She had only given up her career, her dignity, her very identity just to support him and his career. The children were a plus, obviously – she even thought this when they were being horrible – but, in retrospect, she did wonder what else the last ten years of dedication had got her.

She was so immersed in her showdown rehearsal, it took her a moment to register the presence of a second person in the flat. She was sure she had not noticed anyone else arriving at the front entrance, but of course Ralph would have to slip in under cover. There was probably a back entrance or an underground car park. Her heart thumping with anticipation, Emily watched so intently her eyes began to water. She brushed at them impatiently and desperately hoped Susie would not decide to draw the curtains. The sky had darkened to ink now and the windows of the occupied flats glowed like a lit stage. Suddenly, Susie and her companion appeared at the window and stood facing each other before falling into each other's arms.

The profile was unmistakable, instantly recognisable to Emily, as the man she knew best in the world.

It was Matt.

Chapter Twenty-Two

Emily looked away in horror. She realised she was panting, as if she had been running. Leaning forward and resting her hands on her knees seemed to help a bit, so she stood like that, legs trembling, while she tried to absorb what she had seen. The pain was physical, she noticed with detached interest, a crushing ache in her chest. Slowly, she forced herself to raise her head, to look back at the lit window but Susie and Matt had moved away, and – in the seconds since she had looked – the curtains had been drawn. Well, they would be, wouldn't they? Flickers of hope that somehow she had misinterpreted what she had seen, were dismissed, replaced with incomprehension and then a slow-burning anger.

God knows Susie was an evil witch, but to cheat with her husband and then to bloody well take the love of her life too, just when she had begun to find him again? What else did she want from her? Perhaps she should just hand over the keys to her home, her wardrobe maybe, even her children. That said, from what she knew of Susie, she didn't seem the maternal type. No, okay, just the Jimmy Choos then, except that the woman definitely had smaller feet than her. Bitch. In her increasing anger, Emily even entertained the fantasy of going and hammering on the flat door, confronting Susie and quite possibly punching her on that oversized nose. But of course she would have to acknowledge that even bloody Susie couldn't make Matt do anything he really didn't want to. No-one ever had yet. And that meant he actually wanted to be with Susie. By now the embrace had probably moved on to something even more unthinkable.

A bleak tidal wave of misery engulfed her. Avoiding bursting into tears was increasingly difficult and the effort was giving her a headache. Following the urge to simply leave, she started plodding back towards the station. Even though tears were now falling unbidden, she was ignored by the evening crowds that streamed around and occasionally brushed against her as she walked.

Back on the train, she wondered how to hide what had happened from Nessa, who was far too good at knowing what was going on. She remembered the story of Pandora's box, where Pandora was unable to resist the temptation to peek into the box given to her by the gods, releasing all the evils of the world. In the story, Pandora was at least left with Hope to comfort her. For Emily though, her Pandora moment was without the chance of redemption, with the final removal of any possibility that she and Matt would fan their relationship back into life. The tiny spark of happiness that had begun to grow in the back of her mind since he reappeared was extinguished.

'Headache,' she explained tersely, when Nessa raised her eyebrows at the sunglasses she was wearing even at nearly midnight.

'Hangover already, eh?' said Nessa, unconvinced. 'You must have had a good night.' Fortunately, her friend didn't press for an explanation. Brushing her teeth, she regarded her pink, puffy eyes. Even now the tears leaked out and ran down the sides of her nose. Hay fever might be a better cover story for tomorrow, she thought. Lucky it was the right time of year.

Lying in bed, relieved at being hidden by the darkness, she prodded her memories for an explanation. There were no reassuring ones. From the time he came back into her life he must have been lying. She was an idiot to have made herself vulnerable to him again.

He and Susie had professed not to know each other when they met at supper that evening. Was that true? She certainly no longer believed that another journalist broke the story of Ralph's affair. It would have been Matt and Susie together.

Why else was Susie's identity not revealed? They were protecting her from the press pack Emily had had to face. Susie had probably even got a fee. He had comforted Emily so tenderly when he came to warn her that the story was coming out and all the time he was manipulating the whole situation and never mind the damage to her. Good grief, the fact they had a history together was probably just a tool he used to get his story. A wrenching sob escaped, but she had done enough crying over Matt. She had done enough ten years before, she would waste no more tears on him now.

By the time dawn broke, she had made up her mind. With all hope of a future with Matt dashed, her own misery was assured. The only vaguely positive outcome for the whole mess was for her to take the path least likely to cause anyone else unhappiness. She supposed that meant resurrecting her marriage to Ralph. At least that way the children would be happy and, probably, he would be happy too. Providing she dedicated her life to providing for his every need. Maybe if she had been better at doing that he wouldn't have been tempted to have an affair with Susie. Taking the masochism further, she even managed to convince herself to feel sorry for him. He must be feeling bruised that Susie had dumped him for Matt. Assuming he even knew. Perhaps Emily had misjudged him. Perhaps the whole fling had been just that. Ended when he had told her it had. She even managed to make herself feel bad for doubting him. On that bleak thought, she slept at last, fitfully, through a long rambling dream, where she had taken another path in her life. She and Matt were together, content and settled. They were living in a little cottage, working alongside one another, both writing, companionably. In the final stretch of sleep before the alarm tore her awake, she even dreamed they had a son. Ten years old, handsome, funny and energetic, he was climbing a tree in the garden, laughing at her as she begged him to be careful.

He looked just like Matt.

Chapter Twenty-Three

When Emily dropped the children off at their schools the next morning, she carried on – for the first time in ages – to the constituency office. Hopefully there would be some mind-numbing chore to distract her from her misery.

TJ was touchingly pleased to see her. 'Em! We thought you'd got too posh for us.'

'I've always been too posh for you,' she replied. 'But us posh people are too well-mannered to show how posh we actually are.'

'You're right,' he joked. 'You hide it *really* well.'

'Just give me something to do,' groaned Emily. 'I'm bored witless.'

'Join the club. This place is like a morgue now Ralph's hit the big time. Before we were grateful for a crummy fête opening to raise his profile, now we're inundated with requests for the great man to attend constituency events and we don't see him from one week to the next. I've had it, frankly.' He sighed.

'You're not really leaving?'

'Did I say that?' replied TJ.

'No, but …?' she continued. She knew it had been on the cards but now it was possible, she was gutted.

He shook his head. 'I'm not saying I've made up my mind but – well, yes, maybe I'm looking. Things have changed so much. You know I've been looking for a chance to stand for parliament myself where I can make more of a difference.'

She nodded, remembering her little chat with Ralph on the subject.

'As a matter of fact,' he continued, puffing up slightly, 'There's that safe seat coming up in Maresbury, Somerset and your husband has had a word in a couple of ears. I've been encouraged to think about allowing my name to go on the selection list.'

'Well, I think that's a great idea,' she said. 'You would make a fantastic MP. You've got so much experience of constituency work now, it's about time Ralph paid his dues to you.' She looked sad. 'I'll miss you appallingly of course.'

'After our talk the other day, I suppose I assumed I'd be losing you anyway,' he confessed.

'You misjudge me,' she said. 'I'm here now aren't I?' But she knew TJ was right. When she carried out the pledge she made last night, she would be home only for ribbon cutting duties and perhaps the occasional weekend. Ralph would want her in London, and that was where she would be, with a dutiful smile plastered on her face.

'I really am going to miss you,' she repeated.

'Me too.'

They grinned at each other. 'And now,' continued TJ grandly, 'the raffle tickets await!'

'No, please,' she begged, 'not ticket folding duty.'

'"Duty" is the word,' TJ said gesturing at a black dustbin in the corner, filled to the brim with clumps of prize draw tickets. Separating the booklets, checking they each had contact details and folding them individually was a hated task. Today though, the repetitive job was curiously soothing and she allowed her sleep-deprived brain to switch off while she did it, killing time until she needed to gather up her strength to be normal and cheerful in front of the children again.

The following weeks were simultaneously endless and rapid. There was a heat wave. The children became increasingly fractious as their final term in their current schools drew to an end.

Emily braved sports day without Ralph who pleaded a crucial international aid conference. There was intrusive interest in her presence without her husband, a frank appraisal of her, particularly from the other wives, which she found uncomfortable. Preferring a low profile under the circumstances, she demurred at the parents' races. This, in her paranoid state, seemed to incur even more disapproval with tutting parents and staff clearly feeling they were being denied their chance to observe a celebrity by proxy in the detail they felt they were entitled to.

In addition, Emily had a sticky interview with the head teacher when she announced Tash would be leaving at the end of term and Alfie would not be taking up his place in the autumn after all. The head teacher, Mrs Formby, was generally known for being pretty sour-looking at the best of times, but her face contorted as if she was on the business end of a cattle prod when she heard the unwelcome news. Emily didn't know whether to laugh or run away.

'Well, I can't approve of the children having their education interrupted like this,' she said, as if Emily had proposed taking them to Butlins for the rest of their childhood rather than just moving them to a different school. 'The school will suffer of course,' Mrs Formby continued. 'Funding, as you know, is entirely reliant on the number of children in a class.'

Emily really couldn't let her get away with this. 'But surely Mrs Formby, such a popular and well regarded school as this must have a waiting list of children desperate for a place?' Hah, that got her, the old bag.

'It's not as straightforward as that,' said Mrs Formby, but declined to elaborate, preferring to keep an irritating, "it's far too complicated for mere mortals to understand" stance. Emily knew perfectly well the real reason Mrs Formby was so cross was because she was looking forward to queening it over all the other local head teachers who didn't have the Prime Minister's children on the school roll.

Tash's reaction was a lot more difficult to deal with. 'Muuummy!' she wailed in despair. 'You said we wouldn't have to move!'

'I'm not sure I said exactly that darling,' she replied, thinking that, actually, she might very well have done. It was the sort of conversation she would be entitled to expect Ralph to be present at. Both parents should have to take the flak on these occasions. They had seen him just once that week, briefly, and were not due to see him again until after the end of term when the Summer recess would also close parliament and give everyone a welcome breather.

Gerald had given up making complaints about the challenge of explaining to the media why the family were together so little and Emily knew he was working terribly hard to buy her the time in the constituency she had begged for.

'It'll be fine darling,' Emily reassured Tash with no inner confidence at all. Tash was due to start secondary school the year after next and Emily was really concerned at getting her into a nice London school where she would feel safe and make friends. Wherever she went, Emily suspected it would be a shock after this cosy, little village school. Her preference would be to look for a private girls' day school. She was scared Ralph and his bloody cabal of advisors would tell her it was necessary to lob Tash into the nearest huge, dysfunctional comprehensive school with a reputation for teen pregnancy and knife crime, just to make some party political point.

'What about my friends?' said Tash, tightly. Her eyes were brimming and her attempts to rein in her distress were even more upsetting for Emily than the drama queen antics her daughter usually went in for.

'You'll still see them, darling,' explained Emily. 'They can come and see us in London, and – in any case – you'll soon have new friends.'

'I don't want to go,' said Tash grumpily. 'Daddy didn't ask us what *we* wanted,'

'Don't tell me, tell him,' retorted Emily, wearily.

The weariness intensified over the following weeks, a deep fatigue that sleep did nothing to help. In fact, sleep was elusive and when Emily did finally succumb, she woke exhausted from upsetting dreams. Mainly they were about Matt and Susie together, laughing like hyenas at various examples of Emily's distress. The distress was generally to do with Ralph who, in her dreams, was there but unable to see or hear her, whatever she did.

Getting up in the morning was more and more difficult. She remembered that, when the children were babies – especially Tash who was really demanding – she would tackle the sleep deprivation with food, munching her way through endless pieces of toast for the energy to carry on. It worked, to a degree, but she got pretty fat.

This time, eating was even harder than sleeping. She would try to eat with the children, who seemed to need feeding every few minutes, but everything made her feel sick and the physical act of chewing seemed impossibly wearing. Instead she lived on cups of tea and the occasional banana. Soon her clothes were hanging off her, which made her hope she was looking glamorous and skinny. She should do, having returned to a weight she hadn't been since her early twenties. Sadly, she knew she didn't look as good as she had then. Instead, her eyes were sunken, her skin pale and she had to be careful about standing up too quickly because her head was inclined to spin. What a catch, she thought, looking at herself in the mirror. A weary, defeated waif looked back at her.

No wonder Matt preferred Susie.

Come to think of it, no wonder Ralph preferred Susie.

Sometimes only a proper wife would do though. She'd had a call from his new secretary that morning, to check Emily was still planning to attend a Westminster lunch where wives were expected to come and make polite conversation while the husbands dealt with the important stuff. It had seemed easier to say yes than think of an excuse not to, but now she actually had to go, the fatigue at the thought of a trip to London was crippling.

Chapter Twenty-Four

*Make sure to do your homework before your
guests arrive. It is your role to make introductions
and to ensure, not only that you bestow your
guests with their correct title, but also that you
remember and recount a few facts about each guest
so you can set the conversational ball rolling.*

FELICITY WAINWRIGHT, 1953

The lunch, in the yellow dining room at Number Ten, was for
a select group of fifty or so. The bored diplomats' wives were
clearly old hands, knowing each other well and apparently
sharing the same hairdresser, beautician and hunky personal
trainer who probably provided them all with 'personal
services' too. All were immaculately manicured and coiffed.
The unspoken dress code was as for a society wedding, and
Emily felt out of place in her droopy black tunic, with no
boobs to fill the low neckline. It had been a safe bet before
her weight loss, now she just looked like a dreary widow –
which was fine, because that was what she felt like.

Making laborious conversation with the Portuguese
ambassador's wife about Harrods versus Selfridges, Emily
felt the hairs go up on the back of her neck.

'Mrs P,' came a cheery 'humour the idiots' voice, behind
her right ear. Emily turned slowly.

There, looking as reassuringly big-nosed as ever, was
Emily's nemesis.

'Hullo Susie,' she croaked with devastating wit. The idea,
Emily decided, was to stymie the woman with her rapier
sharp intellect and incisive comment. 'Fancy seeing you here,'
she continued, leaving Susie in no doubt of her cunning plan.

'You too,' said Susie, 'it's been ages,' she continued, as if not meeting was an unfortunate problem which had arisen despite their best efforts to get together.

They both stood, smiling around at the other women in the room, desperately searching for a topic of conversation – apart from the obvious. Even in the depths of her own misery she couldn't help noticing Susie looked encouragingly rough. Weight loss had left her face looking pinched and her nose bigger than ever. The smile was bright but it didn't reach her eyes and the overall effect was a certain brittle nerviness. Emily wondered what the problem was.

In the end, Susie broke the conversational impasse. Under cover of the general hum of conversation, she leaned in towards Emily and muttered, 'I'd just like to say how sorry I am about the whole me and Ralph situation. It was just one of those "bigger than both of us" things.' She smiled reassuringly, but Emily noticed the corners of her mouth twitched with tension.

'So, it's over now then,' said Emily.

Susie winced as if she had experienced a stab of pain. 'Absolutely,' she said. 'Absolutely it is. I mean Ralph's great, really he is,' she stared into the middle distance dreamily, 'but it was just impossible, what with everything.'

Emily resisted the temptation to ask what 'everything' consisted of. She would like to think Susie was referring to her and the children but suspected she wasn't, entirely.

'So, are you single?' continued Emily, not wanting remotely to know.

'Well,' confided Susie chummily, 'I can't say I don't have someone – how shall I say? – in the offing …'

'Jolly good,' said Emily faintly. The whole 'tell her who's boss thing' was not going particularly well. A vivid replay of Susie's clinch with Matt flashed into Emily's mind. She reeled slightly.

'Feeling all right, Mrs P?' quacked Susie. 'It's rather warm in here.'

'Fine, fine,' Emily muttered. 'So, tell me more about this sexy new possibility of yours,' she asked, with forced jollity.

'Oh, okay,' replied Susie with a conspiratorial smile. 'He is yummy. As a matter of fact, it's someone you know.'

And now she had to pretend she didn't already know who this "yummy" bloke was. Better and better. Emily felt a line of sweat forming on her upper lip. It really was very hot and airless. 'So, who is he?' she asked to get it over with, so they could go on and talk about Matt.

'Well,' said Susie, pausing for effect. 'You'll never guess, it's Matt Morley, that journalist who did the profile on Ralph.'

Emily pretended to think. Better not make too much of a meal of it, she reminded herself. She was hardly likely to have forgotten a man who had spent days with them just a few months ago.

'Oh yes,' she said vaguely. 'Seems like a nice bloke.'

'Well I think so,' said Susie complacently. 'We met at your supper party. Strange thing is, we didn't really click at that point. I thought he was lovely even then actually,' she confided, 'but if anything I thought he was more interested in you!' She laughed gaily at the ridiculousness of the thought.

'So, how did the two of you get to know each other?' asked Emily, deciding to ignore her incredulity.

'Well it was slightly odd, actually,' said Susie, carefully, not meeting Emily's eye. 'I suddenly got a call out of the blue from him, just a few weeks ago. I had my suspicions at first, what with him being a journalist and the stuff with – you know – with Ralph and so on ...' she flushed slightly. 'Anyway, we met a few times and – no hidden agenda – he was very caring. Wanted to just make sure I was okay, which was really sweet wasn't it? So anyway, there's definitely a connection. You just know these things don't you? I honestly don't know if it's anything serious. We are both grown-ups with a certain commitment to our careers over everything else,' she finished, pompously.

Really? thought Emily. She was dying to dig deeper but couldn't think what to ask without seeming overly interested. Secretly, she admitted to herself, she had been hoping that Susie's obvious decline was down to being "done wrong" by Matt. As that was apparently untrue then she could only surmise it was because Susie was harbouring a deep, secret, unresolved longing for Ralph. Bad enough that the ghastly woman was lusting after her husband, she was clearly just casually toying with Matt's affections at the same time. Emily couldn't decide which riled her the most.

Reliving her memory of the clinch in the window, Emily ground her teeth. Looking around for a diversion, she was pleased to see the Filipino ambassador's wife, Amparo, edging towards her. Emily had met her before and had felt sorry for her. Chosen for her exquisite looks and not, apparently, for her education, the poor girl was thirty years younger than her vain, pompous husband, and spoke practically no English.

'Amparo,' said Emily warmly. 'Susie, this is Amparo, the wife of his Excellency, UK Ambassador for the Philippines.'

Susie took the girl's hand and gave her a little curtsey.

'Amparo,' Emily added naughtily, 'this is Susie, my husband's whore. Actually my husband's ex-whore if we are being strictly accurate. In fact, I say "whore" which suggests he paid her for sex, which I think he probably didn't, because, speaking as his wife, I confess he's always been a bit tight with the cash.'

Susie's face was a hilarious mask of dumbfounded shock. Amparo, uncomprehending, giggled prettily and smiled her hello at Susie.

'Emily!' came a stern voice, from behind. She spun around, but it was just Ralph.

'Hallo darling,' he said cordially for the benefit of anybody listening, but his hand on her elbow gripped hard enough to hurt, and he propelled her away from the scene of the crime with uncompromising speed.

'What the bloody hell do you think you're doing?' he hissed.

'Burying the hatchet with your ex-mistress,' said Emily guilelessly. 'I thought you'd be pleased, all things considered ...' She regarded him thoughtfully. 'You're being very masterful by the way. Rather sexy actually, you're quite the leader of men.'

Ralph looked perplexed. 'Are you drunk?' he muttered, looking shiftily around the room to see who was watching.

Judging from his expression, pretty much everyone was.

'Listen,' said Emily, suddenly serious, 'I'm doing the faithful wife thing, standing by my man and all that bollocks, so don't push your luck and expect one hundred per cent diplomacy as well.'

Ralph looked aggrieved. 'No,' said Emily firmly, 'don't give me that look. Just imagine what a liability I could potentially be, I could take a toy boy or hang out in nightclubs without any knickers on, courting the paparazzi, so just be bloody grateful.'

'She's right,' said Gerald nervously. Neither of them had seen him arrive, but there he was, rubbing his hands together in the way he did when he wasn't sure what was going to happen next. He cleared his throat. 'Actually,' he added apologetically to Emily, 'I'm glad I've caught you. The office has been taking a lot of media calls. Interview requests.'

'Well, just tell them I'm too busy,' said Ralph impatiently.

'Erm, it's Emily they want actually,' said Gerald. 'She's a bit of a hit.'

'How marvellous,' said Ralph sourly. 'Perhaps she should stand for PM.'

Gerald looked embarrassed. 'It's rather good actually, reflects well on you if Emily is popular. Bit like Prince Charles and Lady Di were ... at the beginning,' he qualified.

And we all know how Prince Charles felt about being upstaged by his wife, thought Emily.

'Anyway,' continued Gerald with forced enthusiasm, 'Emily's quite the Twitter star too. She's got more followers than Kirsty Allsopp now, so,' he asked her, 'could we sit down and go through it all? Decide on some key messages – think about your profile, who to go for, that sort of thing ...?'

'No thanks, Gerald,' said Emily firmly.

'No?' Gerald quavered.

'No,' she repeated firmly. 'I really, really can't bear it. In the past – when I was allowed to be me – I was a journalist too, as Ralph doubtless remembers.' She glanced across at Ralph, whose face said 'so what?'

Emily carried on. 'Because of what we did to other people, intruding on their privacy, we couldn't see why anyone would court media attention.' It was Matt she had discussed it with. They had agreed, as they agreed on most things – the important stuff anyhow. 'We could never understand how people could bear to do it, but we used to say that if we, the journalists, ever became the story, then we would have failed as journalists anyway.' She looked at Gerald, pleading with her eyes for him to understand. She thought she could see a degree of sympathy – but it was hard to tell with Gerald's face.

'Not even "Good Morning with Lola and Mitch?"' he said with what he fondly assumed was a persuasive tone.

'Nope, sorry.'

'BBC Newstime?'

'Not even ...'

'How about "I'm a celebrity get me out of here"?' he wheedled.

'Certainly not.'

'Well,' huffed Ralph, 'I really think you might consider it.'

'You're just cross they didn't ask you,' she retorted.

'Don't be ridiculous,' he blustered. 'I'm the PM. I wouldn't dream of doing anything so undignified.'

'Oh but it's all right for me to do it though?'

'Children, children,' interrupted Nessa, appearing from nowhere and grabbing them both playfully by the ear.

Ralph detached himself, obviously considering this undignified too and Gerald, grateful for the diversion, made his escape muttering something about discussing it further when Emily wasn't quite so busy.

'Nessa!' exclaimed Emily, throwing her arms around her old friend. 'It's been ages. What brings you here?' She didn't think she had ever seen Nessa at Westminster.

'Oh, I'm just the "plus one" to someone much more important than me,' she said, evasively, glancing after the retreating Gerald. 'I just thought it would be fun to come and make sure this one's behaving himself,' she added, nodding in Ralph's direction.

Emily felt more cheerful than she had for days. It was so entertaining to see Ralph being treated like a twit. 'I don't think he's got any choice,' she told Nessa, 'he's too busy to get up to anything too much and anyway Sexy Susie's dumped him by all accounts.'

'Shh,' said Ralph, furiously. 'She did not,' he added.

'What? You mean you dumped her?' needled Nessa. 'It's all a bit "High School Musical" isn't it? Having arguments about who dumped who first.'

Emily thought it highly likely Ralph's eyes were going to pop out of his head. Or possibly that he was going to burst a blood vessel, he had gone so purple. In a rare flash of altruism she decided to come to his aid.

'Hark at you with the High School Musical stuff,' she said to Nessa to distract her. 'How on earth do you know about all that?'

'Hanging out with your daughter,' admitted Nessa. 'I could do Robert Pattinson as my Mastermind specialist subject. Actually either that or questions on that ghastly riding programme, what's it called ... Saddle Club?'

'You watch that with her?' exclaimed Emily. Nessa nodded ruefully.

'I'm surprised she hasn't asked you to adopt her,' admitted Emily. 'You're a much better mother to her than I am, listening to all that tosh so patiently. Personally, I can hardly bear to be in the same room ...'

Nessa demurred, laughing, but was unable to hide a tinge of embarrassment. 'Good God,' Emily said, recognising it, 'she *has* asked you to adopt her, hasn't she?'

'No!' exclaimed Nessa. 'Well,' she admitted, 'Tash has asked me to be her sort of honorary grandmama.'

'Well I have to hope you said "yes",' said Emily, meaning it.

'I said I would be delighted,' confirmed Nessa. 'Tash is a child with a lot on her mind,' she added, giving Emily a penetrating look. 'I am happy to be there for her and the last thing I want to do is lose touch with her – or any of you come to that – when you move to London.'

'Never,' said Emily, giving Nessa another hug. It was an unwelcome reminder of what they were giving up, for the sake of Emily's and Ralph's marriage. 'But you're here now,' she noted. 'That lunch date must have been quite a draw.'

It was a totally unsubtle prod, but Nessa just gave her a mysterious smile and declined to elaborate. 'Indeed it was,' she purred. 'And I am bound to say the whole internet dating thing is working out famously, with some highly unexpected results ...' she added with a raised eyebrow.

'Oh?' prompted Emily.

'Weeell, let's just say, the dating site played an important part in getting us together, but that it's a surprisingly small world ...' Nessa said, tapping the side of her nose.

Good grief, thought Emily fleetingly. *Don't tell me Nessa is going out with Matt as well. Obviously he is a busy boy.*

'Anyway,' announced Nessa, who had clearly decided she had said enough on the subject of her love life, 'you may be moving to London but you won't be excused from the constituency work you know.'

'I suspect Ralph will be excused an awful lot of it,' said Emily, talking quietly so he wouldn't hear.

'All the more reason for you to be around my dear,' said Nessa firmly. 'The constituents frankly think more of you than they do of Ralph anyway.'

'Nonsense,' protested Emily, but she knew Nessa was partly right. The real career complainers much preferred the surgeries where Emily was deputising. Not only was she more sympathetic, she was an awful lot better at following up and getting things done. She wasn't quite sure how she was supposed to achieve everything. Life as a Prime Minister's wife was going to be tough on several fronts, as if she hadn't already realised. If, before, Emily felt she was answerable for the needs of too many people, her husband, his career, the constituency and children – not necessarily in that order – it was now going to get a lot worse. That said, Emily was relieved Nessa was reminding her how much she would still be needed in Sussex. It was home, and an excuse to spend time there was more than welcome. If only she could keep Tash and Alfie there too …

'What about schools for the children?' asked Nessa, putting her finger right on it as always.

'Okay, I think,' said Emily wearily. The whole thought of finding alternatives for their cosy village primary made her feel exhausted and depressed. Worse still, security issues were now a factor, meaning sending them to anything close to the equivalent of the local school had been deemed impossible.

'I think I've found quite a nice prep school for Alfie to start at in the autumn,' she said to Nessa. 'Trouble is it's impossibly posh. You have to be a duke or a pop star with social ambition to get a place. All the children seem to be called either Marcus Earl of Shropshire or Moonbeam Coochie Face – poor little gits. Very international though.

Lots of embassy children attend as well, which is nice.' She didn't add that it made her heart bleed to think of those youngsters who had been parachuted into a London school from all four corners of the globe, just to be snatched out of it again, away from their friends, as soon as their father was posted elsewhere. Still, she thought, the alternative was probably boarding school from the age of four which was marginally worse.

'And Tash?' prompted Nessa, gently interrupting Emily's bleak train of thought

'Mm. That's a bit more of a struggle,' admitted Emily. 'She's pretty bright so I want to send her somewhere that'll kick her arse when she needs it – being congenitally lazy like her mother. Trouble is, one so desperately wants to avoid those hideously competitive academic hothouses. One I looked at last week had more than half the fourteen year olds already taking their GCSEs, and ninety per cent of the sixth formers down for Oxbridge.'

'Not a bad start in life,' prompted Nessa. 'It was good enough for me.'

'Oh yes, true,' said Emily, remembering that Nessa had once confided she was an Oxford graduate, having attended in an era when the idea of women like her going to university rather than finishing school was unusual. Nessa was certainly intellectually superior to her husband but had learned early on to keep her intelligence hidden and, marrying so soon after graduation, it was assumed a career was out of the question.

'I wouldn't say Tash was as brainy as all that, though,' Emily said. 'And I suspect if they ever stop competing with each other intellectually it's only to compete over who is precocious enough to become anorexic first. When I went around there were even a couple of girls Tash's age who looked worryingly thin to me.'

'Anywhere else?' prompted Nessa.

'Some,' Emily replied. 'One the security people refused to consider because it had too many entrances and would have cost tax payers the entire national debt of a small African country to police. Another one was just so unbearably snooty. I'm thinking about St Catherine's but Tash is determined to hate it ...' Emily trailed off despairing.

'She'll be fine,' reassured Nessa. 'And as for Alfie, he would withstand nuclear attack. He'll survive anywhere.'

'Too true,' said Emily, thinking longingly of the village school with the oak tree in the playground.

The next thing was to pack up the house which overwhelmed Emily totally. She had never undertaken such a large life change with so little enthusiasm she realised. Still barely eating, she kept finding herself staring into space in the middle of a room, packing paper in one hand and a pile of shirts in the other. Her decision making was shot to pieces. It was taking her an insanely long time to sort each drawer, and she was agonising tearfully over throwing anything out. Even manky old single socks at the back of Alfie's chest of drawers made her weep, their stains and holes reminding her of how impossible it was to get him to put on his shoes before running out into the garden. In Number Ten the surprisingly poky flat had no direct access to outside space at all. Emily could imagine both children becoming thin and pale, starved of exercise and fresh air. Ralph had promised lots of trips to Chequers but Emily doubted very much if that would present them with the casual, grubby outside life they had loved in Sussex.

They would keep the Sussex house of course, but Emily knew perfectly well they would be lucky to get back there often. To lose it altogether would be easier, she thought in some ways, than having to rip out its soul and relegate it to the status of holiday home. Sorting through the kitchen stuff was impossibly hard in Emily's befuddled state. With every possession having to be categorised as chuck, pack or keep, she found herself tenderly wrapping the orphaned lids of long since lost Tupperware boxes whilst chucking the only corkscrew that actually worked into the bin by mistake.

When Emily woke one morning already crying, after a night where hours of heart-pounding wakefulness were broken up by snatches of nightmare, she knew she had to get some help. It was Nessa in the end who insisted on making her an appointment with her GP.

'I can't,' complained Emily, sobbing helplessly. 'He's an old fart. He'll think I'm going mad – which I probably am – and anyway it's just too indiscreet. He'll be onto the press before I am even out of the door. I can see the headlines now. It'll be "PM Pemilly mad wife in attic shock".'

'Mm,' replied Nessa, 'quite apart from the fact you are not locked in the attic and even Ralph wouldn't think to put you there, do you honestly think your own doctor would shop you to the press? And not just any media but the sleazy tabloid end of the market? If you think he would, then I think we can add paranoia to your list of exhaustion, depression and anxiety.'

'I'm not anxious,' said Emily, declining to deny the bit about depression and exhaustion.

'No?' replied Nessa. 'Hold out your hand.' Emily copied her in holding her arm outstretched. Unlike Nessa's, her hand quivered and shook. No amount of effort would still it.

'I rest my case,' said Nessa. 'Now, give me the phone.' Emily meekly obliged. The idea of talking about her desperate state was appalling, but Nessa was right.

On the phone Nessa had to calmly but firmly explain that she was making the appointment with Emily's co-operation but that no, Emily couldn't speak to the receptionist herself, as she was in no state to do so. This seemed to convince the woman on the end of the phone, who offered an appointment in just two hours, a huge change from the usual wait of three to five days that was the norm. Emily had always felt this was a strategy to manage resources. Generally, whatever was the matter surely most people would have either died or got better in that time?

Against her expectations, crusty old Dr Gladwin was very inclined to take Emily's condition seriously. Apologising to him for bursting into tears as soon as she sat down, Emily explained through her sobs how she had been barely able to eat or sleep since – well, she didn't say since she saw Matt with Susie – but just let him know it had been a couple of weeks. He took her pulse, which Emily knew was permanently racing, and looked stern.

Far from telling her to buck up and pull herself together as she had expected, he asked a few more gentle questions and then sat back in his chair. 'Well, it's perfectly clear we can't leave you in this state for much longer,' he said. 'I am going to give you something to help you sleep, that's the first thing – just a mild sedative,' he explained before she interrupted. 'And I'm going to start you on a low dose of antidepressants.' Emily nodded obediently. 'They won't take full effect for a couple of weeks I am afraid, but in the meantime, you need to take something for the anxiety too.'

'I'll be rattling,' joked Emily weakly, but with relief stealing in at the idea that someone was helping. 'You're right though, I need to do something. But anti-depressants? Really?'

'Oh yes,' said Doctor Gladwin. 'They're awfully fashionable nowadays, all the best people are taking them,' he joked. 'Not that I want you to just take drugs, effective though they are. No, it's important that you talk about why you are in this state. We all deal with anxiety-inducing events in different ways. Some of us are unlucky enough to develop unhelpful strategies to deal with it that's all. You've got yourself in a muddle over recent events – and who could blame you?'

Emily blinked. Strange that he should know so much about her private life. But that was it, wasn't it? As Ralph's wife she had no private life. Not any more. Mind you, lovely Doctor Gladwin thought her distress was Ralph's affair and the election. They hadn't helped but he surely couldn't have known the real problem. Emily hoped not anyway. The last thing she felt strong enough to do at the moment was to explain how she was condemned to a miserable life of duty, married to the wrong man because the right one was sleeping with her bitter enemy. Who wouldn't be depressed?

'Well I hope you were discreet,' was Ralph's response when Emily told him about her appointment and the drugs she had been prescribed. Nessa had kindly filled her prescription but if the pharmacist had raised an eyebrow when he saw the name on the form, Nessa wasn't going to be mentioning it to Emily. She was paranoid enough about intrusion as it was.

'Don't you think its bit over the top though, darling?' Ralph had gone on. 'All these drugs, I mean what have you got to be depressed about?' he continued rhetorically. 'What woman wouldn't want to be married to the Prime Minister of the UK for heaven's sake?' he said without a trace of irony which made Emily smile for the first time in days.

'Seriously though darling, I know it was a shock for you this whole unfortunate, er, "indiscretion" with Susie. It must have upset you, obviously, and I've apologised as you know.' Actually Emily didn't remember that he had. 'Granted, the stress of the election must have had an impact on you, but what on earth can you possibly have to be anxious about now?' he concluded with more than a hint of resentment.

'I'm sorry,' Emily said, desperately gritting her teeth so she wouldn't cry. 'I honestly don't know why I'm not coping. I suppose I'm worried about the move, the packing, the children's schools ...'

'Of course,' sighed Ralph. 'You're right. I'll get you more help.' He thought for a moment. 'The best person to put on the case is TJ of course. He's a whizz at logistics and planning and he could probably do with something to get his teeth into.'

The plan appealed more than many others. TJ was an easy person to have around, although the downside was the probability that Emily and the children would be stuck in London all the sooner with his efficiency brought into play. And that would be a good thing overall, admitted Emily to herself, with the new school year approaching. 'Yes,' she said slowly. 'Okay then.'

Chapter Twenty-Five

'Emily lovie,' came the dear familiar voice, just as she was finishing her breakfast coffee. Today she had even been able to choke down half a piece of toast after a record five hours sleep and was consequently almost chipper about facing the day.

'TJ,' she replied, with a rare genuine smile. 'How are you?'

'Oh fine thanks, lovie,' he replied. 'Now, the sainted Ralph,' he paused for a nanosecond of irreverence, 'has asked me to help you get things sorted. What I've done is organised the removal boys for tomorrow. They'll pack too. This morning I need you to use these,' he waved a pack of stickers like semaphore, 'to mark up what goes where. Blue is for Number Ten, green is to stay here, yellow is for stuff going into store ...' Emily let him witter on for a bit longer, tuning back in as he said, '... so the interior designers will meet you tomorrow morning. I've taken the liberty of getting them to make up some mood boards – I'm sure you'll love them.'

'For what?' asked Emily, stupidly.

'Well, for Number Ten,' said TJ in his 'humour the idiots' voice. 'It's the norm for the PM's wife to have a say ...'

'I don't want to,' said Emily firmly. 'I'm sure everything is fine as it is and heaven knows it's going to take lot more than a few thousand pounds worth of taxpayers' money to make it feel like home for me and the children.' TJ looked disappointed. He was obviously keen to get stuck into the interiors part of the role. He fancied himself as quite an authority.

'Okay,' she relented, 'all I'm saying is let's get in there before we just change everything for the sake of it, there's altogether too much change going on at the moment anyway.'

'Okey dokey,' replied TJ brightly.

Okey dokey? thought Emily. *Good God, is that what people say to unhinged people – probably is, actually. Mad people and old people – and especially old, mad people*, she speculated. Then she realised she had drifted off again. TJ was still talking.

'... So with the schools more or less sorted, the other big issue is your new image. Now my very good friend – ex-boyfriend actually – is a buyer at Liberty and he has kindly offered to set you up with a couple of personal shoppers. I can't tell you their names yet because it's all hush hush but they dress the best, that's all you need to know. The emphasis is obviously on British designers. Vivienne Westwood is an obvious choice but a bit, how shall we say, outré. Also, it's nice to support the young designers too isn't it? Not to say you need to dress entirely British all the time, or even all designer, come to that, in fact the team is obviously keen that you support the high street retailers as well. The voters need to see you in the everyday life stuff too, just to show you still have the common touch, and I'm bound to say Em, you're so lovely and slim, I am sure you could carry off "high street" just fine ...'

Emily decided to simply wait until TJ stopped talking. It was amazing how long it took.

'No,' she said at last.

'No to which bit?' enquired TJ solicitously.

'The bit about getting someone else to dress me,' she explained. 'Call me precocious, but I've been managing to dress myself since I was about three – five if you count shoelaces – and I have no desire to be infantilised now.'

TJ looked blank, clearly wondering how to approach this unacceptable impasse.

'However,' Emily continued, 'I appreciate I may need to do some shopping.'

TJ smiled. Things may be okay after all.

'So,' Emily continued, 'I will do so, in my own time, and with my own opinions.'

He looked concerned again.

'I'll probably ask Nessa to give me a hand,' added Emily, relenting just a fraction.

He sighed with relief. 'Cool,' he said. 'Of course Gerald will be pleased to know Nessa is involved.'

Why? thought Emily.

Whether it was the sleep or the toast, or even the buoying effect of TJ's entertaining gossipy bitching about mutual friends, Emily was able to finish the stickering hours before the lorry arrived to move everything.

The removal men were cheerful enough, happy to be made continuous cups of tea by none other than the wife of the country's leader. 'She seems lovely and normal,' she heard one of them mutter to another after she handed over the fourth round of teas with a plate of chocolate digestives. 'Won't last long,' replied the other. 'She'll get the airs and graces quick enough. I mean look at the last one. Imelda Marcos eat your heart out.' She felt this was a little unfair, but, was ashamed to admit, she had thought very little of her predecessor in the previous hectic weeks. What had become of her? Emily should want to know as the same fate inevitably awaited her one day.

The ex-PM, of course, had launched on his hugely lucrative lecture tour and autobiography already. Emily had heard this highly indiscreet memoir was due to be published in time for the Christmas market, although she seriously doubted it was the man himself who was writing it. His wife, on the other hand, had an even more difficult role to forge than she'd had when her husband ran the country.

Emily had watched with detached interest – well, it hadn't seemed so personally relevant then – as the poor woman had been forced to give up a high-flying career in PR. Undercover journalists from a Sunday red top had caught her out making amusing but indiscreet comments about other members of government. The advisors had moved in swiftly and she had been forced, by the middle of the following week, to make a public and humiliating little speech, prettily pledging to give up her career in order to support her husband's career, given that the country needed him to be entirely focused on his work. Emily had felt the woman's pain to say nothing of the employees at her firm who were all, presumably, out of a job. She didn't even have the 'spending more time with family' euphemism to fall back on, given that she and her husband had, to their intensely private and painful regret – also laid out for public examination in the press – never managed to have children of their own. No wonder the poor woman had turned to shopping as an outlet for her new narrow life as consort, or 'concubine' as Matt had insisted on calling her at the time.

Desperate though her own situation was, as a consequence, she could have some sympathy for the party which had clearly been determined to learn the lessons of the opposition. There was to be no chance for Emily to balls up, she thought. Being buried alive – at least career wise – was the safer option. She had been wondering briefly about finding work anonymously. She could perfectly well write under a pseudonym, but the press had developed a keen nose for outing anonymous bloggers in the last couple of years. Given that they had chosen to be anonymous for good reason, being 'outed' had been catastrophic for most, leading to lost or damaged careers, red faces all round and – in one case – terminal damage to a marriage. Mind you, that one was a highly entertaining diary of a serial adulterer – written from experience it transpired. She was surprised it hadn't turned out to be Ralph.

Matt and Emily had watched the whole early blogging rise with interest, and Matt had encouraged Emily to use one as an outlet for all the observations she was too diplomatic to say in her paid work. Very recently she had started doodling on her laptop, putting down a few lines observing her own thoughts. It felt good to write again, to exercise her brain, but she was too craven or too cautious to put her material out in the public domain, even anonymously. If nothing else, she had told herself, it might be useful material for when she found herself a counsellor to speak to as she had told Doctor Gladwin she would. He had offered to refer her locally, but she had declined, telling him she would find someone in London as there was a better chance of making regular contact with them that way. He had made her promise she would. It was another thing on the list but not one she felt she could delegate to efficient but gossipy TJ.

By September, Emily had run out of resettling things to do and the day to day reality of her new life yawned before her like a prison sentence.

The school, St Hughes, had finally been chosen and uniforms bought. Emily had been reasonably happy in the end, finding a little co-educational prep school meaning Alfie and Tash could go together, not that they would see much of each other in the course of the school day, but Emily was comforted by the thought they could seek each other out if they wanted or needed to.

Although sibling bickering continued, worsening if anything, Tash and Alfie had shared a new affection for one another since Alfie's illness. Emily frequently found Tash tenderly reading Alfie a story and he was inclined to give his sister a quick hug providing he imagined no-one else was watching.

Miss Bennett was the teacher in Alfie's class and Emily loved her on first sight. 'He's not reading yet,' she admitted when she brought him into the classroom on the first day of term. 'Thank heavens for that,' Miss Bennett had exclaimed in her broad Yorkshire accent. 'He's only four, the poor little scrap, why would you be teaching him to read for goodness' sake?'

'I just thought he's probably going to be with a lot of quite advanced children,' admitted Emily, sharing a look with Miss Bennett that spoke volumes about competitive and intense pre-schooling.

'There can be a bit of that,' agreed Miss Bennett, 'not that I frankly see the need or the benefit – Horatio!' she barked suddenly, 'we don't pull Anastasia's hair, do we?'

Horatio thought about launching a rebuttal but was quelled with a stare of some majesty, Emily noted with approval.

'Take that one,' Miss Bennett muttered to Emily out of the side of her mouth, 'arrived in our nursery class last term knowing the names of all his dinosaurs – and spelling them too – although he's still wetting his pants most days. And,' she added, 'he's a little bugger as you can see. But then he had three different nannies last term alone and never sees his daddy, poor love.'

Alfie, Emily decided, would be absolutely fine with Miss Bennett.

Tash, she was more worried about. She no longer confided in Emily about her life as she had in Sussex. There she would tell Emily about every minute of her school day – with the exception of anything relating to its academic content.

At St Hughes, Tash would return home silent and unresponsive. Emily didn't think it was the school work that was bothering her as she tackled her homework with few complaints, which was unusual in itself. The school also confirmed that she was managing well academically. 'We do tend to find that children coming from the state sector are working at a lower level than St Hughes' children when they first arrive, but Natasha is a credit to her old school – well advanced for her age,' commented her class teacher when Emily raised it with him.

When pressed, Tash mentioned the names of a couple of girls she had made friends with but was uninterested in Emily's suggestion that they might want to come back for tea one day.

'Why would they want to do that, Mum?' she retorted. 'Our life is weird, okay? I would rather just see them at school when I can at least pretend to be normal.'

That said, Tash's perception of 'normal' seemed to have become considerably grander, Emily noticed.

'Can't we go skiing at Christmas?' she asked one day in November. 'Everyone else goes. God, we never do anything,' when Emily gently explained that now was hardly the time for the PM's children to be taking glamorous holidays while the rest of the country struggled through a recession. And then there had been the 'I must have a mobile phone I'm the only one without one' conversation.

'You're too young,' Emily had explained reasonably.

'The other girls aren't too young, and Sophia is younger than me,' argued Tash, infuriated. 'How am I going to let you know where I am all the time if I can't call you?'

'But I know where you are all the time,' countered Emily reasonably.

'That's the trouble,' retorted Tash darkly. 'I'm never allowed any freedom because of Daddy.'

'Tash,' explained Emily, at the very end of her patience, 'for heaven's sake stop being such a drama queen. The reason you are not allowed to wander around the country on your own is not,' she enunciated slowly and clearly, 'because Daddy is the Prime Minister, it – is – because – you – are – nine.'

Exasperated, Emily had recounted the conversation to a classmate's mother the following morning.

'Don't I know it,' sympathised India, 'my oldest went on about it for months until I gave in when she was eleven, apparently she was the last one in the world to get her own phone. And then the little missy sent me fifteen spectacularly inane texts on the first day – turns out she didn't know anyone else with a mobile to send them to!' she snorted with laughter.

It had taken half a term for Emily to summon up the courage to talk to India, a dauntingly glamorous woman in her early forties with two children at the school. She was one of very few mothers turning up at the school gates. Mostly it was the nanny mafia who studiously avoided eye contact with parents and chatted amongst themselves in a tower of Babel-like variety of Eastern European languages.

India had been extremely friendly and funny when Emily first struck up a conversation and admitted she would have spoken earlier if she hadn't been so sensitive about toadying up to the PM's wife. 'Soooo not done,' she admitted apologetically and, from then on, they occasionally sloped off for a coffee and a chat after school drop off.

Emily was always terrified of saying something she shouldn't and even a casual gossip and chat seemed fraught with danger. As a result of her matiness with India the other mothers at the school gate regarded Emily with an even more unfriendly mixture of envy and aloofness. She knew that a charm offensive would overcome the barriers but was so weary and emotionally fragile, she retreated into shyness instead, doubtless giving the impression that she was stuck up.

Despite her tentative friendship with India, Emily – like Tash, she suspected – was lonely most of the time. Ralph was only the attentive husband when the eyes of the world were upon him. On the rare occasions when they were alone together he was polite but distant. They were like flatmates who didn't particularly like each other, but kept up a diplomatic front. There was little conversation, even about the children.

Although Ralph was in his element at the very centre of the

action, he had been looking drawn after a couple of months in post, tackling the ever deteriorating economic situation. To make it worse the jubilation of victory had been replaced by a tetchy expectation of great things now the party with all the promises had been put into power.

As the autumn wore on, and the relationship between the two of them cooled further, Emily began to suspect Ralph had resurrected his relationship with Susie. Even with her and the children living at Number Ten, he was frequently absent from family life for days on end. Taking to sleeping in his dressing room with the excuse that he didn't want to disturb her by coming in late, she had noticed that, on at least a couple of nights a week, the bed was not slept in at all. At the same time, the silence from Matt remained absolute. Was he still seeing Susie? After calling her a whore, there was no chance Emily could casually ask her. She couldn't help thinking Ralph might be cheating again but was aware her fragile mental state was probably making her paranoid and she didn't want to interrogate him for fear he would tell her she was imagining it.

When the term ended, Emily decided, she would take the children back to Sussex for a long break over the holidays, which were longer now that they were both at private school. They could have Christmas there and see if pretending hard enough to be a happy family could turn them into one. Emily was also keen to see more of Nessa, who was true to her word in coming to London much more than she had before, but her trysts with her mysterious boyfriend left time for little more than a quick cup of tea and an occasional hurried shopping trip with Emily, who craved more of her friend's time but was desperate not to appear needy.

The children were delighted with the plan and came straight home from school to pack after an interminable final assembly with prize giving, speeches, carols and mulled wine for the parents – most of whom Emily saw for the first time.

In just twenty minutes Alfie arrived in the sitting room breathless and with his little backpack overflowing. 'Let's go home now,' he said. Emily sorted through his bag with amusement. There were no clothes of course, not even a change of underwear. Alfie's essential 'going home' items apparently consisted of his toy doggy – one ear torn and chewed nearly off – his plastic dinosaurs and a rubber snake mixed in with a selection of scruffily well-read Thomas the Tank Engine books and a lump of Blu-tack.

'Perfect, darling,' she said fondly. 'We're just waiting for Tash now then.' He ran off to hurry her up while Emily arranged to get their real bags down to the car where the driver was waiting.

Chapter Twenty-Six

After a whole autumn of neglect the house smelled musty and unloved. Even the lock in the front door seemed to have forgotten its relationship with the key and Emily had to wrestle and pull for several seconds before it allowed her to push it open with a squeak of underuse.

Most of the furniture had stayed in the end, but it was like a stage set with personal possessions largely absent, books gone from shelves and the contents of cupboards sparser than before. The children ran to their rooms with whoops of joy and Emily heard them thundering about upstairs, shouting to one another. Within minutes, Alfie was contentedly sprawled in front of the television and Tash was hogging the phone, hooking up with her friends.

Nessa had been in, switching the Aga back on and stocking the fridge with essentials, Emily noticed with gratitude. She would put in a big supermarket order tomorrow, she thought, sliding the big old Aga kettle onto the hotplate. Actually, perhaps she had better do it this evening as the precious pre-Christmas delivery slots tended to get booked up pretty quickly. This little detail reminded Emily how little she now did on a daily basis to run the household. In London a housekeeper would be appalled to see Emily bothering with such things and yet what else was she good for? She was looking forward to running the house, getting ready for a lovely Christmas and worrying about all the logistics that made it special. Not being allowed a career, the domestic goddessery was her only outlet. Hell, she might even dust off the Felicity Wainwright Household Management book, it was bound to have some comments on how to "do" Christmas correctly.

Over supper Tash informed Emily what she, Tash, would

be doing in the few days leading to Christmas. As a result of her phone marathon, she had lined up a schedule of sleepovers leaving no time for anything else. 'Not Thursday night,' was Emily's only comment. 'We've got tickets for the panto.'

'But can't Megan come with us?' wailed Tash.

'I doubt I can get her in, they've been sold out for weeks,' Emily reasoned.

'But Daddy runs the country,' Tash replied, 'surely he can sort it out.'

Emily laughed in spite of herself. 'I'll try,' she promised, 'but I think Daddy's a bit busy with world peace and the public sector borrowing requirement at the moment.'

Really, she admitted to herself, Tash was becoming quite a monster.

Over the next few days Emily cocooned her family in the house, enjoying the familiarity – and the solitude. The constant pressure in London, she realised, was partly because they were never truly alone as a family. There was really the most extraordinary lack of privacy even in their own flat, with aides frequently interrupting the supper and homework routine with batches of papers that Ralph apparently 'simply must see', on his return from whatever vital meeting he was attending.

Susie was frequently one of these aides, Emily noted. She had also noted the return of Susie's *joie de vivre* lately, this blossoming happening to coincide with the improvement in Ralph's temper – more evidence, she thought, that their affair had resumed. Prodding her psyche with this idea, Emily discovered that she cared very little if it had, other than to wonder what had happened to Matt. If anything, her anxiety had improved recently, especially now they had come back home.

Of course it could be the drugs.

As the days ticked down towards Christmas day, the feeling of escape lessened and the anxiety returned. It was about seeing Ralph again but worse than that, she was grieving because it was the last, but the last of what she was not sure. The choice, when she dared to think about it, was stark. This was either the final Christmas the family would ever have in this house, their home with all its precious memories, where Emily had always fully intended they would stay forever. Or, alternatively, it was the last Christmas they would spend as a complete family. As she squirmed in bed throughout the early hours, her head constantly looking for a cool part of the pillow, the latter option seemed the best of the two. By Christmas Eve, Emily had come to two conclusions; the first was that this Christmas would be the best ever; the second was that she would sit Ralph down and tell him the marriage was over.

Matt had barely registered it was Christmas. Desperate to bury himself in work he had encouraged his editor to commission him for every article the paper's shrinking in-house team was unable to cover itself. With family commitments and 'to do' lists growing longer by the day, the other staff grew used to having Matt churning out vast quantities of copy on every subject, even if his sombre presence reminded them all of the Grinch. Previously happier working alone in his flat, he came into the office more often now, soothed by the normality of chatter about holiday plans, though he had none himself.

The other advantage – or disadvantage – of being in the office was that he was constantly surrounded by the outpourings of the national press. Piles of newspapers, their own and their rivals, jostled for space and several television screens were constantly on, tuned permanently to the major news channels. To see Ralph was a distraction which barely interrupted his thoughts but to catch a glimpse of Emily was to throw him totally. He pored over every picture of her in the newspapers, usually where she was turning up to events on Ralph's arm. He searched her face for information ... was she well? Happy? Looking tired? He craved reassurance that she was okay, frustrated that he could do nothing but watch from the sidelines.

Chapter Twenty-Seven

The rituals of Christmas preparation were soothing. Tash, in particular, was clingily desperate that all the correct procedures would be observed, from the decorating of the tree with the shabby and random selection of decorations acquired over the years, to the final ceremonial placing of the wreath on the front door knocker.

The family Christmas tree – always a fresh, real one – would be in the kitchen, placed in front of the French windows. Since Ralph had become an MP they had also had a more formal Christmas tree in the hallway, with co-ordinated decorations on a changing yearly theme. This would be seen and admired by the various guests attending the series of drinks parties held to thank the local party faithful. This year by unspoken consensus, the hallway tree was forgotten. The party faithful had all been invited to an alternative drinks party at Number Ten, a considerably more glamorous option which had proved extremely popular. It had not been necessary to make excuses for the absence of an invitation to Ralph's constituency home. As far as Emily was aware, no-one had questioned its omission, but she suspected if anyone had, quiet words about the 'strain' and 'exhaustion' Emily was suffering would have been muttered to excuse it.

More likely to excite comment had been the absence of Emily at the Number Ten Christmas events. The office had not pressed for her to be there and she had been quietly thankful. She kept herself busy at the Sussex house instead, taking comfort in baking the kind of things she would normally just buy. The kitchen was filled with the scent of cinnamon and candied peel as she turned out mince pies, Christmas cake – which was rather too late in the day really, but lots of brandy would help – and even star-shaped biscuits to hang on the tree.

The last was a particular success. Tash and Alfie worked contentedly side by side at the scrubbed kitchen table. Tash, with her tongue poking out from the corner of her mouth, iced careful lacy patterns on the biscuits and Alfie conscientiously placed little silver balls onto the icing before it dried. In unusual accord, they then threaded ribbons through and hung the stars on the tree.

Next year, thought Emily, we'll have a dog. The children had wanted one for years but Ralph had always said 'no'. A golden retriever, she decided. The star biscuits would have to be hung only on the upper branches then of course. She would look for a puppy in the New Year. With no other adults in the house, the dog would be company for her in the evenings, and an excuse to go for walks too. She really must get fitter, although at least now she was skinny. Thinner than ever in fact, with her ribs showing on her chest and thighs that would no longer meet, she noticed with detached interest on getting out of the bath that morning.

As Emily sipped her tea, watching the children finish decorating the tree, she wondered vaguely about the financial situation. Ralph would have to pay maintenance presumably. It would look terrible for him if he didn't cover his responsibilities as a father, but she wondered if it would be enough. Would they have to move to a smaller house? They didn't really need one this size. There was a whole upper floor they didn't currently use, although Emily had always had it in her mind that the children might like to have their bedrooms up there when they were older. It would make a fabulous teenage den.

No, she decided, they would move out of this home over her dead body.

If she needed to she would get a job. She should do that anyway. Surely the separated and ultimately divorced wife of the Prime Minister could finally do whatever job she liked? Would journalism still want her though, after all these years in the wilderness? She would have to look through her address book and do a bit of networking. With this thought, Matt came – unbidden – into her mind. A sudden wave of longing and loneliness swept over her. She brushed a tear from her eye before the children could see. For days she had been tortured by images of Matt and Susie enjoying a romantic child-free Christmas together at Susie's flat, making love in front of an open fire and drinking champagne together. She told herself it was unlikely as her suspicions over Ralph and Susie continued. Ironically this thought was less hard to bear, but – one way or another – the pain went on.

It had been arranged that Ralph would return to the constituency house on Christmas Eve but regular telephone bulletins from his office announced later and later departure times from London. In the end, Emily had no choice but to persuade the children to go to bed, promising them that their father – like Father Christmas himself – would arrive silently in the night, but only for good boys and girls who went to bed when they were told.

They observed the final ritual of hanging stockings on the high marble mantelpiece in the sitting room and leaving out a glass of sherry, a mince pie and a carrot for the reindeer on the coffee table. Doing so, Emily had a pang of reminiscence of past years when Ralph and Emily would roll back from a drinks party late on Christmas Eve, tucking an already sleeping Tash into her bed and then arguing amiably about who would swig the sherry which was not the drink of choice for either of them. Emily would argue even more vociferously against having to bite into the raw carrot. Ralph would generally end up generously playing Rudolph, she remembered. They *were* happy, she reassured herself. The marriage had worked once.

'I'm glad we're home for Christmas,' said Tash, when Emily went to kiss her goodnight.

'So am I darling,' agreed Emily.

'Do you think ...?' Tash paused.

'What darling?' prompted Emily, dreading what Tash was going to ask.

'Do you think we could live here again? All the time, I mean?' she asked at last.

'Daddy needs to be in London darling, you know that,' said Emily.

'Yes but we don't,' said Tash simply. 'Daddy's never around anyway. What would be the difference?'

What indeed, thought Emily as she went downstairs. God forbid that the children would know too much about these awful adult dilemmas but Tash, in her nine year old way, knew everything. As far as Emily could tell, her daughter was telling her to "go for it" and she was relieved. Although she was dreading the process, especially the conversation she would need to have with Ralph, the way forward was clear. It was going to be all right.

Chapter Twenty-Eight

Emily fell asleep before Ralph arrived. When she heard the children sneaking downstairs to collect their stockings the following morning – she guessed it was around half past five – she worried that they would find their father in the guest room. To her relief, when she turned her head, she saw him beside her in bed, fast asleep. His jaw was slack and the bags under his eyes more apparent than she ever remembered seeing them before. Without its careful combing, she noticed she could see his scalp more clearly than ever through the hair at the front of his head.

'Daddy!' Tash and Alfie exclaimed, as they burst into the room with their full stockings. Mayhem ensued as the stockings were emptied and examined in the bed.

'What about our big presents?' asked Tash after an indecently short time.

'Let's get downstairs then,' said Ralph with a pretend sigh, looking ostentatiously at his watch. He had a point. It was barely six o'clock.

'Tell me we don't have people joining us for lunch or anything,' he pleaded with Emily as they trailed downstairs.

'Just us,' she reassured him. 'We can stay in our pyjamas all day if we want to.'

'Sounds like bliss,' replied Ralph, giving Emily a rare squeeze of approval. She smiled, but then the corners of her mouth turned down against her will. She busied herself with the kettle until the tears that had sprung to her eyes drained away again.

'Wait!' commanded Ralph, as the children both circled the pile of presents under the tree, prodding and squeezing as they went. 'We're going to need a cup of tea, to say nothing of breakfast.'

'Mine's the biggest,' observed Alfie delightedly.

'Mine'll be the best though,' countered Tash, giving him a shove.

'Children, children,' rebuked Emily as she came over with steaming mugs, passing one to Ralph. 'Right, come on then, who's first?'

The pile of presents disintegrated quickly under the onslaught, resolving itself into drifts of torn wrapping and towers of brightly coloured boxes.

'Daddy!' shrieked Tash when she unwrapped the present Emily had chosen for her to get from her father. 'Thank you, thank you, thank you, it's exactly the Nintendo I wanted – how did you know?'

Ralph gave Emily an amused look over Tash's head and mouthed his thanks. 'It's my job to get things right,' he told Tash, 'and luckily I have a fantastic team around me that makes sure I do.'

'That's it,' said Alfie, regretfully at last, stirring the pile of wrapping paper with his toe.

'Not quite,' said Ralph. 'There's a little one, now where's it gone ... ah! Here it is.' He handed Emily a little square box, exquisitely wrapped in embossed paper with a striped silk ribbon. Under his gaze, she read the little label attached.

"To the mother of my children, for the loyalty I don't deserve, with my heartfelt love and respect forever, Ralph." Tears sprang unbidden to her eyes again and she surreptitiously wiped them on her dressing gown sleeve. 'Goodness,' she said, 'what can it be?'

She quickly unwrapped it to reveal a dark green box with gold writing on it.

'This is the jeweller my engagement ring came from,' she exclaimed.

'I know,' said Ralph. 'Open it.'

Inside, nestling in black velvet was a pair of exquisite jewelled earrings. Each one was a tiny spray of flowers, the curving stems in gold with emerald-studded leaves, sapphires for petals and diamonds at the centre.

'Forget-me-nots,' said Emily reverently. 'They're beautiful.' And they were, quite the most charming, probably Victorian, objects that Emily had ever seen. She was astonished Ralph had chosen something so perfect on his own.

'You had help, didn't you?' she teased.

'On the contrary,' rebutted Ralph. 'There are certain things a wife is entitled to expect her husband to manage on his own. This is one of them.'

'Well, they're absolutely perfect. You did a good job.'

Ralph ducked his head modestly. 'No less than you deserve,' he said softly and kissed her chastely on the forehead.

'Yuck, kissing,' complained Alfie.

It was late evening before they had the chance to be alone and have the conversation they were both dreading. Ralph, playing the dutiful husband, piled the last plates into the dishwasher and then joined Emily in the sitting room in front of the fire. By the time he had opened the wine and poured them both a glass, Emily was crying, tears running down her face and off her chin into her lap.

'It's no good is it?' she said.

'No,' replied Ralph gently. She looked up into his face, and was astonished to see tears in his eyes too.

'We could just keep on like this,' she suggested desperately. 'Today's been all right, hasn't it?'

'We can't,' said Ralph sitting down and taking Emily's hand into his. 'I did think we could for a long time but it's the one thing I'm not prepared to lie about,' he explained. 'I don't care about appearances anymore, I just want people to be happy. At the moment none of us are happy, not even the children and especially not you. That's the bit I really can't bear.'

Emily blinked. For a moment it was like she had the old Ralph back, the one who would do the right thing rather than the easy thing. 'I could fall in love with you all over again when I hear you talk like that,' she joked sadly.

'I've never stopped loving you,' he replied. 'And that's why I can't stand what I'm doing to you, dragging you along in my wake, making you live my life and I know it's the life you never wanted. I want to let you go, to be yourself again, like you were when I fell for you in the first place.'

'Could I be like that again?' asked Emily, like an animal who suddenly notices the cage is open but doesn't believe that freedom is really possible.

'Absolutely,' said Ralph. 'I fully expect you to be an utter embarrassment to the government – and me personally,' he said. 'It's the least I deserve. And anyway,' he added, 'if you do decide to behave like a total liability, the electorate will probably feel quite sorry for me. It'll do my popularity ratings the world of good.'

Emily gave him a playful shove.

'How will it all work though?' she said, barely daring to hope but feeling excitement welling up along with the sadness.

'Basically, I can't see that much will change,' said Ralph purposefully. Clearly he had thought it all through. 'You will live here with the children. I can either have them join me at the weekends or – if you agree – I can come here.'

'What about Susie?' Emily asked.

Ralph denied nothing. She knew he wouldn't.

'I hope the children will get to know her,' he admitted. 'I hope you will too. She's a good woman.'

'She's been a snotty cow,' said Emily. 'But she's had a hard time,' she conceded. 'And she's better suited to being a Prime Minister's wife than I am. Plus she desperately wants to be, which is the other big difference between us …'

'Well, steady on,' said Ralph with a trace of panic in his

voice which amused Emily. 'I haven't flipping proposed, or anything … One thing at a time after all.'

'You do want to marry her I take it,' pressed Emily.

'Yes,' Ralph replied, with new resolve. 'Eventually, I really think I do.'

'And does she want you?' continued Emily. 'For richer, poorer, sickness, health, opposition and government – the whole steaming package?'

'She says she does …' replied Ralph, a smile stealing, unbidden, across his face.

'Well you'd better ask her then hadn't you? Before she changes her mind,' said Emily, sensibly. 'Anyway, what will the Party make of it, do you suppose?'

'Frankly, I really don't care.'

'You should tell her we've discussed this,' said Emily.

'I said I would go to her,' Ralph admitted. 'Once we had talked, you and me.'

'You should,' urged Emily, and this time it felt right that he would go.

The following morning, after a conversation that continued into the small hours, along with tears and laughs over fond memories, and lots of reassuring hugs, Emily woke alone.

Chapter Twenty-Nine

Nessa stormed into the coffee shop like the wrath of God. A lesser man would have dived for cover, but Matt regarded her calmly over his double espresso and waved for her to sit down opposite him.

'What the bloody hell are you doing just sitting there?' snapped Nessa, with uncharacteristic bluntness – even for her.

'You asked me to come,' said Matt reasonably, folding his newspaper and putting it, unhurriedly, down on the table.

'Only because you're being such an idiot I simply can't bear to watch it any more. I've got better things to do with my time you know,' she continued. 'I'll have a large skinny latte by the way.'

'Cake?'

'Do I look like I need cake?'

'Yes, you do actually,' said Matt who was a big believer in its calming effects on irate women.

'All right then,' she muttered. 'If you're having some.'

By the time Matt returned with the coffee and two large chocolate brownies, Nessa had taken some deep breaths and overcome at least some of the fury which had been rising in her since she'd extracted Matt's mobile number from Gerald and texted him a summons.

She gave Matt a beady look. He was calm, she granted him that, but she reckoned he would emanate calm in front of a firing squad so that meant nothing.

'You've lost weight,' she accused.

'Just as well we're eating cake then,' agreed Matt equably.

'I'm not here for my health, you know.'

'Nor am I.'

'I just want you and Emily to get over yourselves and stop making each other so desperately unhappy.'

For the first time, Matt's composure cracked. 'I wish ...' he said and then stopped, a muscle twitching in his jaw. 'How is she?'

'Bloody awful,' said Nessa, tersely.

He bowed his head.

'I suppose you've heard she and Ralph have split up,' she added.

'Of course,' replied Matt. 'At least, I have my sources and there's no mistaking the subtext in the material coming out of the press office over the last couple of weeks ...'

'And you've contacted her?'

'No.'

'I bloody *know* you haven't,' interrupted Nessa, furious again. 'She and Ralph finally do the sensible thing, you're free, Emily's free, what on *earth* is the problem?'

'Well, if you know I haven't contacted Emily I expect you also know she's made it perfectly clear she doesn't want me to,' said Matt, irritation creeping into his voice.

'I know nothing of the sort ...'

'You surprise me,' retorted Matt. 'You seem to know a mighty large amount about everything else.' He glared at her, but Nessa, satisfied she had him where she wanted him at last, just waited for him to continue.

'Look,' he said with heavy patience, 'I am relieved she has had the courage to get herself out of that charade of a marriage. I'm happy for her. Truly. The reason I am so happy is because I love her and – yes – of course we *all* want the best for the people we love,' he indicated Nessa with a nod. 'Sadly,' he continued, 'my love for Emily is not reciprocated. I believe once it was,' he paused, and placed his hands flat on the table. 'I do believe she loved me once, but ... I ... did some things which I regret. There was,' he paused, searching for the right word, '"damage" to her perceptions of me. A future with Emily is simply not to be. Her choice, not mine.'

Nessa's eyes softened. 'Okay, sunshine,' she said more gently, 'I think you'd better tell me how you've come to that idiotic conclusion so we can sort this mess out once and for all ...'

Over the following weeks Emily felt fragile but relieved, as though she – like Alfie – was recuperating from a serious illness. She contented herself with the day to day tasks of putting food on the table at regular intervals and keeping the washing basket from overflowing. The domestic chores had a soothing regularity and she clung to them like a life-raft of sanity.

She was vaguely aware of the delicately worded press campaign which was being managed assiduously in the background. Far from the proactive information management of recent months, the strategy, as she understood it, was for Gerald's office to bounce back any enquiries about Ralph's domestic life with platitudes whilst simultaneously promoting his career successes and sneaking Susie into the picture, first as an indispensable aide and gradually, as someone with a more fundamental connection to the PM. This, he maintained, would build Ralph's perceived success in preparation for the slow realisation amongst the public that the marriage was over and that Susie had shuffled sideways into the limelight in her place. Hopefully it would be so slow and without incident that there would be no front page splash moment where all was revealed. In the meantime, Emily was relieved that the strategy called for her to contribute nothing but simply to disappear into the Sussex backwater, invisible, and waiting to launch her new life like a moth from a chrysalis.

Undoing the mammoth task of moving to London seemed easy in comparison with setting it up. Emily had a tense meeting with the head teacher of the local school again and was amused that the woman was almost entirely unable to hide her smug pleasure that she would have the PM's children after all, although she did her very best to suggest to Emily that the whole issue was hugely inconvenient.

Emily was in no hurry to have the original contents of the house moved back from London, relishing instead the minimalism and calming lack of clutter, although the children had been quick to insist that their own piles of junk be lovingly packed and transported back to their Sussex bedrooms. She was relieved at this. It meant their visits to see their father were very clearly in the 'staying away from home' category.

She was also grateful that Ralph made a huge effort to ensure he had time to spend with them both. In fact, they were spending more quality time with him now than they had in years.

No-one mentioned Susie.

Despite the calm of the domestic routine, Emily was still grateful for the effect of the anti-depressants. Mostly the numbness they induced meant that she could think about Matt's betrayal – his second, albeit ten years after the first – at an emotional distance. She did find herself wrestling with the way he had jumped into bed with Susie so very soon after repeatedly declaring his love for her. Was it for some devious journalistic advantage? If it was, there was no sign that he had taken it. No, the whole thing made no sense in the context of his other behaviour over the previous few months. It had to have been a deliberate betrayal. She agonised, night after night, replaying every conversation, every gesture for alternative interpretations.

No, it was deliberate betrayal, she repeatedly concluded. Why else had he failed completely to get in contact with her? She had not seen him since the night before the poll, when he took Alfie to hospital and proposed to her again. Weeks

227

later, she had seen him for the very last time in the window of Susie's flat. The damage was absolute, but Emily couldn't let it go. There was something missing and if only she could tell what it was, she felt she must surely be able to find some peace and move on.

Matt had been impressed and amused by Nessa. He admired her loyalty and her persistence and – even though he couldn't be persuaded by her arguments – he was pleased Emily had a loyal friend like Nessa in her life. Without Ralph and the entourage that went with him, he worried that Emily would find herself increasingly isolated. For the millionth time, he wished she would let him do more than worry from afar.

Not having anything else in his social diary, he took little persuading to meet photographer Kevin and his journalist mate, Simon, for a beer.

'So, it's the biggest scoop I've ever had,' explained Simon. 'They're good lads basically. We were at school together. I knew perfectly well they'd been sent off for Jihadi training last year, although of course they had to deny it. Now they've been told to go back out and they're prepared to take me and Kev along with them. No journalist has *ever* had this kind of access to the radicalisation process before. It's gold dust.'

Matt nodded, impressed. 'So, why are you telling me?'

'His missus won't let him go,' explained Kevin.

Simon nodded, regretfully. 'It's the kids. She's gone a bit funny since we had the last one. Post-natal depression. She needs me here really so I've had to rein back on the warzone stuff. Mind you, I need to keep getting the commissions too. It's not easy being freelance when you're just starting out and staff jobs are hard to come by …'

Matt nodded.

'Will you do it?'

He nodded again.

'I'd better get back home,' said Simon, looking at his watch. 'I said I'd take the kids to the park to give her a break ... You're a lucky bastard,' he added.

'You're the lucky one,' said Matt.

Matt's editor took a different view.

'You're a bloody idiot,' he announced when Matt told him he would be overseas and, most likely, out of touch for a few months.

'Why the hell can't you just settle for the cushy political commentator number like normal people your age?' he asked, peevishly. 'Get up late, have lunch with a sycophantic spin doctor, destroy some minister's career by pointing out what a lowlife he is and still make it home in time to put the kids to bed? Why not just have that?'

'I don't know,' said Matt, honestly.

'Instead, you're going to travel out to the arse end of nowhere with a rabble of psychotic losers who fancy themselves as Muslim warriors because they've been spending too much time playing violent computer games and watching nutters ranting about the infidel on YouTube ...' he trailed off. 'They'll probably kidnap you and demand a ransom for God's sake. I don't employ you to get abducted and murdered by a bunch of religious zealots.'

'You don't,' agreed Matt. 'Actually you don't employ me at all. I'm freelance.'

'Really?' said Mike. 'I was wondering why you weren't giving me any notice ... Anyway, like I said, if you get yourself kidnapped you're on your own. Doesn't matter how many weeping women turn up begging us to pay.'

'No weeping women,' promised Matt.

'Thank God,' said Mike, who had a morbid fear of crying females. 'Although I've got no idea who I'm going to get to cover for you.'

Matt reached into his top pocket for the business card

Simon had given him and handed it over. 'Try this guy,' he said. 'He could do with the work.'

'Is he cheap?'

'Probably,' replied Matt, on his way out of the office.

'Come back in one piece,' said Mike to the closed door.

Just hours later, Matt was packed and ready to go. He chucked the multi-way adapter into the laptop case and zipped it with finality. He and Kevin weren't scheduled to fly out until the morning. To pass the time in the interim, they had a date with much alcohol, a large curry and – most likely – a shared bottle of whiskey to see them through the early hours. Where they were going there would be no alcohol. It would be their last drink for months – possibly forever.

'Well?' said Nessa interrogatively, as she stirred her coffee.

'Well what?' responded Emily.

'Well, what are you going to do next?'

'I rather thought I might finish my coffee, possibly have another slice of toast and then the whole panoramic vista of the day stretches ahead of me, with such exciting treats in store as getting dressed, putting a load of washing on, ordering the groceries – actually perhaps not all of the above. It's probably not good to have too much excitement in one day ...'

It was the bleakest part of winter, with Christmas gone and the first bank holiday several months away. Emily wondered about telling Nessa that January was the month with the highest incidence of suicides. Then she thought better of it. Nessa was pretty sensitive about Emily's mental state and might take it as a veiled cry for help or something silly.

'I mean,' said Nessa heavily, 'what on earth are you going to do about Matt, you silly girl? I'm quite out of patience with you now, sitting on your bum wallowing in your misery when you need to be sorting out your love life.'

'How do you know about Matt?' said Emily, astonished.

She knew for a fact she and Nessa had never discussed him before. She hadn't even met Nessa when she and Matt were together the first time round.

'Mainly, darling, I'm not an idiot,' snapped Nessa.

Emily blinked. She had never seen Nessa so uncompromising and stern. Usually she could count on her for gentle moral support and encouragement, not this right royal telling off. 'I wouldn't dare suggest you were,' she said seriously, 'but I thought Matt was a bit of a secret, that's all.'

'Not now, darling, and you seem to be the only person denying it.'

'I don't follow,' said Emily, who genuinely didn't.

'I didn't press you to identify him when we talked before, but since then you seem to be completely ignoring the man's confession of undying love in the national press and I, for one, would like to know why, given that you and Ralph have managed to perfectly legitimately disentangle yourselves from one another.'

'We're not divorced yet,' said Emily, 'but if Matt has been writing me love letters for the world to see I'm blowed if I've had them.'

'The article!' exclaimed Nessa, nearly tearing her hair in frustration. Emily had never seen her so exasperated.

'Oh you mean the profile of Ralph?' remembered Emily. 'Never read it. Anyhow it must have come out ages ago, just after the election if I recall. He's been shagging my husband's lover since then,' she pointed out.

'But you never read it,' established Nessa doggedly.

'Nope,' confirmed Emily, not seeing the point.

'Well, it's about time you did,' snapped Nessa. 'Now, where's that Gerald?'

As if stage-managed, the doorbell rang and Nessa bustled to open it.

'My house actually,' muttered Emily but not loud enough for Nessa to hear. She might get even more of a telling off, the mood Nessa was in.

'Gerald darling,' she said kissing him peremptorily on the mouth. Emily stared, dumbfounded.

'You and Gerald?' she said, blankly.

'Yes dear,' said Nessa. 'For months. You really have had your head up your own arse, haven't you?' she observed before turning back to Gerald who was gazing at her dreamily. 'Now, Gerald, could you please be a love and make sure the office sends Emily a copy of that Matt Morley article that everyone got so excited about?'

'Gladly darling,' sighed Gerald, clearly in Nessa's thrall. 'As a matter of fact, I've got a set of post-election cuttings knocking about in the car, shall I get them?'

'I will,' replied Nessa. 'Now you get Emily to give you a cup of coffee, and then we must go. There are a lot of extra-curricular activities at this hotel we're going to, I want to make sure we have time to have fun with them all,' she winked at Gerald who blushed and grinned like a schoolboy.

'What an amazing woman,' he said reverently, as they wandered into the kitchen together.

'Amazing,' agreed Emily, noticing that Gerald had no hint of a stammer. He had even completely stopped saying 'um' and 'er' since she saw him last. 'So, you and Nessa ...?'

'Yes,' admitted Gerald blushing. 'I didn't think she'd be interested in me but ... when I saw her profile online, it was such a coincidence, I already thought she was amazing from the day I met her with you last year and I just decided ...' his grin told her everything she needed to know and more.

'Good for you both,' she said warmly.

Nessa barely allowed Gerald long enough to leaf through the cuttings she brought to find the article by Matt before she hustled him off for their dirty weekend together, leaving his barely touched coffee steaming on the side.

The article was long. It spread across several pages, starting with the front cover of the supplement where she could see – even though it was a poor quality photocopy – that they had used a full page head and shoulders shot of Ralph looking noble. The headline was 'Planet Pemilly – Matt Morley asks: Can we truly judge a man by the company he keeps?'

Emily placed the article carefully in the middle of the kitchen table and regarded it. Then, she loaded the dishwasher with the breakfast things and wiped the surfaces, glancing at it all the while. When she had run out of things to do, she reached for it – but then changed her mind. Dragging the kettle onto the hob, she made herself a cup of coffee, measuring it out with unusual care. Then, and only then, she sat down at the kitchen table and began to read.

First she speed read it from beginning to end before reading it through again carefully and slowly. Finally she revisited a couple of parts that she was most drawn to, studying individual sentences forensically to extract every nuance. The drive of the article was an exposé of the machine which controlled how Ralph was presented to the voters. It was like watching a heckler at a magic show revealing how the magician does his tricks. It was brutally revealing but – Emily had to admit – completely true. Somehow the photographer, Kevin, had managed to capture a shot of Ralph with the children in the kitchen doing his "happy family life" thing. Emily was in the background, slightly out of focus, but looking sideways at Ralph with an expression of frank despair on her face. The image was mesmerising. There was even a little fact box detailing her life before her marriage to Ralph and then – with a jolt of recognition – she read the final sentence. She rubbed her eyes and then read again, holding the magazine up to the light to make sure she wasn't seeing things that weren't there.

Eventually, she sat back and sipped her coffee. She noticed her hands shaking and clutched her mug a little harder to still them. Just as she was taking the last thoughtful gulp, staring sightlessly out of the window at the wintery garden, the doorbell clamoured, making her jump.

Chapter Thirty

The figure she could see through the etched glass was too tall for the postman and lacked the red jacket. Even as her mind tried to make sense of what she was seeing, her heart told her who it was. That was why it pounded in her chest as she reached for the latch to open the door. The last time she had seen that profile it had been through the window of Susie's flat.

At first, she only gazed, drinking in every detail of his appearance; his unshaven face, tanned from a recent trip abroad by the look of it, his blue linen shirt washed soft with a slightly frayed collar. He had always been without vanity, she remembered, only buying new clothes to replace something that needed throwing away.

After a long, silent evaluation she reached for him, intent, concentrating as she ran her hands through the thick, wavy hair on his head, continuing down his back, feeling the muscles beneath the fabric of his shirt and then nuzzling his neck, breathing him in. As she did so, he moved at last, encircling her fiercely in his arms, pressing her against his body.

Her feet were no longer taking her weight and he lifted her back inside the house, pushing the door closed behind him. In the hallway, they gave themselves to a more detailed exploration. Matt slid both hands inside her dressing gown and down the length of her naked body. With one hand in the small of her back, supporting her, and the other cradling her breast, he finally found her mouth with his. Emily allowed herself to sink into the kiss, and to think of nothing but the warmth, the touch and the smell of him as her senses overwhelmed her.

After a long moment, as they continued to kiss, she

fumbled with his shirt buttons, desperate to feel his bare skin against her own, but her fingers slid off, clumsy with nerves. Reading her mind, he stepped back and started to undress. Then, looking around the hallway where they still stood, as if seeing it for the first time, he swore under his breath and picked her up. Cradling her as if she weighed nothing he climbed the stairs, pausing momentarily on the landing between Emily's bedroom and the spare room where she had rebuffed him all those months before.

'I'm damned if I'm going to take you to a bed you've slept in with Ralph,' he growled, as he kicked open the spare room door and laid her tenderly down. He was panting but Emily doubted it was from carrying her up the stairs. She was breathless too.

'Now, don't move,' he said, as he removed her dressing gown and gazed down at her body with heavy-lidded eyes, whilst systematically removing his own clothes. Finally naked, he left her in no doubt that he was more than ready to take her in that bed or any other.

'Where are the children?' he murmured as he slid down beside her, then started slowly and thoroughly exploring every inch of her with his hands, mouth, tongue and teeth.

'With friends,' she gasped, as he slid his fingers inside her willing body, 'not back until teatime.'

'That should be long enough,' he murmured, 'to be going on with at least.'

As it happened, it was only just enough time. After they had made love, first urgently, then again, exquisitely slowly, they fell asleep wrapped around one another. Waking later, they got up to take a shower together, which led to another session, leaving Emily with her legs shaking and her body feeling deliciously as though every limb had been filled with lead.

'What are these?' interrogated Matt, finding her anti-anxiety medicine in the bathroom cupboard.

Emily told him.

'You won't need that rubbish now you're with me,' he said. 'And you're too bloody skinny, what the hell's that all about?' he added, his brusqueness failing to hide his concern.

'Am I disgusting?' said Emily in a small voice.

Matt sighed, 'I don't care what you weigh, you stupid woman. You can put on ten stone and grow a beard for all I care. I'll still adore you and want you constantly, but you need to eat more – and I'm going to make sure you do.'

True to his word, he wrapped her back up in the towelling robe and settled her in the Lloyd Loom chair in the corner of the kitchen. Checking out the fridge, he collected eggs, butter, milk and bacon and then slapped some bread on the hob to toast.

'Bacon and scrambled eggs do you?' he asked Emily who now felt absolutely famished. She nodded gratefully.

'You look about ten years old sitting there,' he observed, smiling at her scrubbed freckled face and wet, tangled hair from the shower.

'That casts a rather dodgy light on what you've just spent the last few hours doing to me, doesn't it?' she replied.

'Don't be cheeky or I'll insist we do it again before I feed you,' he joked sternly. It wasn't until he found a bowl to break the eggs into and placed it on the table to beat them that he saw the photocopied article.

'What are you doing with this?' he said, pointing at it with the whisk.

'I only got it this morning,' admitted Emily. 'I was reading it when you got here.'

'You mean you haven't seen it before?'

'Actually, no.'

'I can't believe you didn't read it when it was published,' said Matt, staring unseeing into space. 'That would explain ...'

'Well, yes it would, I'm so sorry,' said Emily quietly. 'I can't believe your editor passed that quote ...'

'"*When you give someone your whole heart and she doesn't want it, you cannot take it back. It's gone forever,*"' said Matt quietly. 'Sylvia Plath, as – of course – you know. My editor owed me a favour. It cost me quite a few favours, actually.'

'You remembered,' said Emily. 'I've still got it. The signed copy of her poetry you gave me. It was so soon after we met. I was boring on about her and you were the only man I'd ever met who'd ever read any of her stuff ...'

'I assumed ...' he began again. 'I knew you'd understand what I was saying so then – when I heard nothing from you ...'

'You could have called,' she said, knowing she was being a little unfair.

'I didn't want to put you through any more pain. I felt I was starting to bully you. Of course I wanted you to leave Ralph for me but you were so determined in the hospital, and then, when you didn't contact me after this,' he indicated the article again, 'I decided the right thing to do was support you in continuing with your marriage. By leaving you alone, that is. I was watching over you though. Watching the press. I've always had that option, of course. I've always done that ... all these years,' he admitted.

'You didn't take long to hook up with Susie,' chastised Emily gently. 'It's hard to imagine you were *that* heartbroken.'

'Who says I hooked up with Susie?' said Matt, looking puzzled.

'She did. Or at least, I think she did,' said Emily, trying to remember their conversation at the reception. Had she actually said? 'It was sort of – well – she said she was interested ... plus I saw you both. You were definitely hugging.'

'I hug a lot of people,' said Matt. 'And I don't deny Susie made it clear she was up for something if it was on offer,' he said, remembering, 'but it definitely wasn't.

'Look,' he continued, 'when I found out you and Ralph were determined to make a go of it, I contacted her to make sure she was all right. She's pretty flaky, I was worried she might do something stupid, especially she's obviously been in love with Ralph for years, I could see that from the first time I met her. I might have put my arms around her, sure, but – good grief – not Susie ...!'

He rubbed his scalp through his hair in a gesture she knew so well. 'You do believe me?' he asked, staring into her eyes.

'Yes,' replied Emily. 'I do, of course I do,' and she did. The gnawing grief and pain she had felt for months, thinking of Susie with Matt, simply floated away, leaving her dizzy with relief.

'Actually,' she said, 'Susie's as much of a victim of this whole situation as I was, in a way. Just being around a man as charismatic as Ralph is a dangerous game and we all fell for it one way or another.' She considered, for a moment. 'I think I may have been a little harsh,' she added, remembering calling Susie "a whore" the last time they met.

'Really?' joked Matt. 'But you're right,' he agreed, 'although Susie is better equipped to be in Ralph's world than you ever were. They are creatures from the same mould. They deserve each other – in every sense of the word,' he said. 'You were miserable with him but she was miserable without him,' he added rescuing the toast and putting the eggs on the hob.

'She said you were miserable too.'

'Yeah,' agreed Matt shortly. 'I was.'

It wasn't until they were tucking into their meal, Matt watching Emily with approval as she buttered her third bit of toast, that she thought to ask, 'So, why did you come here today?'

'Well, it was your text, this morning,' said Matt, remembering how it pinged through just as he went to switch off his phone prior to take-off. He had practically had to fight his way off the plane and the airline was furious at having to find and remove his luggage.

'Wasn't me,' said Emily. 'I've lost my phone.'

'Well someone definitely has it. Here, look,' he said, handing her his phone.

She peered at the mystery text. It simply said: "Please come. I can't bare to be apart from you."

'"Bare?"' quizzed Emily raising an eyebrow.

'Yeah, I wondered about that.'

At that moment, the back door crashed open and Alfie ran in. 'Beat you!' he shouted back at a person or persons unknown behind him.

'Hi Matt, hi Mummy,' he said casually. Turning the TV on, he then threw himself onto a beanbag where he immediately adopted a vacant stare and shoved a thumb in his mouth.

'You're here,' said Tash approvingly to Matt as she came through the door her brother had left swinging open. Like Alfie, she showed no surprise at his presence. 'Going upstairs, Mum,' she muttered as she wafted vaguely through the kitchen, stopping briefly in the doorway to the hall. 'Are you staying then?' she asked Matt.

Matt and Emily glanced at each other.

'Yes,' they both said, together.

'Cool,' replied Tash.

Epilogue

A year later ...

*Although the food is important, more important
still is a daintily laid table, with crisp white linen
and polished silver. Standards in this area should not
be allowed to fall below the very highest level.*
FELICITY WAINWRIGHT, 1953

Tash chucked the handful of cutlery onto the bare pine table with a clatter. 'Do we have napkins, Mum?' she asked.

'God knows,' Emily told her. 'Even if they're clean they'll need ironing and I can't be bothered with that. Bung the kitchen towel on the table. That'll do.'

Looking idly out of the kitchen window as she stood at the sink scraping carrots, she noticed a man in a dark suit and sunglasses, picking his way through the plants at the end of the garden. He had his finger in his ear and appeared to be talking to himself.

She sighed. 'Ralph? Is that one of your security bods lurking in the shrubbery?'

'Fraid so,' he replied, fiddling with the foil on the bottle of wine he was supposed to be opening. 'Two more out the front, by the way.'

'Shall I take them a cup of tea, do you think?' asked Matt, slipping his arm around Emily's waist as he came to stand beside her.

'That'd be nice,' she agreed. 'The poor things, having to work on Easter Sunday. Give them some chocolate biscuits too and ask them if they'd like some lunch later – there's going to be loads. And for goodness' sake don't sneak up on them,' she added. 'They're all armed remember.'

'Here we go,' said Ralph, passing Emily a glass of white wine. 'Cheers.'

'Cheers,' she said, taking a tiny sip and then leaving it casually on the kitchen window sill. 'You'd better take poor Susie a glass. I think she's having a hard time out there.'

Susie was in the garden with Alfie and the new golden retriever puppy, who, at four months, was already a gangly teenager with razor sharp teeth and a propensity for chewing shoes. He liked them best with the feet still in.

'You can stroke him,' Alfie was telling Susie, 'but don't pat him on the head like this, because, to him, it just feels like hitting,' he explained. The puppy who was lolling on the lawn with one ear inside out, basked in the attention, licking Susie's hand and finishing with an affectionate little nip.

Susie stifled a yelp and surreptitiously wiped her slimy hand on her jeans. Only recently Emily had persuaded Susie that jeans at the weekend were perfectly acceptable but, even now, she noticed with amusement, they were the darkest blue denim with an ironed crease down the front.

'Can I help?' said Susie, escaping into the kitchen with relief.

'Sure,' said Emily, 'it would be lovely if you could lay the table for me.'

'How many are we?' asked Susie, counting the knives and forks Tash had dumped down.

'Us lot, plus TJ and Philip, Gerald and Nessa,' said Emily, counting on her fingers. 'I'll feed the security boys on trays because I know they won't want to come inside.'

'All the usual suspects then,' commented Susie.

'Family,' said Matt. 'A pretty unconventional one too, lucky for us,' he continued. 'Did you see Emily's article on the new nuclear family in the paper last Sunday?' he asked Ralph. 'Very well received it was, the editor's already commissioned another piece. A bit more of that and my wife-to-be will be well on the way to keeping me in the style to which I'd like to become accustomed,' he joked.

'It was stating the obvious really,' said Emily modestly. 'There was quite a bit about the role of the step-parent,' she told Susie. 'I used you and the children for inspiration. I hope you don't mind, I just think you manage it really well,' she said.

'Gosh, thanks,' gushed Susie, 'I'm really lucky they're such nice children, I'm sure the whole "wicked stepmother" thing only happens when they're ghastly brats.'

'They are, when they're with us,' said Matt, affectionately ruffling Tash's hair. She tried to look sulky, but her adoration of Matt was too obvious.

'Do you think you'll add to the family when you and Ralph tie the knot?' asked Emily, who was finding herself quite preoccupied with the subject.

'Don't think so,' said Susie, 'Ralph's quite enough to manage on the "child front" and anyway I can't see how I could possibly combine babies with all the PM's consort stuff. I'm up to my eyes at the moment with this wives' visit when Ralph hosts the international peace conference next week.'

'Gosh, are you doing the official consort bit?' asked Emily, surprised.

'Sort of,' chipped in Gerald who had just arrived with Nessa. He pecked both women on the cheek shyly. 'Of course it can't be official until the decree absolute and wedding announcement but it is remarkable how well the changes are being perceived and accepted by the various target audiences. I mean it's only been a few months after all.'

'Not remarkable at all,' commented Nessa, who had already managed to get a drink in her hand. 'Just a credit to your extraordinary PR skills darling,' she said, giving Gerald an approving squeeze around his contentedly expanding waist.

'Just TJ and Philip to come now,' observed Emily, 'which is good because lunch is pretty much ready,' she added, just as the doorbell rang.

TJ looked more grown-up that she had ever known him, and every inch the prospective MP in his impeccably cut suit, having come straight from church.

'Hello both of you,' said Emily, giving the couple a quick hug. 'TJ, Ralph's in the sitting room. I know he wants to hear about your candidacy. Well done by the way. When is the by-election?'

'Three weeks' time,' said TJ making the fingers crossed sign as he went off in search of his mentor.

'And how are you finding it?' Emily asked Philip.

'Mm,' said Philip, the master of understatement. 'We're ready for Maresbury, but is Maresbury ready for us?'

'They chose TJ as their candidate didn't they?' reasoned Emily. 'And it's a pretty safe seat from what I've heard.'

'It is,' agreed Philip. 'I just hope it's not me that buggers it up for him.'

'Why would it be?' she asked, giving him a reassuring hug, 'although I should probably give you a copy of my ten commandments for politician's wives.'

'Better still,' interrupted Nessa, 'you should give him that hideous "How to Run a Perfect Household" book I found in the jumble sale. Do you remember?'

'How could I forget?' joked Emily. 'You'll find it a laugh actually Philip, I'll dig it out for you after lunch.'

'If I find it first I'll chuck it on the fire,' said Matt, 'you haven't still got it, darling? The damned thing's pure poison.'

'I'd no idea you'd read it,' teased Emily, wrapping her arm around his waist as they stood looking out at the children in the garden.

'Ours would have been nearly eleven now,' said Matt quietly. 'I still wonder what he would have looked like. Pretty handsome I reckon, with you for a mum.'

'Well,' said Emily carefully, 'you had better hope our genes are a good mix because we'll be finding out soon enough.'

Matt looked puzzled, 'What?' he said, and then, as Emily raised an eyebrow, a slow smile spread across his face.

'When?' he said at last.

'Ooh, well, if my calculations are right,' said Emily, 'you'll be getting an early Christmas present from me.'

'Seven months?' Matt said, wonderingly, turning her to face him, his hand on her still flat tummy and a huge grin spreading across his face.

Emily nodded, gazing into the eyes of the man she loved. Yes. Here was the man she was meant to be with. The happy ending they had been waiting eleven years for had come at last.

About the Author

Sarah Waights

Sarah wrote her first book when she was five. With a father in the forces and the diplomatic corps she spent the best part of her childhood in UK boarding schools, joining her parents in exotic destinations during the school holidays.

After obtaining a degree in music she gave up classical singing and took up a career where she could indulge her love of writing. After several years in public relations, campaigning, political lobbying and freelance journalism she realised her preference for making things up and switched to writing novels instead.

She takes an anthropological interest in family, friends and life in her West Sussex village where she lives in a cottage with roses around the door, along with her artist husband, their children and other pets.

Never Marry a Politician, Sarah's debut novel, was a runner up in the 2014 Good Housekeeping Novel Writing Competition.

http://www.sarahwaights.com
https://twitter.com/SarahWaights

More from Choc Lit

If you enjoyed Sarah's story, you'll enjoy the
rest of our selection. Here's a sample:

How I Wonder What You Are

Jane Lovering

Book 4 in the Yorkshire Romances

**"Maybe he wasn't here because
of the lights – maybe they were
here because of him ..."**

It's been over eighteen months
since Molly Gilchrist has had a
man (as her best friend, Caro,
is so fond of reminding her) so
when she as good as stumbles
upon one on the moors one
bitterly cold morning, it seems like the Universe is having a
laugh at her expense.

But Phinn Baxter (that's *Doctor* Phinneas Baxter) is no
common drunkard, as Molly is soon to discover; with a
PhD in astrophysics and a tortured past that is a match for
Molly's own disastrous love life.

Finding mysterious men on the moors isn't the weirdest
thing Molly has to contend with, however. There's also those
strange lights she keeps seeing in the sky. The ones she's only
started seeing since meeting Phinn ...

Visit www.choc-lit.com for more
details, or simply scan barcode using
your mobile phone QR reader.

Too Charming
Kathryn Freeman

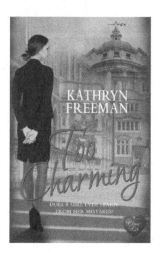

**Does a girl ever really
learn from her mistakes?**

Detective Sergeant Megan
Taylor thinks so. She once lost
her heart to a man who was too
charming and she isn't about to
make the same mistake again –
especially not with sexy defence
lawyer, Scott Armstrong.
Aside from being far too sure
of himself for his own good,
Scott's major flaw is that he defends the very people that she
works so hard to imprison.

But when Scott wants something he goes for it. And he
wants Megan. One day she'll see him not as a lawyer, but as
a man ... and that's when she'll fall for him.

Yet just as Scott seems to be making inroads, a case presents
itself that's far too close to home, throwing his life into
chaos.

As Megan helps him pick up the pieces, can he persuade her
that he isn't the careless charmer she thinks he is? Isn't a
man innocent until proven guilty?

Visit www.choc-lit.com for more
details, or simply scan barcode using
your mobile phone QR reader.

The Rest of My Life
Sheryl Browne

You can't run away from commitment forever ...

Adam Hamilton-Shaw has more reason than most to avoid commitment. Living on a houseboat in the Severn Valley, his dream is to sail into the sunset – preferably with a woman waiting in every port. But lately, his life looks more like a road to destruction than an idyllic boat ride ...

Would-be screenplay writer Sienna Meadows realises that everything about Adam spells trouble – but she can't ignore the feeling that there is more to him than just his bad reputation. Nor can she ignore the intense physical attraction that exists between them.

And it just so happens that Adam sees Sienna as the kind of woman he could commit to. But can he change his damaging behaviour – or is the road to destruction a one-way street?

Visit www.choc-lit.com for more details, or simply scan barcode using your mobile phone QR reader.

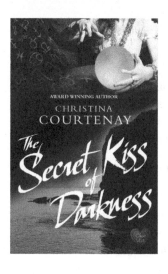

The Secret Kiss of Darkness

Christina Courtenay

Book 2 in the Shadows from the Past Series

Must forbidden love end in heartbreak?

Kayla Sinclair knows she's in big trouble when she almost bankrupts herself to buy a life-size portrait of a mysterious eighteenth century man at an auction.

Jago Kerswell, inn-keeper and smuggler, knows there is danger in those stolen moments with Lady Eliza Marcombe, but he'll take any risk to be with her.

Over two centuries separate Kayla and Jago, but, when Kayla's jealous fiancé presents her with an ultimatum, and Jago and Eliza's affair is tragically discovered, their lives become inextricably linked thanks to a gypsy's spell.

Kayla finds herself on a quest that could heal the past, but what she cannot foresee is the danger in her own future.

Will Kayla find heartache or happiness?

Visit www.choc-lit.com for more details, or simply scan barcode using your mobile phone QR reader.

Introducing Choc Lit

We're an independent publisher creating
a delicious selection of fiction.
Where heroes are like chocolate – irresistible!
Quality stories with a romance at the heart.

See our selection here:
www.choc-lit.com

We'd love to hear how you enjoyed *Never Marry a Politician*. Please leave a review where you purchased the novel or visit: **www.choc-lit.com** and give your feedback.

Choc Lit novels are selected by genuine readers like yourself. We only publish stories our Choc Lit Tasting Panel want to see in print. Our reviews and awards speak for themselves.

Could you be a Star Selector and join our Tasting Panel? Would you like to play a role in choosing which novels we decide to publish? Do you enjoy reading romance novels? Then you could be perfect for our Choc Lit Tasting Panel.

Visit here for more details…
www.choc-lit.com/join-the-choc-lit-tasting-panel

Keep in touch:
Sign up for our monthly newsletter Choc Lit Spread for all the latest news and offers: www.spread.choc-lit.com. Follow us on Twitter: @ChocLituk and Facebook: Choc Lit.

Or simply scan barcode using your mobile phone QR reader:

*Choc Lit
Spread*

Twitter

Facebook